THE GUARDIAN

BOOKS BY JOSHUA HOOD

STANDALONE NOVELS
The Guardian

THE TREADSTONE NOVELS
Robert Ludlum's The Treadstone Resurrection
Robert Ludlum's The Treadstone Exile
Robert Ludlum's The Treadstone Transgression
Robert Ludlum's The Treadstone Rendition

THE SEARCH AND DESTROY SERIES
Clear by Fire
Warning Order

THE
GUARDIAN

JOSHUA HOOD

**BLACK
STONE**
PUBLISHING

Printed in the United States of America

First edition: 2023
ISBN 978-1-6651-0957-4
Fiction / Action & Adventure

Version 1

Blackstone Publishing
31 Mistletoe Rd.
Ashland, OR 97520

www.BlackstonePublishing.com

CHAPTER 1

Staff Sergeant Travis Lane stepped outside the hangar, the East African sun hot as a blast furnace against his skin. During his twelve years as an Air Force Pararescueman, Lane had conducted combat operations in some of the world's most unforgiving environments and had thought he knew a thing or two about privation. But Camp Lemonnier had been quick to prove him wrong.

Located on the southern side of the Djibouti-Ambouli International Airport, a rifle shot from the Gulf of Aden, the camp was close enough to both Yemen and Somalia that it was the perfect choice for prosecuting America's war against the terrorist groups that plagued the Horn of Africa. But its tactical advantages aside, Camp Lemonnier was an undeniable shithole—the kind of place a soldier's morale went to die—and since his arrival three months earlier, all Lane could think about was getting back to the States.

Already sweating, he decided to forgo his usual stretches and, after starting the timer on his watch, pushed himself into a jog. Lane ran east, his surgically repaired knee tight as a bowstring. Ignoring the pain, the twenty-nine-year-old PJ slipped past the candy-striped sawhorses and *NO Foot Traffic* sign that guarded the entrance to the cargo apron, and once clear of the fence, he looped around the tail of a recently arrived C-130.

The exhaust from the turboprops scalded his lungs, but Lane kept running, weaving his way through a line of olive-drab forklifts that criss-crossed the flight line like mechanized ants. Feeling his knee loosening up, he increased his pace, and leaving the superheated tarmac behind, he followed the gravel path south toward the razor-wire-topped wall that encircled the Joint Special Operations Command compound.

He nodded to the men guarding the gate and glanced inside as he ran past, the sight of the bearded operators mingling around the tactical operations center sending his thoughts back to his time with the elite 24th STS. Before joining the Air Force, Lane hadn't known the differences between a rescue squadron and a special tactics squadron.

In fact, all he'd known about Air Force Pararescue was that, like most special operations, the PJs had come of age in the dark days of Vietnam, but while the SEALs and Rangers were out in the jungle taking the fight to the enemy, the PJs were rescuing pilots shot down behind enemy lines.

But more important than a PJ's training was his mindset. His willingness to rope into a hostile area, fight his way through the enemy, and provide the medical care required to keep the injured alive until the cavalry arrived to get them out.

These things we do, that others may live—that was their motto. The oath written in blood that had captured Lane's attention so many years ago.

Making it through the PJs' grueling two-year pipeline had damn near killed him, but Lane had succeeded, and after donning the coveted maroon beret, he'd felt ten feet tall. Invincible. It wasn't until he went to Afghanistan and saw the operators from the 24th in action that Lane realized the best was yet to come.

On paper there was nothing to separate one special tactics squadron from another, but Lane and the hardened few who'd survived the grueling selection process of the 24th found themselves in rarefied air. As members of the Air Force's only Tier One team, the men of the 24th STS were the best of the best. The tip of the spear whose lethality and medical proficiency had earned them the right to join the operators from SEAL Team Six and Delta Force on America's most classified missions.

Lane had spent the next five years putting foot to ass for the good ol' US of A, but then on a nighttime hostage-rescue mission in northern Iraq, everything had gone wrong. He could remember little from that fateful night. The heat of the explosion when the RPG hit the tail rotor. The screams of the pilot and the kaleidoscope of earth and sky as the helo spun toward the ground.

Then everything went black.

His next memory was of the hospital in Germany, of staring at the swollen mass of purpled flesh that had been his knee and looking at the faces of the doctors as they told him his time as an operator was over.

They'd offered him a medical discharge. A chance to get out of the Air Force before completing his term of service, but he'd never been a quitter and he wasn't about to start. Determined to reclaim his spot on the team, Lane threw himself headfirst into physical therapy. It took nine painful months to get fully back on his feet and another three to get back in good enough shape for a tryout, but halfway through the required reentry physical, he knew his surgically repaired ACL wasn't going to hold up.

With his hopes of rejoining the 24th crushed, Lane had two options: take a team leader position with one of the rescue squadrons or get out. Usually, he would have done whatever it took to stay in, but the years at war had ground him down, and Lane had been thinking of a life outside the Air Force when he'd gotten the fateful call from his sister, Abby, four months ago.

"There's something wrong with TJ. I don't know what to do," she said, her normally cheery voice pinched over the line.

"Abby, slow down and tell me what's going on," Lane begged.

"I don't know," she said. "He hasn't been the same since Mosul . . . He's angry all the time, and all he does when he's home on leave is drink."

"I thought he quit drinking," Lane said.

"He did but started up again after I filed for divorce." She sniffled. "I'm scared, Travis . . . scared that he's going to do something stupid. Get himself hurt . . . or worse."

Growing up on adjacent farms and with no other neighbors for miles around, the two families had been understandably tight. In fact, he and TJ had been raised more like brothers than friends. But while Lane was more levelheaded, TJ was all gas and no brake. A gap-toothed Evel Knievel who had to turn everything into a competition.

Whether he was riding dirt bikes, playing sports, or doing something trivial like feeding the cows, losing was not an option for TJ. The constant competition was exhausting, and when Lane decided to join the Air Force, he was looking forward to the break, but TJ had other plans.

"I'm coming with you."

"Do you even know what a PJ is?" Lane had asked.

"Nope."

"It's like the hardest job on the planet," Lane said, "and you haven't done anything to train for it."

"Well, if you can do it, so can I," TJ replied, flashing an impish grin.

True to his word, he'd followed Lane into the Air Force, and while Lane had struggled through the two-year pipeline, TJ had made it look easy.

Out of training, they were assigned to different units, and while Lane continued to find his footing, TJ quickly developed the reputation of a fearless, sometimes reckless operator. The fact that everything came so easy to TJ had pissed Lane off, but he kept pushing. Kept honing both his body and his mind, and by the time they both showed up at Green Team, Lane had come into his own.

As difficult as it had been for Lane to get there, nothing in his life had ever been harder than watching his *then* brother-in-law fail. In retrospect, the problem was obvious: TJ had gotten cocky, and his immaturity combined with his innate recklessness made him a liability. After one too many safety violations, TJ was cut from the training.

Lane had tried to console him, tell him that he'd done his best, but TJ's ego couldn't handle it. To cope, his brother-in-law had pushed both him and Abby away, turned to the bottle and the comfort of random women instead of his family. For Lane, TJ's cheating on Abby had been the last straw. An unforgivable sin, and their relationship had never been the same.

"TJ's a grown man," he said. "I'm sure he'll be fine."

"No, Travis, he won't," she sobbed. "You have to help him."

"What do you want me to do?"

"He's got one more deployment, and then he's done," she said. "I know you want to come home, but if you could just—"

"Just *what?*"

"Look after him," Abby pleaded. "Make sure he doesn't do anything stupid . . ."

Lane wanted to tell his sister no. Tell her that he was a PJ, *not* a damn babysitter, but the fear in her voice cut through his resolve like a knife. The pain reminded him of when she'd called to tell him that their father had lost his battle with cancer six months prior.

"Abby, even if I wanted to help, I'm not in TJ's unit," Lane said. "I can't just—"

"Yes, you can," Abby said, her words coming fast. "Chief Master Sergeant Holland just took command of one of the rescue squadrons—"

"How do you know that?" Lane demanded, his voice hard as iron.

"Because I talked to him."

"You shouldn't have done that, Abby."

"I know, but, Travis, I'm desperate. Our marriage is over, but I still care about him. Please, you have to do this for me," she begged. "You and TJ are all I have left."

Abby's words sliced through him like a straight razor, and despite his mountains of misgivings, Lane gave in. "Fine, I'll talk to Holland, but no promises."

The memories began to unravel as he started on the third mile and the pain from his knee began spreading to his thigh like a beaker of spilled acid. Lane's body screamed at him to stop or at least slow down. Unfortunately, PJs, like all special operators, were a competitive lot, and as the oldest man on the team, Lane knew that the moment he stepped into the ready room, one of the younger operators would be dying to know the "old man's" time.

Biting down on the pain, he rounded the old French ordnance locker that marked the start of the fourth and final mile, his eyes locked on the distant outline of the HH-60 Pave Hawks that indicated the end of the course. Digging deep, Lane shoved the pain back into its box and surged forward.

The last five hundred meters were the hardest, and by the time he made it to the helo, his right leg was on the verge of locking up and his breathing came in short, ragged gasps. Sucking wind, he stumbled into the hangar and was searching for a spot to collapse when one of the younger PJs came strolling in.

"Good run?" he asked innocently.

"Y-yeah . . . it was great."

"Hmm . . . what was your time?"

Not trusting himself to speak, Lane held up his watch for the younger man to inspect.

"Twenty-six minutes . . . not bad for an old—"

Forcing himself upright, Lane was quick to cut him off. "Say another word and I'll have you raking gravel for the rest of the deployment," he said.

"Roger that."

Lane waited for the man to leave, then limped over to the supply closet for a pair of ice packs and a bottle of ibuprofen. He twisted the cap free, shook four of the pills into his mouth, dry swallowed, and then headed for the room he shared with his brother-in-law. After unlocking the door with the key he wore around his neck, Lane tossed the ice packs onto his rack and hobbled to the bathroom.

Stripping out of his sweat-soaked shorts, he turned on the shower and, without waiting for it to warm up, stepped inside. The water came out of the tap cold as ice, the spray hitting his overheated body like a balm. Savoring the feeling, Lane leaned forward and pressed his forehead to the tile.

Just five more days; then we're back in the States.

Besides the end of the deployment, their rotation back to North Carolina signaled the end of his enlistment, and while the decision to leave the Air Force hadn't come easy, Lane knew it was time. Still, there was a sense of uncertainty that came with getting out. A fear of the unknown that sent a shot of panic rushing through his veins every time he thought about life on the other side.

Standing there under the showerhead, Lane felt his pulse quicken, the shot of adrenaline a prelude to the doubts he knew would follow.

But before they could grab hold, he shoved them away, grabbed the soap, and scrubbed himself clean.

After rinsing off, he climbed out of the shower, grabbed the towel from the hook, and dried himself off before heading back into his room. After spinning the combination into his wall locker, he pulled the door open, his eyes coming to rest on the eight-by-eleven photo stuck to his mirror.

He pulled on his pants and studied the picture. It had been taken shortly after TJ and Abby were married and showed the three of them standing on the wraparound porch of their two-story farmhouse. Lane and TJ were grinning like fools in their maroon berets and jump boots, while Abby rolled her eyes.

The thought that the ten-acre spread would ever be anything but a nuisance had been impossible for him to understand at the time. Especially after all the years he'd spent helping his father keep the damn thing running. But something had changed when his father died, and while Lane couldn't put it into words, he knew that the time had come for him to go home.

Pulling on his assault shirt, he closed the locker door and moved to his bed. He sat down and reached for his boots, his eyes drawn to the dog-eared brochure sitting on TJ's desk.

The pamphlet had shown up a week prior during one of the main calls, and while Lane had seen TJ reading it, he'd never given it much thought, but now it had his full attention. Frowning, he got to his feet and snatched it off the desk, his fury rising as he read the neatly typed mission statement. By the time he finished the first paragraph, his smoldering anger had blossomed into an all-consuming rage. Hands shaking, he was about to tear it up and throw the pieces into the garbage when the door creaked open and TJ stepped into the room.

CHAPTER 2

CAMP LEMONNIER

Djibouti

"What the hell is *this* shit?" Lane demanded.

Caught off guard by the greeting, TJ studied him from the doorway. "Why are you going through my stuff?"

"Answer the question," Lane ordered.

TJ ignored him and crossed to his bed. "We talked about this," he said, taking a seat.

"The hell we did."

"Last week we were talking about the farm and how much money your dad owed the bank before he died. I screwed up by cheating on Abby, and I get why she wants a divorce. But I still love her, and I'll be damned if I leave her dealing with all this financial shit by herself."

"I remember the conversation, but I don't recall you mentioning anything about becoming a mercenary."

"Did you actually read it?" TJ demanded.

"I read enough," Lane snapped back. "Now stop bullshitting me and tell me what's going on."

TJ sighed and rubbed a hand through his blond hair before looking up. "First off, they *aren't* mercenaries. They are retrieval experts who offer their policies to a select clientele. Basically, I'd be doing the same job I'm doing now but for three times the cash."

"Call it what you want, but to my way of thinking, a person who sells his skills to the highest bidder is pretty much the textbook definition of a merc," Lane said, tossing the brochure onto the bed.

"Hey, I was all about staying in," TJ said. "*You're* the one who decided to get out."

Lane opened his mouth to respond, but before the words were off his lips, the speaker in the ready room crackled to life, the prerecorded "scramble, scramble" that came booming down the hall cutting him short.

"We'll talk about this later," Lane said, snatching his HK416 from the wall locker. With the rifle in hand, he stepped out into the hall and double-timed it to the ready room, where he found the pair of newly minted PJs gawking at him from the couch in front of the flat-screen TV.

"We've got a mission," he barked. "Grab your gear and get your asses to the bird. Now!"

The two cherries snapped to, and he waited for them to clear the room before continuing down the hall to the TOC. If the tactical operations center was the eyes and ears of the 82nd's mission in the region, then the combat rescue officer in charge of the team was the brain. The all-seeing eye who monitored their missions from the row of computers sitting on the plywood table.

Slinging the rifle across his broad chest, Lane moved in behind the battle captain, who was staring at one of the screens.

"What do we have?"

"French Commandos just lost contact with one of their Pumas," the officer replied, pointing to the red blip on the screen. "Last contact had them going down ten klicks south of Al Hudaydah."

"Shit, that's Houthi territory," Lane said, referring to the Iranian proxy group that had been fighting the Saudis in Yemen. "What the hell are they doing that far north?"

"No idea, but with their combat search and rescue units tied up in Mali, they are asking for our help."

Lane studied the screen, noting the surging green mass churning in from the south. "What's that?"

"Another dust storm," the battle captain said. "What do you think?"

While Lane was undoubtedly the most experienced PJ in the room, the fact that the officer was asking his opinion caught him off guard. Lane shoved it away and focused on the facts at hand.

Having been caught in a dust storm during a deployment to northern Iraq, Lane knew the dangers that came with the high winds and limited visibility of the dreaded haboob. And that, combined with the very real possibility of a highly capable fighting force waiting for them on the ground, was a recipe for disaster.

But despite his reservations, Lane knew *not* going wasn't an option.

"Tell them we're coming," he said.

Without waiting for the officer's response, Lane turned and sprinted for the door. He burst outside, the light from the setting sun glinting off the pair of HH-60 Pave Hawks spooling up on the tarmac fifteen feet away.

Ducking beneath the rotors, Lane grabbed the plate carrier and helmet he'd stowed in the cargo hold and pulled them on. Snapping the chin strap, he shoved a magazine into his rifle and climbed into the cargo hold, just as TJ reached the door.

"What's going on?"

"A French Puma went off the scope ten klicks south of Al Hudaydah," he advised, plugging his Peltor noise-canceling headphones into the aircraft's communications. "No word on casualties, but there's a nasty-looking storm heading that way, and we need to get there first."

"Any enemy presence in the area?"

"Unknown," Lane said, racking a round into the chamber.

"Well, that sucks," TJ said.

"We've launched with less," Lane replied, pulling a map from his plate carrier. While he marked the grid for the crash site, the door gunners snapped a belt of 7.62 into the minigun, and by the time the pilots finished their preflight checks, the helo was ready to roll.

"You guys ready?" the pilot asked, looking back at the two PJs and two door gunners jammed into the back of the Pave Hawk.

"Good to go," Lane responded.

"Roger that."

The pilot released the brakes and twisted on the throttle while his copilot clicked over to the control frequency. "DJ control, this is Archangel Two-One requesting immediate departure on runway one."

"Good copy, Archangel," a voice said over the radio. "You are cleared for departure. Good luck."

And with that, the Pave Hawk was rolling, its turboshaft screaming like a banshee as the throttle opened and pulled the helo skyward. While the pilots guided the aircraft toward the target grid, Lane requested an update from the TOC.

"Still nothing."

Great.

The helo moved north over the Gulf of Aden, the dying sun spilling across the water like liquid gold. It was a thirty-minute flight to the target area, and Lane used the time to double-check the medical gear and rescue equipment stowed on the bulkhead. Finding everything where it should be, he rotated his night vision down over his eyes and checked the PEQ-15 infrared aiming laser mounted to the foregrip and the EOTech holographic sight on the top rail.

"Feet dry," the pilot advised.

Lane checked the GPS strapped to his wrist and, seeing that the grid was coming up, moved to the door. He pulled it open, the rush of the humid air into the cargo hold fogging his night vision.

"One minute out," the pilot said.

Lane wiped the moisture from the lenses and, bracing himself against the strut, leaned out the open door. While his body adjusted itself to the rise and fall of the helo, he scanned the desert for any sign of the crash site, but with the Pave Hawk traveling at 150 miles per hour, at first, all he saw was the dizzying blur of the ground passing beneath him.

Holding on to the strut, he leaned farther out, the wind tearing his eyes as he scanned the darkness. Then he saw it, the black smoke and flickering flame rising from the palm grove on his left.

"Crash site nine o'clock," he said over the radio.

"Got it," the portside gunner replied.

The pilot brought the Pave Hawk in low, the downdraft from the rotors bending the trees and kicking up a wall of dust. Squinting against the haze, Lane got his first view of the downed helo, the twisted wreck of the aircraft not nearly as terrifying as the approaching line of military-attired figures running through the undergrowth.

"Rope," he shouted to the crew chief.

The man nodded and yanked the fast rope from a large duffel, snapping it to the hoist. While the crew chief checked to make sure it was locked in, Lane shouldered his medical ruck and pulled on a pair of thick gloves.

TJ was the first to the door, and after giving the rope a sharp tug, he flashed the crew chief a thumbs-up.

"PJ in the door," the chief advised over the radio.

While the pilot held the helo steady, TJ moved into position and was about to swing out when Lane grabbed his shoulder. "None of that cowboy shit of yours," he shouted. "We get in, do what we can, and get the hell out."

"Whatever you say," TJ said, his cocky grin telling Lane that his brother-in-law hadn't listened. Then he was gone, swinging out of the bird and sliding down into the darkness.

Cursing under his breath, Lane moved to follow, but before he could get a bite of the rope, a line of tracers came coiling up through the palms. The door gunner shouted a warning, and the pilot stomped the right rudder pedal, the sudden movement sending Lane stumbling toward the door.

Unable to catch his balance, he reached out and grabbed the rope with both hands, his feet sliding free of the bird. Unlike rappelling, where you had both a harness and a carabiner to secure you to the rope, the only thing keeping Lane from a fifty-foot fall was his grip, and with the weight of his gear and the wash of the rotors working against him, it was all he could do to hold on.

He dropped like a lawn dart, the friction from the rope burning through his gloves while he tried to get the line routed between his boots. With the ground rushing up to meet him, he knew that he was seconds away from a pair of broken legs when he finally got the rope where he needed it.

Using all his strength, he clamped his boots together and prepared for impact. He hit hard, but the bolt of pain in his knee was eclipsed by muzzle flashes from the men moving forward through the trees. Limping away from the rope, Lane shoved an HE round into the grenade launcher mounted beneath the barrel of his H&K and sent it arcing toward the advancing enemy.

The grenade exploded, the rush of flame and shrapnel blasting the men off their feet. But the firefight was just beginning, and before Lane could shove another grenade into the breech, more rifle fire came snapping in from the north.

Lane brought the rifle up to his shoulder and fired a three-round burst into the closest fighter. The suppressed *thwack-thwack* of a rifle drew his attention left, where he found TJ ducked behind the husk of a fallen tree. Firing on the run, he slid into cover beside his brother-in-law, the slivers of bark from the impacting bullets peppering his face.

"Took you long enough," TJ said.

Lane ignored him and, after wiping the grit from his eyes, keyed up on the radio. "Archangel Two-Two," he said, calling the second helicopter, "we've got hostiles in the tree line. I need you to clear 'em out."

The words were no sooner out of his mouth than the Pave Hawk came racing low across the treetops, flame spitting from the miniguns mounted to the doors.

With the enemy suppressed for the moment, Lane shoved a fresh grenade into the launcher and rushed to the crash site, the flame from the spilled aviation fuel flaring his night vision. While TJ covered the rear, Lane moved to the cargo hold and glanced inside.

Empty.

A pained moan from the cockpit drew his attention forward, and he slithered through the crumpled hatch.

The copilot was dead, his neck twisted awkwardly to the right and his sightless eyes staring up at the shattered windscreen. The pilot, however, was still clinging to life, but given the blood pooling from the gaping wound in his leg and the front of his flight suit stained black with more blood, it was clear he didn't have long.

Using his knife, Lane cut the man free from his harness and eased him back into the cargo hold. Lane laid him flat and pulled a tourniquet from his kit, looping it over the man's thigh as the gunfight outside the helicopter grew to a crescendo.

Shit, who are these guys?

While TJ directed the helo's gun runs and engaged the enemy with his rifle, Lane pulled the tourniquet tight over the pilot's leg. The man screamed at him in French and tried to push him away, but Lane held him tight and continued spinning the windlass.

Once the bleeding stopped, he cut open the pilot's flight suit and began packing gauze into the wound. While Lane worked to save the man's life, the rest of the team came sliding down from the second Pave Hawk, and Lane could hear TJ barking instructions. "Brown, get the litter ready. Keller, get in there and help Travis."

Lane moved out of the way to let the younger PJ crawl in beside him and took up a position at the casualty's feet. "We've got to get him out of here. Grab his arms."

The younger man nodded, and together they pulled the man free and carefully lowered him to the waiting stretcher. While Brown strapped him in, Lane got on the radio. "Archangel Two-One, patient is critical. I need you to set the bird down south of my location."

"Roger that," the pilot said. "But be advised we've got more hostiles moving in from the east."

Lane double-clicked the mic to indicate that he'd received the transmission, then got to his feet. "Let's move."

Lane waited for the younger PJs to pick up the litter and then took point, his rifle up and ready. Scanning for threats, he led them south toward the LZ, the dust from the approaching sandstorm stinging his exposed skin.

He pushed them hard, and they were almost to the clearing when a figure stepped out of the shadows, the AK against his shoulder spitting fire. Luckily the shots were high, and the bullets snapped over Lane's head and into the darkness. "Fucker." Still moving, he centered his laser on the man's chest and dumped him with three shots center mass.

The bullets dropped the man flat on his back, but a look through the trees showed more were coming. "TJ, get 'em to the helo," Lane shouted.

Without waiting for an answer, he took up a position behind one of the trees, centered his reticle on the forehead of the closest fighter, and pulled the trigger. The rifle bucked, and the man dropped like a marionette with cut strings.

Lane dumped two more of the men and was shoving another HE round into the breech when a figure came running in from his left. He snapped his rifle on target and was about to fire when he realized that it was TJ.

"What the hell are you doing?" Lane shouted. "I told you to get them out of here."

"And let you have all the fun?" TJ grinned. "Not happening."

"You never fucking listen."

"Relax, bro, I got them loaded on the helo and—"

But whatever he was about to say was cut short by a rush of flame followed by the shriek of an RPG leaving its launcher. Lane turned toward the sound and, seeing a trail of white smoke racing through the trees, tried to grab TJ and pull him into cover. But before he had a chance, the 40 mm rocket-propelled grenade slammed into one of the trees and detonated.

CHAPTER 3

Washington, DC

Mia Webb's alarm went off at 5:00 a.m., the electronic beeping echoing loudly off the bare walls of her bedroom. Still jet-lagged from the twenty-two-hour flight from Nairobi she'd taken the night before, she reached out and slapped blindly at her phone on the bedside table.

It took her three tries, but she managed to corral the phone and, after silencing the alarm, rolled onto her back. She closed her eyes, hoping to fall back asleep, but with the dread of the upcoming day pressing down on her like a lead weight, Mia knew that wasn't going to happen.

As she lay there staring up at the ceiling, her mind drifted to the botched raid that had gotten her called back to the States. As a rising star in the FBI's African counterintelligence unit, Mia had always prided herself on her attention to detail and ability to see past the overload of information that could derail even the best lead investigator. Looking back on it now, she was certain that she'd done everything right.

Then how the hell did it all go so wrong?

The ding of her phone pushed the question from her mind, and she unlocked the screen to find a text from her boss.

Director's office 11:00 am. Don't be late!!

Shit.

Mia typed out a quick reply, confirming that she would be there, and then, out of habit, opened the Signal app she and her team used to communicate in the field. Usually, the thread was full of the idle chitchat and gossip that marked the day-to-day lives of those used to working in a tight-knit team, but today it was painfully silent.

For someone not accustomed to failure, the sudden ostracization that followed her summons home was a painful blow. However, it wasn't the quiet text thread but the unanswered message she'd sent to Angelo Garza the night before that sent a chill racing up her spine.

Where are you?

They'd been supposed to meet up for drinks before she flew out, but Angelo had never shown, and sitting there staring at the screen, Mia couldn't help but wonder if he'd abandoned her too.

Unwilling to believe he would do that, she returned the phone to its charger and got out of bed, the hardwood floor cold on her bare feet. She pulled on her workout clothes and then padded off to the bathroom to brush her teeth.

With her brown hair, sun-bronzed skin, and athletic build, Mia Webb liked to think of herself as pretty in the girl-next-door kind of way. But her looks had no bearing on her current profession. No, it was sheer determination and intelligence that had gotten her the job in Kenya. And while there were a few of the old heads who liked to make lewd speculations as to how Mia had made it to the top, Angelo wasn't one of them.

They'd first met at a counterproliferation conference in New York, where he was giving a presentation on the smuggling of African conflict minerals. The lecture was dry and heavy on the PowerPoint slides, but there was something about the handsome UN investigator that piqued her interest.

Perhaps it was his friendly face and easy smile, or maybe it was the passion she saw in his eyes, the determination to help make the world a better place no matter what the cost. Whatever it was—Mia wanted more.

Before their first meeting, she'd had a strict rule of not mixing business with pleasure, but once they were introduced, there was an immediate connection. The ensuing relationship lasted for three years, and while both knew they had something special, once Mia was promoted, they had to cut it off.

She'd worried that the end of their relationship might affect their work, but Angelo was quick to prove her wrong. "We're still a team," he told her. "And nothing is going to change that."

So why didn't he show up in Nairobi?

It wasn't like Angelo not to text her back, and standing there at the sink, Mia felt the anger that had come with being stood up on her last night in-country giving way to concern. The uneasy feeling gripped her like a vise, and Mia's mind began to fill with the hundreds of things that could have gone wrong.

Is he sick? Hurt? Or is it something worse?

Mia didn't have the answers, and as she had enough problems of her own to deal with that day, she decided it best not to create any more. Assuring herself that Angelo was fine, she rinsed out her toothbrush and went to the kitchen, pausing to fill her water bottle before grabbing her gym bag on the way out of the apartment. She closed the door behind her and locked it, then headed to the elevators at the end of the hall.

By the time the elevator settled on the bottom floor, Mia had finished the water and slipped the bottle into her bag, her shoes squeaking as she walked across the marble floor of the lobby. She stepped outside, the sallow glow of the streetlights struggling to pierce the fog that had rolled in the night before.

Mia followed the sidewalk to the end of the block and turned left onto Twelfth Street, the distant wail of a police siren following her up the hill. She walked east toward the distant cluster of industrial buildings that housed Capital Martial Arts and the morning jiujitsu class she hoped would take her mind off the shit show that had been her last mission in Nairobi.

For Mia, living in DC had been a dream come true, the arts and culture scenes that were the hallmark of the nation's capital standing in striking contrast to the thorny shrubs and endless flats of the South

Texas plains where she'd grown up. Not that the constant travel that came with her job left her much time to see the city where she lived.

Still, she wasn't complaining.

Before joining the FBI, the only time Mia had been out of Texas was when her father was teaching her how to fly and they had stopped for fuel in Durant, Oklahoma. But that all changed two years ago when Mia was sent to Africa to serve as the assistant legal attaché in Nairobi.

Officially she was there to support the State Department. In reality she was the Bureau's eyes and ears in the region, and her first assignment was to investigate and assess China's Belt and Road Initiative.

Launched in 2013, B&R was China's attempt at establishing a unified world market—a twenty-first-century spice road—that would exclude both the United States and Russia. The core of the operation was to establish a series of land and sea routes that would connect Asia with Africa and Europe, but to accomplish their goal, the Chinese first needed to modernize the sorely outdated infrastructures of their African partners.

It was a monumental undertaking, and after reading up on the project during the flight over, Mia couldn't help but think that the plan was destined to fail. However, the newly paved roads and the construction cranes that dotted the skyline during her drive from Jomo Kenyatta International Airport to the US consulate in Nairobi were quick to prove her wrong.

How had the Chinese been able to pull it off?

That was the question Mia had been sent to answer. One that began and ended with a shadowy private military company called Crimson Ridge.

According to the dossier compiled by the CIA, Crimson Ridge had originally been a South African–based security company that hired former soldiers to provide static security for the oil fields and pipelines that crisscrossed the African mainland. But when the Chinese showed up with their pallets of cash and eagerness to get to work, everything changed.

Before arriving in Nairobi, the Chinese had begun projects in Kazakhstan and Indonesia, and while their successes hadn't been as fast as they wanted, they had been able to easily identify which palms needed greasing. The same could *not* be said when it came to the myriad of war-ring factions that operated in Africa, and rapidly losing patience, the Chinese turned to Crimson Ridge for help.

The man who was brought in to break this logjam was Gavin Roos, and once he was on the ground, he didn't use words but the barrel of a gun to gain the necessary compliance. Shocked by the violence left in his wake, the Kenyan government issued a warrant for Roos's arrest, but by the time a judge finally signed off, the wily South African was nowhere to be found.

Desperate to get Roos before he fled the country, Mia had squeezed every informant and snitch she could get her hands on, but with every lead came an insurmountable mountain of red tape. The problem was that while her new posting came with a temporary bump to GS-14—a pay grade usually reserved for supervisors and other top-level positions—it did *not* come with the corresponding authority.

Which meant that before Mia could launch a tactical operation to apprehend Roos, she had to clear it with her boss back in DC, who would then run it past the State Department. It was a bureaucratic nightmare, and Mia could feel her chances of catching the man slipping away, until she received a call from one of her most trusted sources.

"There is a man in Busia I think you should speak with," he'd said over a meal of *nyama choma* at the Kenyatta Market.

"Who is he?"

"His name is Emmanuel Otieno, and rumor is he is helping the man you seek get across the border into Uganda."

"How do you know this?" she demanded.

"From the forger working on his papers," he replied.

"How long do I have?" Mia asked.

"Difficult to say," the man said, holding out an empty hand.

Sighing, Mia drew a wad of cash from her pocket and slapped it into his palm. "How long?"

"The documents will be delivered at four p.m."

"Four p.m.?" Mia demanded, looking at her watch. "Shit, that only gives us six hours."

"Yes, so you better hurry."

Pressing another wad of cash into the man's hand, Mia got up from the table and headed outside. She pulled out her phone and called her boss, but it went straight to voice mail.

Shit.

Unwilling to allow Roos to escape again, she made the decision that would prove to be her undoing and called Colonel Samuel Maina, the commander of the Kenyan General Service Unit.

In retrospect it was a hasty decision, but at the moment Mia thought it would be easier to beg forgiveness than ask permission, and an hour after making the call, she was in the back of one of the GSU's Bell helicopters, heading toward the tiny border town.

While not as reliable as the National Police Service, the GSU was the only unit in the country that had the firepower and the training to take down a high-value target. Plus, after losing two of their men during a shoot-out with Crimson Ridge, they were out for blood.

The objective was a walled compound on the edge of the village, and upon landing and meeting up with the rest of the team at the regional outpost, Mia handed out the hastily made briefing packet.

"The target is Gavin Roos," she said, holding up the picture of the South African merc.

"And the rules of engagement?" Colonel Maina asked.

"We return fire *only* if fired upon," she said. "No civilian casualties, am I clear?"

"Crystal," the colonel said.

"Good, then let's kit up."

Ten minutes later Mia was sitting in the back of the lead van, an FBI-issued M4 carbine slung across her body armor. The driver kept his foot on the gas, and they raced through the town, the dust kicked up from the convoy choking the merchants hawking their wares in the market.

"Target is coming up," the team leader yelled. "Right-side drop."

Mia nodded, racked a round into the rifle, and closed her eyes. She took a deep breath to settle her nerves and opened her eyes to see one of the assaulters sliding open the right-side door.

A second later the driver slammed on the brakes, and then they were moving, Mia's rifle up while the breachers rushed toward the iron gate. They slapped their charges into place and backed off, a burst of rifle fire from the main house sending the wide-mouthed onlookers standing in the street running for cover.

"Burning," a man yelled.

Mia opened her mouth and waited for the charge to blow, her hands pressed tight against the FBI-issued Peltors that protected her ears. The noise-canceling earmuffs were rated for eighty-two decibels, more than adequate for most charges, but not knowing the thickness of the metal gate, the Kenyans had resorted to the time-tested formula of using *P* for *plenty*.

"Fire in the hole," one of the men yelled in French.

The charge detonated in a blinding flash of orange. The flame was followed a microsecond later by the thunder roar of the concussion that rolled over Mia like an invisible wrecking ball.

The flat-handed smack of the overpressure left her dizzy, and she was trying to clear her head when the assaulters flowed through the breach, their AKs chattering as they advanced on the main building.

Still dizzy from the blast, Mia fell in behind them and was angling for the cover of a rusted truck when a figure stepped into view, the rifle on his shoulder spitting fire. Throwing herself behind the vehicle, Mia rolled to her knee, the bullets snapping harmlessly overhead.

With no time to think, she brought her own M4 onto target, flipped the selector to fire, and dumped three rounds into the man's chest.

Her target went down in a spray of blood, and Mia got to her feet, her hands shaking from the rush of adrenaline. Ignoring the tremors, she hustled toward what was left of the front door, but by the time she got inside, the gunfight was over—and the men who'd been occupying the house were lying in pools of their own blood.

"Where's Roos?" she demanded.

"He's not here," the men said, shrugging.

Dammit.

The low hum and flashing yellow light of a street sweeper ended the memory, and Mia paused at the curb to let the machine pass. While she waited, her mind shifted to her boss and how she was going to explain what had happened. How Mia had managed to let what *should* have been a simple snatch and grab turn into a raging gunfight.

They were the right questions; unfortunately, she didn't have the answers, and standing there watching the bristles scour the asphalt, Mia couldn't help but think that her career was over.

CHAPTER 4

NORTHSTAR MINE

Ubili, DRC

Gavin Roos leaned against the fender of the Land Rover, the sallow glow of the truck's headlights illuminating the bare-chested porters slogging through the ankle-deep mud. Even in the darkness, they were a miserable-looking lot. Their sunken eyes and waxen skin gave them the look of walking corpses, but the grizzled South African didn't give a shit about their health.

No, all he cared about was getting the burlap sacks they carried on their shoulders loaded onto the back of the six-wheel Ural-4320 before the sun came up. After that they could slink back to their shitty lean-tos on the far side of the mine and die for all he cared.

Roos shook out another cigarette from the sodden pack of Gunstons and lit it off the butt of the one in his hand. He took a greedy drag and held the smoke deep in his lungs, the rush of nicotine into his bloodstream doing little to calm his ragged nerves.

Christ, I need a drink.

Remembering the bottle of Johnnie Walker he'd left inside the converted shipping container that served as his office, Roos turned and headed back down the hill, his mind drifting over the lifetime of bad choices that had brought him to the Democratic Republic of the Congo.

Growing up poor in the slums of South Africa, Roos had found himself on the wrong side of the law at an early age. At first, his crimes were born of necessity, like stealing food from the local Woolworths so he'd have something to eat, or clothes from the Maponya Mall so he'd have something to wear.

It was chickenshit stuff. Stealing to survive.

But by the time he turned seventeen, Roos was in it for the cash and making good money boosting cars and selling them to the local chop shops. Then he got busted popping the steering column on a BMW someone had left parked on the street, and it was game over.

Luckily, he didn't have a record, and the magistrate offered the age-old deal: join the army or go to jail.

It was a no-brainer.

When he went in, his only concern was keeping his nose clean, finishing his enlistment, and then getting out. But to his surprise, Roos found a home in the South African Army, and after four years of serving with the infantry, he decided to try out for the 5th Special Forces.

He was good at his job and on his way to becoming a team leader when he was approached by Jan Botha, a headhunter for a local PMC called Crimson Ridge, who asked Roos to meet him at one of his favorite Johannesburg watering holes. Until then, he'd never thought about leaving the army. But Botha was good at his job, and halfway through their second pints of Castle Lager, Roos was interested in hearing more.

"How'd you like to leave all this and make some real money?" Botha offered.

"How much?" Roos asked.

"Fifteen hundred dollars a day."

Roos whistled.

Compared to the 212,000 rand he was making as a freshly promoted staff sergeant, it was a huge number. Life changing. But if Roos had learned anything during his time on the streets, it was that if someone was offering him that amount of money, there had to be a catch.

"What kind of work are we talking about?" he asked.

"Primarily site security for clients in the natural resources sector."

"Fifteen hundred dollars a day to guard a mine?" Roos asked. "Why so much?"

"Well, that's not *exactly* right," Botha said, leaning in closer and lowering his voice. "You see, our firm caters to clients who operate in the mineral-*exploration* sector, and the wages are reflective of the inherent risk involved in these ventures."

There it was.

"So, this is not *exactly* legal?" Roos asked.

"In the eyes of the South African government—no," Botha said. "But then again, the work isn't *in* South Africa, so . . ."

Roos had his reservations about the job, but in the end, the money was just too good to pass up, and he'd signed on. He embraced his new trade and spent the next four years killing so that those back in civilization wouldn't feel the pinch of the pump. From fighting Somalian pirates in the Gulf of Aden to ambushing rebels in the mud-stained Niger Delta, Roos used superior firepower and a growing penchant for brutality to keep the oil flowing.

He'd been on track to finally rotate back to South Africa for a bit of the good life when Botha had sent him to Nairobi. With their unlimited budget and history of human rights abuse, Roos couldn't have picked a better benefactor than the Chinese, and when a land dispute with one of the tribesmen turned violent, Roos settled the matter by burning the man's village.

Shocked by the violence, the Kenyan government filed a warrant for his arrest. Roos was forced out of the country, which was how he and his men had ended up in North Kivu and *not* back home in South Africa.

Bunch of bullshit, Roos thought.

Compared to the gleaming pumping stations and spindly derricks that marked the oil fields Roos was used to, the mine was an ugly and primitive place—a two-acre strip of bare earth and roughly dug pits that had been hacked out of the jungle. But beneath the mud and brackish water lay the largest untapped reserve of columbite-tantalite the world *didn't* know about, and that made it almost the most valuable piece of property in the world.

And it was his job to keep it that way. A fact reinforced by Alexander Sterling the day Roos had arrived at the mine.

Since signing on with Crimson Ridge, he'd worked for all kinds of bosses. Some were good, some were bad, but they were all narcissistic pieces of shit. It wasn't that Roos judged them for it. No, he was a pragmatist and quick to realize that it took a specific kind of man with a very specific kind of personality to be able to come into a dirt-poor country with the sole intention of raping it of natural resources. But out of all the big men Roos had met, he'd never run across anyone like Sterling.

The man was as ruthless as he was rich, and despite his carefully cultivated persona as an international philanthropist and human rights activist, Sterling was a soulless son of a bitch. During their one and only meeting, he had been quick to get to the point.

"Botha tells me you are a hard man, so I will be direct," Sterling said, his clipped British accent on full display. "There are only two things that I care about. The first is that you are willing to do whatever it takes to ensure the ore shipments stay on track and under the radar."

"And the second?"

"That nothing you or your men do is ever traced back to me. You succeed, and I will make you richer than you could have ever imagined," Sterling said, his eyes dark as a shark's. "Fail me, and I will kill you."

There was no doubt in his mind that Sterling would end him if he failed at his task, which was why Roos was still fuming about the previous night's security breach. How Angelo Garza had even found the mine, much less gotten close enough to take pictures, was beyond him. But the man had pulled it off, and to Roos that could only mean one thing.

We've got a fucking rat. But who?

Roos didn't know, but he was determined to find out.

Cursing under his breath, Roos quickened his pace, the rain soaking through the Gore-Tex jacket he'd bought in Kinshasa, the wet suck of the mud threatening to rip his boots from his feet as he slogged past the scrum of workers huddled around the fires they'd built in the empty fifty-gallon drums.

He was almost to the conex, his mind on the bottle waiting for him inside, when the radio on his hip hissed to life. "Boss, you there?"

"Yeah, what's up, Pieter?"

"We've got a problem with the patient."

"Shit, is he dead?"

"No, but he's out of surgery, and the doc is trying to transfer him to Kinshasa."

That meddling bastard.

"You tell that prick that Angelo Garza is staying here," Roos barked into the radio.

"That's exactly what I told him," Pieter said, "but the little shit locked himself in his office. Said he was going to call Mr. Sterling."

"That fucking twat," he snarled. "I'm on my way."

By the time Roos made it to the infirmary, his legs were on fire and his already foul mood had darkened to a simmering rage. *This fucking place . . .* He opened the door and stomped inside, tracking the mud he'd collected on his way across the freshly shined floor.

"Excuse me," the nurse said from behind her desk, but he ignored her and continued to the back, where Pieter stood pounding on an office door.

"Dr. Lars, open the—"

"Out of the way," Roos snarled. He booted the door and stepped inside, his hand dropping to the Browning Hi-Power holstered at his waist. "Where the hell is he?" he demanded of the man sitting in front of him.

The doctor leaped to his feet, his eyes wide behind his thick glasses. "G-get the hell out of here."

Roos ignored him, and seeing the satellite phone on the desk, he drew the pistol. "You know the rules, Doc," he said. "No unauthorized phones at the mine."

"As a doctor it is my job to—"

Roos cut him off with a backhand to the face, the blow from the heavy pistol crushing the man's nose. The doctor dropped to his knees, and Roos stepped over to him, pressing the pistol to his forehead.

"Your only job is to do what I fucking tell you," Roos said. "Is that understood?"

The doctor nodded, blood from his shattered nose gushing through the hands pressed tight to his face.

"Good, now how long until the patient is awake?"

"H-his injuries were quite severe," the doctor stammered, "and I . . .
I think it best if we keep him sedated for another—"

"How *fucking* long?" Roos screamed.

"Tomorrow . . . I will bring him out of sedation tomorrow."

"Any more delays, Doctor," Roos said, leaning in close, "and I will
hold you *personally* responsible."

"I—I understand."

"Good. Then I will see you tomorrow morning," Roos said, turning to the door.

CHAPTER 5

Atlantic Ocean

Travis Lane lay on his back, the world silent and cold around him. One minute he was locked in a dreamless sleep, and the next he was back in Yemen. There was a vividness to these nightmares that he'd never known. The chatter of the machine guns and the boom of the grenades caused his body to flinch. But it wasn't until he heard the earsplitting shriek of the incoming RPG that he was jolted awake.

Lane sat up, his heart hammering in his chest as he scanned the unfamiliar space. *Where the hell am I?* Slowly the world drifted back into focus, the horrors of the battlefield giving way to the hypnotic hum of the C-17's engines and the flag-draped coffin in the center of the cargo hold.

Then it all came rushing back.

Lane had tried to pull TJ down before the RPG hit, but just as he was reaching out, the openhanded slap of the concussion sent him flying. The blast must have knocked him out, because when he woke up, he was back at Camp Lemonnier, his body aching from the impact of the explosion.

"Where's TJ?" he'd asked the orderly.

The man's face told him everything that he needed to know.

TJ was dead.

Now looking around himself and suddenly feeling sick, Lane grabbed one of the white airsickness bags that were standard issue on most military cargo aircraft. He ripped it open and vomited until there was nothing left and then rose to his feet. He wiped his mouth against the back of his hand and walked over to the black trash bag tied off to the strut near the cargo ramp and tossed in the white bag. When he turned around, the loadmaster was standing there with a bottle of water.

Lane took the bottle and cracked the top. "Thanks, brother."

"We take care of our own," the other man said.

"Yeah." Lane nodded.

He drained half of it in one long pull and then headed back to the nylon bench that was his seat. He sat down, his eyes locked on the silver coffin just visible beneath the flag. He'd never been able to forgive TJ or even look him in the eye after he'd broken Abby's heart—cheated on her despite everything she'd put up with. It was one thing for him to put up with TJ's shit. But his betrayal of Abby was something else altogether.

And yet his sister had surprised him. "If I can forgive him, then so can you," she'd told him during one of his weekly calls home.

Forgiveness.

There had been times at Camp Lemonnier when being around TJ had felt like it used to—at the range or following one of the requalification jumps the team had to do to stay current. But while Lane had been aware of the opportunity to mend their fractured relationship, he'd let it slip away.

The truth was he'd always thought he had plenty of time to make it right, but sitting there in the back of the C-17, he realized that he'd been wrong. "Man, I'm sorry," he said, leaning forward and placing his hand on the coffin in front of him.

Overwhelmed by the sudden rush of emotions, Lane's voice broke, and he trailed off, his eyes hot with tears. Wiping his face, he leaned back against the bulkhead and thought of the picture of the farm he'd kept in his locker. The usually crisp image that had gotten him through some of his darkest times was starting to fade, causing Lane to think of everything he'd lost during the last year—first his father, then his career, and now TJ.

What was the right thing to do?

He didn't know, but by the time the C-17 touched down at Pope Airfield, of one thing Lane was certain—he was going to save the family farm, no matter what it cost him.

While the pilot taxied to the far side of the airfield and dropped the ramp, Lane got to his feet and ran a hand over his rumpled uniform. Pulling on his beret, he took a deep breath and turned toward the opening, where Chief Master Sergeant Holland and the honor guard were formed up in front of the low-slung hangar.

Holland barked an order, and the men snapped to attention, the medals on their dress blues glinting in the sun as they marched across the tarmac. Lane waited for them at the top of the ramp and snapped a crisp salute as they filed into the cargo hold.

Together, they all lifted TJ's coffin from its mount and carried it down the ramp and into the back of the waiting van—the only fanfare the low whine of the C-17's engines spooling down. Lane offered a final crisp salute before the van doors were closed and held it until the vehicle pulled away.

Then he was alone with Holland on the runway.

Like most of the silent professionals who made up the ranks of AFSOC, or Air Force Special Operations Command, Holland was a stoic man. Typically a warrior with ice in his veins and gunpowder in his heart, this time he made no attempt to hide his emotions.

"He was a hell of an operator," he said, clasping his arm around Lane's shoulders.

"That he was."

"I know you've already put in your paperwork to get out," Holland said, "but is there any way I can change your mind? Maybe offer you a permanent spot on the rescue side?"

"Afraid not," Lane said. "It's time for me to go home."

"Well, if you ever need anything," Holland said, offering a hand, "I'm just a phone call away."

"I appreciate that, Chief," Lane said, shaking the man's hand.

Then he turned and stared across the flight line, the uncertainty of his future mirrored by the impenetrable wall of pines in the distance.

CHAPTER 6

Nashville, Tennessee

Lane swung the Jeep off Interstate 40 and turned south toward the halo of light that marked the twenty-four-hour Exxon station a half mile down the road. It had taken him three hours to get everything he owned packed up and into the back of his '85 CJ-7, and then he was on the road.

He'd been driving for eight hours, and according to the map he'd bought at the AutoZone outside Asheville, he should have been on the other side of Nashville by now.

But he wasn't, and as he pulled into the parking lot, the dash lights blinking like a Christmas tree, Lane was coming to the realization that the old CJ was not the best vehicle for this long a trip. In retrospect, *not* taking the time to ensure the Jeep was roadworthy after it had been sitting in storage for the past four months had been a bad idea. This was reinforced by the half-empty case of motor oil and the plastic bags full of busted hoses and dry-rotted belts that littered the back seat.

They sure don't make 'em like they used to, he thought.

However, in all fairness, when Lane bought the old CJ from a fellow PJ who was transferring duty station, he'd been thinking not about its roadworthiness but about how much the coeds down at NC State liked riding around with the top off.

Lane pulled up to the pumps and, afraid that the Jeep might not crank back up if he cut it off, left the engine running while he climbed down to the diesel-soaked pavement. He stretched his legs and gathered the empty Red Bull cans, protein bar wrappers, and half-finished Gatorade bottles into a plastic bag before dumping it into the trash can.

The housekeeping taken care of, he unscrewed the gas cap, pulled the nozzle, and flipped the lever. He shoved the nozzle home, locked the handle, and left the old analog pump clicking like a slot machine as he grabbed a handful of paper towels from the dispenser and unlatched the hood.

When he was growing up on a farm, a new car was a luxury the family couldn't afford. While other kids bonded with their fathers over games of catch or during trips to the fishing hole, in Lane's house bonding meant sitting out in the garage while his old man worked on whatever piece-of-shit car he'd picked up from the auctions in Memphis.

It wasn't an easy childhood, but it had taught Lane the value of hard work, and more importantly it had given him the skills required to keep the old Jeep on the road.

He lifted the hood, secured the prop, and fished the penlight from his pocket. Holding the light in his mouth, Lane swatted at the swarm of mosquitoes that settled over him and then leaned in to check out the wrap of Gorilla tape he'd used to patch the radiator hose.

The tape was holding, but a careful look into the radiator showed the water level low. After checking the oil, Lane tossed the paper towels in the garbage and, with the pump still slowly ticking, headed to the store for a gallon of water.

He opened the door and stepped inside, the blast of AC a welcome reprieve from the sultry suck of the southern night. Wiping the sweat from his forehead, Lane was heading to the rear of the store to grab another Red Bull from one of the coolers when the mouthwatering smell of fresh fried chicken stopped him dead in his tracks. Instantly forgetting about the energy drink, Lane pivoted to his right and followed the scent to the counter, where a timeworn woman in a grease-spattered apron was pulling a fresh batch of fried chicken from the fryer.

"Can I help ya?" she asked, shaking the chicken into the warmer.

As a member of the 24th, Lane had the diet of a professional athlete, and everything he ingested, from the food he ate to fuel his body to the supplements he took to protect his prematurely aged joints, was designed for peak performance. Standing there, savoring the smell of the chicken and the sight of the turnip greens and mashed potatoes mounded beside it, Lane couldn't remember the last time he'd chosen a meal for the taste and not the calories. With his stomach growling like an angry bear, he figured now was as good a time as any to start.

"Yes ma'am," he said.

Lane ordered a to-go plate, his mouth watering as the woman filled the Styrofoam carton.

"Anything else?" she asked, closing the lid and putting it into a plastic sack.

"No ma'am," he said, reaching for his wallet.

"You pay up front."

Lane nodded, grabbed a stack of napkins and a fork from the dispenser, and then continued back to the cooler for a jug of water and his third Red Bull of the night.

He carried his purchases to the front of the store, where a makeup-caked girl was leaning against the cigarette rack, her eyes glued to her phone. He set everything on the counter and smiled at her as she moved forward to ring him up.

"That everything?" she asked.

"Think so," he said, tugging his wallet from his back pocket.

"That'll be twenty-two fifty."

He handed her one of the hundreds he'd gotten from the ATM at Bragg and told her to put the change on the pump before heading back to the Jeep. Tossing the Red Bull and chicken dinner into the passenger seat, he used the jug of water to top off the radiator and was replacing the cap when he noticed the pump had shut off.

Securing the hood, Lane wiped his hands on his pants, a frown spreading across his face when he realized that eighty bucks hadn't filled up the tank. "Well, that sucks," he said, suddenly realizing that what money he'd saved from his deployments might not go as far as he hoped.

Looks like I'm going to need a job, ASAP.

With that somber thought in mind, Lane got into the Jeep and

pulled away from the pump, nosing the vehicle into one of the parking spots near the store. He grabbed his food, climbed out, and set the
Styrofoam container on the hood. Opening the lid, he tore into one of
the pieces of chicken, the crunch of the skin and the explosion of herbs
and spices catapulting him back in time.

His mind drifted back to the farm and that warm summer evening
when he'd first glimpsed his calling. The day had started like it did on
any other farm: getting up before the sun to feed the animals, having
a quick breakfast, and then heading off to school. When he'd returned
home, there were more chores and then more animals to feed and pen
up before the family could sit down and eat.

On most nights, while their mother was cooking dinner and their father
was enjoying a short break with a cold beer on the porch, Lane and his
sister would give the horses a quick ride around the corral before putting
them up. But this night Abigail had wanted to take them out to the pasture.

"Race you around the hay bales," she'd said.

"You're on."

Abby was a year older and a better rider, so it was no surprise that she
beat him. But what was unexpected was when the normally docile mare
she was riding began to whirl and snort on the way back to the barn.

Lane had tried to grab the reins, but before he had a chance, his
sister was flying through the air and landing hard on the ground. It
wasn't the first time either one of them had been thrown from a horse,
and Lane was expecting her to bounce quickly to her feet, but instead
she lay there, unmoving and silent, a crimson stain spreading slowly
from beneath her flaxen hair.

"Get up, Abby," he begged. "Please get up."

When she didn't respond, Lane leaped onto the horse and went gal-
loping back to the house, yelling to his father to call 911. Leaving her
there was the hardest thing he'd ever done, and the ten minutes it took
before the ambulance came racing up the drive seemed interminable.
But when the EMTs came leaping from the back, their faces were calm
as they jogged across the pasture to save Abby.

Lane had never felt so helpless as he did at that moment, and as he watched the EMTs strap his sister's limp body to the spine board and carry her back to the ambulance, he made a vow that it would never happen again. But even at that young age, he was quick to realize that making a promise and keeping it were two entirely different things. Not sure how to proceed, Lane turned to the strongest man he knew—his father.

"Dad, how do I learn to help people who can't take care of themselves?"

It was this question and the subsequent conversation that set Lane on his path to join the military, and even though he was way too young to enlist, his dad agreed to take him to all the local recruiter offices, where Lane asked each recruiter the same question: "Who are the toughest guys on the planet?"

He'd come home with a handful of brochures and spent the night reading up on the Army Rangers, Marine Recon, and Navy SEALs. To Lane's untrained eye, they all looked the same—each stoic-eyed warrior depicted on the cover looking just as fierce as the next. Still, as he'd pored over the brochures until the edges were tattered and the paper began to thin, it was the one the Air Force recruiter had handed him that held Lane's attention.

"That's a PJ, son," the recruiter had told him. "They're the ones the SEALs and the Rangers call when they need help."

The blare of a passing truck's horn pulled Lane back to the now. He shook free of the memory and, after tossing the now-empty Styrofoam container into the trash, climbed behind the wheel of the Jeep. He sat there, listening to the distant rush of traffic, wondering if he'd made a mistake leaving the Air Force.

It's a little late for that now, don't you think?

The doubt rushed unbidden into his mind, and Lane had the sudden urge to head back the way he'd come, tell Holland that he'd made a mistake, and take whatever job the man would offer.

No, dammit, he chastised himself. *There is no going back—only forward.*

And with that, Lane shoved the Jeep into gear and pulled out of the lot.

CHAPTER 7

Carson West stood at the window, looking out over the kill houses, rifle ranges, and off-white hangars that dotted Broadside Solutions' two-hundred-acre compound. Located in the heart of the Shenandoah Valley, two hours west of Washington, DC, Mount Jackson was a "blink and you missed it" kind of town. A sleepy four-mile stretch of rolling hills and unimproved pasture that made it the perfect spot for Broadside's stateside headquarters.

But as West was the vice president of operations, it wasn't the location as much as the shortage of qualified personnel to accomplish Broadside's very specific mission that currently had his attention. With that thought in mind, the former CIA case officer turned from the window and crossed back to the half-dozen personnel files lying open on his desk.

West looked down at the folders, scanning the DOD photos clipped inside. At one time the grim-faced warriors with their chests full of medals had been the best soldiers on the planet—highly trained operators who'd cut their teeth prosecuting the war on terror in far-flung hellholes most Americans couldn't find on a map.

But just like the careers of professional athletes, the men's lethal skill sets had a shelf life, and with most of them now pushing forty, what West *really* needed was fresh blood.

"Dammit."

Suddenly exhausted, he dropped into his chair and pulled off his readers. He rubbed his face and leaned back, his tired gaze sweeping across the plaques and certificates of appreciation that dotted the far wall before stopping on the framed photo that had been taken outside the CIA's tactical operations center in Iraq.

The genesis for what would one day become Broadside Solutions was the brainchild of retired CIA case officer Taran Carter, who'd spent time in Iraq helping stand up the country's counterhostage program. Before the US invasion in 2003, kidnapping for ransom had been almost unheard of in the Middle East, but that security evaporated with the fall of Saddam and the de-Ba'athification purge that followed.

In retrospect, the consequences of that fateful decision should have been obvious, but at the time the hawks back in DC were too busy patting each other on the backs to consider what would happen when everyone with any connection to the Hussein regime found themselves suddenly out of a job.

Having been part of Taran's mission in Iraq, West had helped try to sound the alarm, but with typical American hubris, the politicians had ignored them, and a year later what had once been a relatively stable country had fallen into chaos. And with no money to feed their families and no hopes for positions in the new Iraq, the ostracized officers of the former regime lashed out at their "saviors," killing them whenever they could.

But while most of these insurgents were only interested in revenge, a handful of enterprising men realized there was a profit to be made in the kidnap and ransom of the infidels flowing into their country.

By the time West and Carter were getting ready to leave, Baghdad had become as dangerous as Sinaloa, and with the insurgents on track to kidnap more people than the cartels, K&R insurance had become a must-have for anyone who planned to stay alive while doing business in Iraq.

For the big boys of the contracting world, companies like Dyn-Corp, KBR, and Washington Group International, multimillion-dollar kidnapping-and-ransom policies were nothing new. The only problem was that while the insurance company's negotiators were focused on getting the "asset" back for the *least* money, whatever project the hostage had overseen ground to a halt. With the larger companies losing millions of dollars a day in lost production, something had to change, but as most K&R policies lacked the teeth to do anything about it, they were stuck.

Enter Broadside Solutions.

Founded in 2012, Broadside came to market with the goal of giving at-risk companies the ability to take matters into their own hands. Their first offering was an evacuation policy—a low-risk operation in which if a client got into a dicey situation in a *permissive* environment, Broadside would send in a team to assist them in getting out of the country.

While the traditional K&R policies required a lengthy contract and monthly premiums, all Broadside needed from a prospective client was a reasonably priced, nonrefundable deposit in one of their Cayman accounts and the agreement that the rest of the funds would be paid if and when the company required their services. To some in the industry, this was an outrageous proposition, but to others it was like being able to buy flood insurance during the storm.

As West was the vice president of operations, it was his job to use his various government contacts to find the necessary equipment and manpower. It had been an uphill battle getting the first two teams operational, but eighteen months after opening the doors, Broadside had a full client list, and with West's bank account growing fat from the bonus checks that followed every successful mission, he wanted more.

"I've got an idea for another policy," he mentioned during one of the board meetings. "Something reserved for the companies with deep pockets."

"How deep?" one of the shareholders asked.

"Seven figures, minimum."

"And what would they be getting for that kind of money?" Taran questioned.

"An extraction policy," West said. "One that comes with the guarantee that no matter where they are in the world or what kind of trouble they are in, we will send a team of shooters to pull them out. No questions asked."

"Is that even legal?" another shareholder asked.

"Well, obviously we aren't going to break them out of jail," West laughed.

The room fell silent, and suddenly he was afraid that he might have shot for the moon. *Damn, did I go too big?*

Finally, a second shareholder cleared his throat. "It's a hell of an idea, but is it even possible?"

"I guess there's only one way to find out," Taran said.

Besides the manpower and equipment required to take West's idea from inception to execution, Broadside needed the technology that would allow them to track a client anywhere in the world, and while it hadn't been easy—or cheap—they'd managed to pull it off. But though both Broadside's client list and mission tempo had skyrocketed during the previous two years, and West was making more money than he'd ever dreamed of, qualified applicants—*especially* those with medical training—were becoming harder and harder to find.

And despite his friendship with Taran, West was beginning to feel the pressure.

"We've got companies who've been waiting years for a retrieval contract," the usually unflappable CEO had told West the last time they spoke. "Every time I go to a board meeting, all the shareholders want to talk about is how *your* inability to find the right people is costing us tens of millions of dollars a year."

"I'm trying," West had said.

"Well, you better try harder, because if you can't do your job, I'll find someone who can."

"I'll take care of it."

"You've got one month," Taran warned. "One month, and then it's out of my hands."

The beep of his desk phone followed by the cheery voice of his secretary through the speaker brought West back to the now.

"I'm sorry to disturb you, sir, but you've got a nine thirty with Mr. Carter."

"Yes, thank you, Shelly."

West stabbed the speaker button with his finger, grabbed the uncomfortably small stack of folders he'd set aside, and headed out the door. He stepped into the hall and followed it around the corner to Taran's office. Pausing outside, West adjusted his tie and took a breath to calm his nerves before knocking on the door.

"Come in," a gruff voice commanded.

West stepped inside and closed the door behind him before crossing to the massive oak desk that dominated the center of the room.

Taran looked up from his computer, his blue eyes unreadable as his gaze shifted from West's face to the folders in his hand. "Well, how many do you have?"

"I've got two candidates that I think will fill the open slots on the rescue teams," he said, placing the corresponding folders on the desk. "A couple of SEALs from Team—"

"Let me rephrase," Taran said, holding up his hand. "How many applicants do you have for the *extraction* team?"

"One, sir."

"One?" Taran repeated, his voice flat as he glared at West from behind his desk. "Last week you said we had five."

"Well, the SEAL we tested failed the psych exam, and the Green Beret can't sober up long enough to pass the run."

"What about the Rangers?"

"One failed the qualification course, and the other never showed up."

"How the hell does someone not show up considering the money we're offering?"

"I can't answer that."

"Fine. Tell me about this one candidate."

"He's an Air Force PJ," West said. "His name is TJ Owens. He's got the medical knowledge, plus multiple combat deployments. He's a combat diver, jumpmaster . . . you name it, he's got it."

"So can we get him?"

"Well, sir, I did some digging," West replied. "Turns out his wife's family has money problems. They've got a little shit box of a farm that's going into foreclosure, and I went ahead and took the liberty of—"

"How much?" Taran asked.

"One hundred and fifty thousand," West said.

Taran whistled. "You think he's worth it?"

"Compared to what else is out there, I think he's the *only* man for the job." West shrugged. "He's got the medical skills we need to get Guardian 7 back in the game."

"For that kind of money, we're going to need a contract," Taran said. "Something to make sure he doesn't cut and run after the first mission."

"I was thinking the same thing," West said, taking off his glasses.

"With the board breathing down my neck, I *need* you to make this happen," Taran said, leaning forward in his chair. "No mistakes."

"You can count on me."

"Good. I'll call the pilots and tell them to get the jet fueled up and ready to go."

"Already done," West said, getting to his feet. "I'll call you when I'm wheels down in Memphis."

CHAPTER 8

Washington, DC

Finished with her workout, Mia grabbed her bag and headed out to the street, the hollow rumble in her stomach reminding her that she hadn't had anything to eat since her layover in Germany. Knowing there was nothing in her fridge, she headed south on Blagden Alley, the morning breeze cool on the back of her neck.

It was a short walk to La Colombe, and when she arrived, she found an open table near the window. Mia sat down and ordered an egg white omelet and a glass of orange juice. Then, having nothing else to do, she retrieved the copy of the *Times* a previous diner had left on the adjoining table and scanned the front page.

Having grown up in the digital age, Mia couldn't remember the last time she'd read an actual newspaper. She'd always been good with computers, and that, combined with her keenly analytical mind, had made her perfect for investigations. It was a blessing and a curse. A gift that came without an off switch, so while most people would have been content to sit and enjoy the articles, Mia found herself dissecting each story as if it were a mystery waiting to be solved.

She'd made it halfway through the front page when the waiter was back with her breakfast.

"Can I get you anything else?" he asked after setting the plate on the table.

"No, thank you," she said. "This looks great."

Mia took her time, savoring each bite, then sat back to enjoy the scene around her: a couple having breakfast, parents and kids on the way to school. To the casual observer it was just another boring day in DC, but to someone who spent most of the year dodging bullets in third-world hot spots, boring was a nice change of pace.

The *ding* from the table caught her attention, and Mia reluctantly gave up on her people watching and picked up her phone. She typed in her passcode and, seeing that she had a new email, opened her inbox. A quick glance at the sender showed that it was from Angelo, but whatever relief she might have felt from seeing his name evaporated when Mia read the subject line.

Happy Birthday

If it had been her birthday and *if* the message had come from anyone else, Mia would have smiled and typed out a thankful reply. But it wasn't her birthday, and the seemingly innocuous words were their agreed-upon code to let the other know that they were in *serious* trouble.

Oh my God.

The breath caught in her chest, she opened the email, the world suddenly silent as she waited for the image to load. Her mind filled with the thousands of things that could have happened. *Is he hurt? Sick? In jail?* The thoughts ran rapid fire through her head, each one worse than the one before.

She cursed the slow internet connection while pleading with the image to download faster. *C'mon . . . C'mon . . . Please hurry.* Slowly the image buffered, the gray shade of the pixels clearing to reveal a cartoonish birthday cake with red balloons and four flickering candles.

The image caught her off guard. *What the hell is this? Where's the rest?* Forcing herself to breathe, Mia scrolled to the bottom of the page, searching for something, anything, to tell her what was going on—but there was nothing.

Unable to sit still, she dug her wallet from her gym bag and signaled for the waiter. "Can I get my check?"

"Just give me a sec to run this food to that table," the man said.

Mia moved to the register and opened her wallet, but instead of the cash, all she found in the divider was a stack of Kenyan shillings she'd forgotten to exchange at the airport. It was a simple oversight. One that would have barely registered under normal circumstances, but with the waiter still dawdling over the table of diners, Mia was rapidly losing patience.

"Fuck."

The word hit the family-friendly café like a bomb, and the dining room went quiet, the mother she'd been looking at earlier flashing her an angry look. Mia's face reddened, and she mumbled an apology before turning back to the register. She was about to pull out her credit card when she remembered the hundred-dollar bill she kept in her gym bag for this exact situation.

Dropping the bag on the counter, she reached into the tiny key pocket and pulled out the neatly folded bill. Mia slapped it down next to the tip jar and then, shouldering her bag, raced for the door. Outside the café, she slung her bag over her shoulder and broke into a run, heading south down the alley. She took her first right, hoping to cut through, but found her way blocked by the back side of the adjoining buildings.

Shit.

She headed back the way she'd come, her mind whirling as she tried to find a way out of the maze of trendy cafés and eclectic shops that made up the block. After a few more turns, Mia got her bearings and took off down the sidewalk. She could see her apartment building now and pushed herself into a sprint, pausing at the corner just long enough to hazard a glance at the oncoming traffic.

She saw the taxi coming, but instead of waiting, she dashed out in front of it. The driver stomped on the brakes, the squeal of tires on pavement and the angry blast of his horn following Mia down the block.

Fueled by adrenaline, she made the two-block run to her building in record time, and by the time the doorman got out of his chair, Mia was already to the elevators. She pushed the button and heard the distant rumble of the elevator as it began its descent, but unable to wait, Mia moved to the stairwell.

When she finally made it into her apartment, her legs were on fire, but she ignored the pain and threw the bag on the floor on her way to the computer. Mia typed in her password and brought up the email. The picture came up just as it had at the café, and she stared at it carefully, trying to make sense of what Angelo was telling her.

There has to be more. What am I not seeing?

Out of sheer desperation, she dragged the PNG image to her desktop and used the mouse to open the menu. She right-clicked on Get Info and examined the metadata on the screen, her eyes narrowing as she studied the size of the file.

It was big—twice the size of a normal file. *Why?* Then it hit her. *Shit, of course.*

Like most investigators, Angelo was a born skeptic, and to protect his sources and evidence from prying, he always used some sort of encryption when sending emails. One of his favorite methods was steganography: the art of hiding data within seemingly innocuous images. With that thought in mind, Mia opened her browser and, after a quick search, found an open-source PNG stripper.

Unlike the internet at the café, her Wi-Fi was lightning fast, and after downloading the program, she used it to open the file. For a moment there was nothing; then a second black-and-white image popped up on the screen. With the color stripped from the picture, Mia could now clearly see the hyperlink inside the middle balloon. She moved the cursor over the link with shaking hands and double-clicked the mouse.

The screen blinked, and she took a deep breath as the link redirected her to an encrypted file-hosting service that immediately asked for a password. On instinct she typed in her birthday and hit the Enter key. The screen blinked, and she was redirected to a second page with a single file folder.

She opened it and studied the photos inside, trying to make sense of what she was seeing. The first was a high-angle shot of a postage stamp of bare earth that had been hacked into the jungle, followed by pictures of a black star logo stenciled on the sides of camouflaged shipping containers. Then there were hoppers filled with what looked like gray rocks and photos of heavily armed white men with assault rifles and body armor standing guard over a line of emaciated natives working the mine.

Mia had been in the game long enough to recognize mercenaries when she saw them, but who were they, and what were they guarding? She zoomed in on one of the men, recognizing the shoulder patch with the red sky over the black mountains as the same one she'd seen on the Crimson Ridge mercs in Kenya.

Fingers shaking in anticipation, she clicked on the next picture and felt her heart skip a beat when she found herself looking at the last face she'd ever expected to see.

Gavin Roos.

CHAPTER 9

Collierville, Tennessee

By the time Lane arrived in Collierville, it was almost midnight, and the street was pitch black. Unlike the city, the unincorporated areas of Shelby County weren't required to provide streetlights, and even with the Jeep's headlights, the darkness was all-encompassing. Lane eased off the gas and squinted through the gloom, searching the tangle of kudzu that lined the roadway for a sign of the driveway to his boyhood home.

He missed it on the first pass and was forced to turn around and slow down even more, but he felt a small smile crack his lips when he finally saw the dented mailbox with the sun-faded address barely visible on the side. Not wanting to wake up Abby, Lane cut the lights and spun the wheel, the shocks creaking in protest as he started up the drive's incline.

After some coaxing and a lot more cursing, Lane managed to make the summit, and he was just starting down the other side when the moon finally slipped out from behind the clouds, its white light illuminating the entire spread in front of him.

Before leaving for the Air Force, Lane had spent almost every waking hour keeping up with the homestead. If he wasn't mowing the pasture or fixing the fences, then he was painting one of the outbuildings. Back then a person would have been hard pressed to find a better-looking parcel in the county, but as he stared down at it now, the sight of the overgrown pastures and sagging two-story farmhouse looming dark at the end of the drive caught him completely off guard.

What the hell?

He took his foot off the gas and let the Jeep's momentum carry it around the old pond where he'd first learned to swim and past the forlorn barn before he finally touched the brakes.

Lane was trying his best to be quiet, but the sudden flash of the porch light blazing to life told him that his mission had failed. He climbed out of the Jeep and grabbed his bag, the screen door slamming shut as he started toward the house.

He was almost there when a woman with long blond hair stepped out onto the porch, the flashlight in her hand blasting him full in the face. The sight of his sister in her nightgown made him realize that he should have called to let her know he was coming home.

"Travis—is that you?"

"Yeah, Abby, it's me," he said. "I didn't mean—"

But before he could finish his apology, she had run over and put her arms around his neck. "Oh my God, Travis . . . I'm so glad you're here," Abby said, burying her face in his chest.

Lane dropped his bag and held her tight, feeling her shoulders shaking against him. Not sure what to say, he held her close and simply let her cry.

Finally, she took a shaky breath and pushed herself away. "We need to talk."

"Yeah . . . let's go inside."

He grabbed his duffel and followed her up the creaky stairs and into the house, his boots echoing loud off the hardwood floor. She led him into the kitchen, and Lane could see the questions in his sister's eyes, but thankfully instead of asking them, she went to the fridge and pulled out two cans of Coors.

Abby tossed him one, and Lane took a seat at the table and cracked the top. He took a deep pull, the ice-cold beer exactly what he needed after the fourteen-hour drive.

"Man, that's good," he said.

His sister nodded and took a seat across from him. "If you'd called, I could have cleaned up a little bit," she said, hitting him with the frown his mother had always used when he tracked mud into the house.

"From the looks of the place, I'm not sure it would have mattered." Lane grinned.

"Hey, you're the one who wanted to keep this dump," she said, taking a sip.

"It's our home, Abby."

"Give me a break, Travis," she said, rolling her eyes. "Growing up, all you did was bitch about how much you hated this place."

"Things change," he said. "I've changed."

"If you're going to get all maudlin on me, I'm going to need something a *lot* stronger than beer," she replied, getting to her feet.

"Where are you going?" he asked.

"I think there's some of Dad's old whiskey in the den," she said, storming out.

Lane watched her go, a confused frown spreading across his face. He'd prepared himself for the tears and the guilt that he knew would follow TJ's death, but his sister's anger had caught him off guard.

What is she pissed about?

He wasn't sure, but knowing that Abby had never been one to hide her emotions, Lane was sure he'd find out when she returned with the booze. Draining the rest of his beer in a long gulp, he got to his feet and tossed the empty into the trash, his eyes drifting to the fridge and the picture of him and TJ standing on the front porch in their maroon berets and shined jump boots.

The picture sent him back to the day Abby had learned he was joining the Air Force.

"Travis, you're out of your mind," she'd exclaimed. "There's a war on. Are you trying to get yourself killed?"

He'd been expecting his father to say the same thing, but instead he'd been quick to take his son's side. "Abby, there's a whole other world outside of this one," he said, "and it's Travis's right to find out where he fits in it."

"Dad, that's the dumbest thing I've ever heard," Abby said.

"Well, if you think that's dumb, wait till you talk to your boyfriend," Lane said, smirking.

"TJ wouldn't do that." She glared. "Not without talking to me."

"Hey, don't shoot the messenger," he said, holding up his hands in mock surrender. "I had *nothing* to do with that."

"I'm going to kill him, and then I'm going to come back and kill you too," she snapped.

Now, the thought of TJ sent his heart sinking like a stone in his chest, and Lane tore himself away from the fridge, grabbed a pair of glasses from the kitchen cabinet, and carried them back to the table. He set them down, his eyes drifting to the stack of envelopes with *Last Notice* stamped on the front. He hadn't noticed them before.

What the hell?

He was reaching for the envelopes when Abby stepped into the room. "Please don't," she said. There was something in her voice that froze him in place, and he stopped, his fingers hovering inches from the top envelope. "What is this, Abby?" he asked.

"We can talk about that tomorrow," she promised. "But right now, can we just . . . sit and be grateful you're home."

He turned toward her, wanting to ask where all the money he and TJ had been sending had gone, but seeing the shimmer of tears at the corners of her eyes, Lane let it go. "Hey, you've been taking care of this place for years now. I trust you," he said quietly.

"With Dad sick and you gone, I really didn't have much of a choice," she said, pouring a generous amount of whiskey into the glasses.

"I'm sorry, Abby," he said. "I should have been here. I should have . . ."

"Tomorrow," she said, holding up her glass. "We can talk about *all* of that tomorrow."

CHAPTER 10

Collierville, Tennessee

Travis Lane woke up at eight, his head pounding from the bottle of booze he and Abby had finished the night before. He lay there, the house quiet around him as he summoned the strength to roll out of bed. With a groan, he got to his feet and eyed the pair of shorts and battered trail runners he'd laid out the night before.

"Yeah, that's not happening," he said, crossing to the bathroom.

While the cold shower wasn't nearly as beneficial as a run, it did the job, and with his mind beginning to clear, Lane pulled on a pair of faded work pants, a gray T-shirt, and his trusty hiking boots. Once dressed, he stepped out of his room, a glance across the hall showing Abby's door was still shut tight.

His sister had never been much of a drinker, but she'd made a valiant effort, and despite her promise of tomorrow, their conversation had inevitably ended up in the past.

"I never stopped loving him," she'd slurred. "Even after we separated and he started acting like an asshole, I still tried to help him."

"I know you did," Lane said, drinking straight from the bottle.

"What about you?"

It was the question he'd been wrestling with since their last mission. One that had followed him across an ocean and two continents, and despite the time he'd spent wrestling with the question, Lane's answer remained half-formed.

"The best way I can put it . . ." he began. Then he stopped and took another pull from the bottle. "Look, Abby, I don't—"

"Travis, I need to know," she said, leaning forward. "I need to know that you don't blame yourself for what happened . . . or blame *me* for asking you to do it."

"I don't blame you, Abby."

"What about TJ?"

"Let's just say I hated him for what he'd become but still loved him for who he'd been."

Maybe it was the booze or the answer, but Abby seemed placated, and their conversation soon veered back to the farm and his plans for the future.

"What are you going to do now?" she asked.

"Tomorrow I'll start trying to get this place back in shape," he said, getting to his feet, "but right now, I'm going to take a piss."

When he'd returned from the bathroom, he found Abby passed out in her chair, her half-empty glass sitting on the table next to her. Lane had finished her drink and then carried her up the stairs, not envying the hangover he knew would be waiting when she woke up.

Now, Lane eased past her door, wincing at the creak of the hardwood as he started down the stairs.

Thankfully a timer had ensured a fresh pot of coffee greeted him in the kitchen. Lane filled one of the stainless-steel travel cups to the brim, grabbed the keys for his father's old pickup from the hook near the door, and then headed outside. Even though the sun wasn't yet over the trees, it was hot, and with the humidity already at 80 percent, the air was thick and oppressive as he followed the gravel path to the barn.

Using the key on the ring, Lane unlocked the side door and stepped inside, the rush of stale air catching him off guard. He flipped on the lights, the blink of the fluorescent tubes showing his father's once-immaculate workbench covered in a thick layer of dust and cobwebs.

Adding a much-needed cleaning to the list of things he needed to

do, Lane crossed to the gun safe next to the chop saw, spun the combination into the dial, and pulled it open. Setting the coffee on top of the
safe, he pulled out his dad's old Colt 1911. Lane removed the pistol from
its leather holster and locked the slide to the rear. A quick check of the
chamber showed it free of rust, and he grabbed one of the loaded magazines from the shelf, slapped it into the pistol, and dropped the slide.

Closing and locking the safe behind him, Lane shoved the pistol
into his waistband, grabbed the coffee, and, now properly armed, left
the barn for the low carport where his dad's old Chevy pickup sat waiting beneath a paint-spattered drop cloth.

He pulled the cloth free, folded it up, and set it on the shelf before
unlocking the door and climbing behind the wheel. The dashboard lit up
when he turned the key, while the engine offered a halfhearted attempt
at turning over. Ignoring the caution lights, Lane patiently adjusted
the choke and feathered the gas until the big V-8 finally roared to life.

"That a girl."

Lane tugged the truck into gear and backed out of the carport, a
cloud of black exhaust spewing from the tailpipe. He turned the truck
around, the old farmhouse somehow managing to look even worse in
the daylight. Its rotted wood and sagging eaves were a cruel caricature
of its former self.

He guided the truck down the gravel drive and ran over the list of things
he needed from the hardware store on his way to the street. The interstate
was the fastest way to go, but Lane wasn't in a rush and instead guided the
truck through the patchwork of oak-lined back roads. Rolling down his
window, he savored the blow of the fresh honeysuckle into the cab.

Fifteen minutes later he pulled into the parking lot of the hardware
store and, after taking stock of his surroundings, climbed out and headed
toward the contractor's desk.

"What can I help you with?"

Lane pulled the list he'd made from the front pocket of his shirt
and handed it over.

"You got a truck?" the man asked.

"Yes sir."

"All right, give me ten minutes," he replied.

Fifteen minutes later, Lane helped the man load the last of the lumber into the bed of the truck. "I appreciate it," he said.

"No problem, let me know if you need anything else."

"Don't know if I can *afford* anything else," Lane muttered.

He waited for the man to step back inside before pulling away, the truck's dry-rotted belts squealing loud across the parking lot. Lane paused at the Stop sign and, after adding a tune-up to his growing to-do list, was about to pull onto the street when his phone buzzed to life. He pulled it from his pocket, surprised to see Abby's number on the caller ID.

"Didn't expect to be hearing from you already," he joked.

"Where are you?" she asked, her tone putting him instantly on guard.

"Just left the hardware store. Is everything OK?"

"No, you need to get home," she said, her voice tense.

"What's wrong?"

"There's a man at the door looking for TJ."

"What man?" Lane asked.

"His name is Carson West, and according to his business card he works for a company called Broadside Solutions."

"Lock the door and stay inside," he said, stomping down on the accelerator. "I'm on my way."

Lane ended the call and tossed the phone into the center console. He cut the wheel hard over, the lumber banging around in the bed when he pulled a U-turn in the middle of the street. He felt the back end come loose and the truck began to slide, but Lane expertly got it straightened out. Pressing hard on the gas, he blew through the intersection and raced south for the interstate.

By the time he hit the gravel drive, the blinking lights on the dash told him that he'd pushed too hard. However, it wasn't the truck but the man in the black suit sitting on the front porch that had Lane's attention.

He brought the truck to a sliding halt next to the dark-blue SUV parked near the house and slammed it into park. Not bothering to cut the engine, Lane leaped out, his hand dropping instinctively to the butt of the pistol. "Can I help you?" he asked.

"My name is Carson West, and I'm looking for TJ Owens," the man said. "You know him?"

"Yeah, he's my brother-in-law," Lane answered. "But he's not here."

"That's what your sister told me," West said, standing up and starting down the stairs. "Any idea where I can find him?"

"That depends on what you want."

West frowned at him, the rush of blood to his face telling Lane he was on the verge of losing his temper. "Look, slick, my business with TJ is exactly that: *my* business. So why don't you just tell me where he is, and I'll be out of your hair."

"He's dead," Lane said.

"Dead? What the hell are you talking about?" West demanded.

"He was killed on an operation in—"

"That's impossible." West cut him off. "I talked to him three days ago after wiring him money for the contract."

"What money?" Lane questioned.

"The money to keep this house from being foreclosed on," West said, pulling a sheet of paper from his pocket and handing it over.

Lane snatched the document out of his hand, a quick scan of the neatly typed text showing a $150,000 deposit into an escrow account at Patriot Bank.

"What is this?"

"A fucking waste of time," West said, brushing past him and heading to his SUV.

"Hold on," Lane said. "What's going to happen to the house?"

West stopped and turned, his face an angry mask. "Unless you've got some way to raise TJ from the dead, it will go into foreclosure at the end of the week. Now if you'll excuse me, I've got to catch a flight."

Lane stared at the man, his mind spinning as he tried to figure a way out of this situation. *Think, dammit.* But there was nothing more to do, and with West reaching for the door handle, he knew that he was running out of time.

"Wait, I'll do it," Lane blurted.

"Do what?" West asked.

"Whatever TJ signed up to do."

"You?" West sneered.

"I was a PJ too," Lane said, talking fast. "I was on the mission when he was killed, and before that I was with the 24th STS. Just give me a chance to make this right—that's all I'm asking."

West stared at him, his lips pursed in thought. "There's a tryout tomorrow morning. *If* you make it, we'll talk," he said.

"Fair enough," Lane said. "Just tell me when and where."

"I've got a plane waiting at Wilson Air. We are wheels up in an hour."

"Good thing I'm already packed," Lane said.

CHAPTER 11

Gavin Roos stepped out of the orange conex box that served as his quarters and crossed to the infirmary. The rain had stopped sometime during the night, and the sun hung low over the mountains, its light spreading slowly across the mine. Already Roos could feel the heat shimmering through the jungle, and by the time he reached his destination, he was beginning to sweat.

He stepped inside and moved to the heavy metal door where they stored the infirmary's drugs. "Open it," he told the nurse. "And don't give me any of that bullshit about *not* having the key."

The nurse stared at him, defiance burning hot in her brown eyes. Realizing she was about to deny him, Roos stepped close, his voice cold when he spoke. "You're not going to like what happens if you make me ask again."

The nurse took a step back, her face pale as she withdrew the ring of keys from her pocket. She fumbled to find the right key, her hands shaking as she unlocked the door. "There," she said, pushing it open. But before she could step out of the way, Roos shoved her inside.

"Naloxone. Do you have it?" he asked.

"Y-you mean Narcan?" she responded, her earlier fear shifting fast to confusion.

"That's right."

"But why do you—"

"Enough of the questions," Roos snapped, slapping his hand against one of the metal shelves. "Just draw it up!"

"Y-yes . . . yes . . . of course."

The nurse lifted a vial from one of the shelves and then retrieved a syringe. "How much?"

"All of it."

She filled and capped the syringe and then handed it to Roos, who started down the short hall and into the recovery room, where a blond mercenary was posted at the foot of Angelo's bed.

"How is our patient?" Roos asked.

The former Special Forces medic got to his feet, his eyes contemptuous as he looked down at Angelo. "He had a slight fever, but he's responded well to the antibiotics I gave him."

"What about the pain?"

"Dr. Lars has him on a morphine drip," Pieter said, nodding to the IV bag, "so if you were planning on talking to him, you're going to have to wait a bit."

"We'll see about that," Roos said, handing Pieter the syringe.

"What's this?"

"Narcan," he answered. "It's an opioid antagonist, the same thing the doctors in Cape Town use when a junkie shoots up too much smack. It will counteract the morphine and put Mr. Angelo in a more cooperative mood to talk."

"How long will it last?"

"Ask her," Roos replied, nodding to the nurse, who had followed him.

"Two milligrams will last thirty minutes."

Pieter nodded, and after stopping the morphine drip, he flushed the IV line with saline and then injected the two milligrams into the port.

"How long does it take to kick in?" Roos asked the nurse.

"Not long," she said.

Interrogation was a subtle art, one that required equal parts carrot and stick. Usually, Roos would spend days prepping the subject, working to gain his trust, before the questioning began. Unfortunately, time was not on his side, and with the date of the final shipment out of this godforsaken place drawing close, Roos needed answers and he needed them now.

Finally, Angelo began to stir, the placid expression he'd been wearing stretching first to a frown, then lengthening to a scowl as the pain came rushing back. He groaned and licked a dry tongue over equally dry lips.

"W-water . . ." he croaked.

The nurse moved to assist, but Roos brushed her out of the way and turned to the cup and pitcher of water sitting on the bedside table. He filled the cup and stepped back to the bed. "Drink," he said, positioning the straw in front of the man's lips.

At the sound of the mercenary's voice, Angelo's eyes snapped open, the blood draining from his face as he tried to get away. But the restraints around his ankles and wrists held him fast.

"W-what the h-hell is this?" he asked, his voice rough as sandpaper.

"It's water," Roos said.

"That's not what I meant . . . and you know it," he croaked.

"Do you want it or not?"

Angelo stared at him, the emotion in his eyes switching rapid fire from fear to helplessness and then, finally, to anger.

"Last chance," Roos said, shaking the cup.

For an instant it looked as if Angelo were going to refuse, but then the unquenchable thirst that came with the anesthesia took over, and he lifted his head, clamped his lips around the straw, and took a long sip.

Roos let him get a few swallows and then pulled the cup away. Angelo winced when he dropped his head back on the pillow. "How are you feeling?" Roos asked, fishing his cigarettes from his pocket.

"Like I got hit by a bus."

"That pain you are feeling is from the Narcan I gave you to counteract the morphine," he said, lighting the cigarette. "Unfortunately, it's only going to get worse."

"W-why would you do that?" Angelo asked.

"Because despite your best efforts, we were able to recover the contents of your laptop," Roos said, "and I've got some questions that you're going to answer."

"The hell I will."

"This is how it's going to work," Roos said, continuing as if Angelo hadn't spoken. "I am going to ask a question. If you answer with anything but the truth, Pieter is going to hurt you. Do you understand?"

On cue, the mercenary drew the skinning knife from its sheath at the small of his back and shifted closer to the bed. He pulled away the covers and in one smooth motion grabbed the hem of Angelo's hospital gown and sliced it down the middle, exposing the patchwork of sutures and bandages that covered the man's damaged torso.

"First question," Roos said, taking a deep drag and blowing the smoke into Angelo's face. "Who in the hell is Mia Webb?"

"I'm not telling you shit."

With a nod from his boss, Pieter grabbed a handful of bandages and began to squeeze.

Angelo reacted as if he'd been hit by a cattle prod. His back arched and his mouth stretched wide in a silent cry of torture. At first the only sound was the frantic beep of the blood pressure machine on the far wall, and then Angelo screamed, his voice ringing loud off the corrugated metal roof.

He tried to get away, but Pieter held him in place, his grip tightening until the first hints of blood were visible through the white cloth wrapped around his abdomen. Angelo writhed in pain. His bloodcurdling scream combined with the spike of his vitals on the monitor sent the nurse into a panic.

"I'm going to get Dr. Lars," she shouted as she ran from the room.

Roos ignored her and repeated his question. "Tell me who Mia Webb is, and the pain stops."

The man was tough, Roos had to give him that, but there was only so much a human could take, and as Pieter dug his fingers deeper into the wound, Roos knew the injured man would soon crack.

Angelo managed to hold out for another few seconds before the pain consumed him, and he screamed out the answer. "S-she's a nobody," he cried. "Just some girl I used to date."

It was a lie and a bad one at that. But it was to be expected.

"The bandage," he said to Pieter. "Rip it off."

Pieter did as he was told, and Roos stepped forward. "In your moment of need, you send an email to 'some girl' you used to date? I don't think so."

"It's the truth."

Roos nodded and puffed on the cigarette, waiting until the tip glowed an angry red before pulling it from his lips. He exhaled and then slowly lowered it toward Angelo's exposed abdomen.

"Is that your final answer?"

"Go to hell," Angelo said defiantly as fear flickered in his eyes.

Roos shrugged and slowly ground the cherry into the center of the wound, the hiss of burning flesh muted by Angelo's guttural moans. He was there, right on the verge of answering the question, but before he had a chance, the doctor came stomping into the room.

"Let him go before you kill him!" he shouted.

"Fuck off," Roos barked.

"For God's sake, look at his blood pressure. The man is about to stroke out."

Roos glanced at the monitor, but the flashing red lines on the screen told him nothing, so he turned to Pieter for confirmation. "Well?"

"He's right. I don't think his heart can take much more."

With Angelo fading, Roos switched tactics and turned the interrogation to the one answer he *needed* to know. "Who told you about the mine?"

"I . . . I don't know his name," Angelo gasped.

"Pieter."

"N-no, please," Angelo whimpered.

Roos stopped Pieter with a wave of his hand, his face softening as he leaned forward. "You want the pain to stop. All you have to do is answer the question."

"He never told me his name," Angelo gasped. "He reached out to me, said he worked for NorthStar."

"NorthStar?" Roos repeated.

"That's what he said."

"Where did you meet?"

"At the H-Hotel Cap Kivu," Angelo got out.

"And the man never gave you his name?"

"No . . . I . . . swear."

Roos studied the man's face, part of him believing that Angelo was telling the truth. *I've got to be sure.* "Pieter," he said.

Again, the man stepped toward the bed, and again his hand closed around another fresh bandage. He tightened his grip and dug his fingers into the wound, twisting and pulling until Angelo's face turned white and his breathing was little more than a short intake of air.

"Shut that machine off before I put a bullet in it," Roos yelled.

While the nurse rushed over to the heart rate monitor, he nodded to Pieter, who let go. The room went silent, the only sound Angelo's ragged breathing. Roos took a final drag from his cigarette, then crushed it out on the table, studying Angelo with a practiced eye. He was on the ropes, and one look at his wild eyes and sweat-soaked face told Roos that all it was going to take was one final nudge to send him tumbling over the edge. Still, the question remained: Which way would Angelo fall? Would he lie, or would he tell the truth?

Realizing there was only one way to find out, Roos leaned in close and spoke softly in the man's ear. "Tell me his name, and I'll make the pain stop—lie to me, and Pieter is going to start using his knife."

Angelo looked at him, a small spark of anger flaring in his eyes, and for an instant Roos thought he was going to hold out. But then Pieter stuck the tip of his knife beneath the neat line of sutures crisscrossing the man's abdomen and began to cut.

The puckered flesh opened like a crimson flower, and at the sight of the blood rushing from his abdomen, the American crumbled. "Winston," he screamed. "His name is Winston Sawyer."

The name hit like a bullet from a high-powered rifle, and Roos cursed himself for not seeing it sooner. *Sawyer. Of course it was Sawyer, you fucking idiot—who else knew about the mine?*

Digging his sat phone from his pocket, Roos was turning to leave when Angelo reached out and grabbed his hand. "T-the pain . . . you p-promised to make it stop."

"Of course," he said.

Roos stepped away and grabbed a pillow off the chair, then tossed it to Pieter. "Put him out of his misery."

The man caught it in the air and stepped forward.

"W-what are you doing?" Angelo asked.

"Keeping my word," Roos said, and then he was moving to the door, dialing the number he'd been given while Pieter pressed the pillow over the American's face. Roos waited at the door for Angelo to stop kicking and then stepped outside. He studied the number for a moment, hesitant to call his boss, but knowing he didn't have a choice, Roos hit the call button.

The phone rang twice before Jan Botha answered with a gruff "Yes?"

"Boss, we've got a problem."

CHAPTER 12

Washington, DC

An hour after leaving the café, Mia was driving south on Ninth Street, her hair still damp from the shower. Gone were her gym clothes, replaced by a charcoal-gray business suit that she wore buttoned to hide the Glock 19 holstered to her waist. She stopped at the light and glanced up at the rearview to check her makeup.

Finding everything in order, Mia turned her attention back to the road, tension creeping into her muscles at the sight of her destination at the end of the block.

Located at 935 Pennsylvania Avenue NW, the J. Edgar Hoover Building lorded over the block like the neighborhood bully. It was a massive structure, two million square feet of raw concrete and cold steel that evoked a shudder every time she saw it.

I hate this place.

Mia pulled into the parking garage and, ID in hand, stopped at the security checkpoint. She rolled down the window and handed it to the armed security contractor, who took it inside the guard shack while a second contractor produced a pole mirror and walked slowly around her car.

While the two guards went about their business, Mia turned her attention to the copy of the *Washington Post* sitting in the passenger seat. The instant she'd seen the picture of Roos, she'd known something bad had happened, but it wasn't until she'd googled Angelo's name and seen the grainy picture of the bullet-riddled Land Cruiser with the headline "UN Investigator Feared Dead in North Kivu" that her worst fears were confirmed.

The headline had hit her like a punch to the gut. Her first thought was that this had to be a mistake, that there was no way Angelo was dead, but if there was anything she'd learned during her time with the FBI, it was that there was no such thing as coincidence. Not having a subscription to the *Post*, she couldn't read the entire article. That had to wait until after she'd printed out the pictures and headed back downstairs, where she'd swiped the doorman's copy before heading to the garage.

She'd read the article twice when traffic was stalled, but the details were sparse, and the only real information she gleaned was that Angelo had been missing for almost twenty-four hours when a local farmer stumbled upon the Land Rover and a body inside. According to a government spokesman, they were still in "the preliminary stages of the investigation" and expected to know more soon.

But Mia knew that was a lie, because with the rebels controlling most of North Kivu, what was left of the government was holed up in Goma. Which meant there would be no investigation—no justice for Angelo—unless she could convince her boss to let her go to the DRC. Unfortunately, considering the botched raid in Kenya that had gotten her recalled in the first place, Mia knew the chances of that happening were extremely low.

Still, I've got to try.

Finally, the guard returned with her ID, and after the mirror man confirmed that her car was deemed to be free of any bombs or whatever the hell it was they were looking for, the gate was raised and Mia drove down the ramp.

Five minutes later she'd badged through security a second time and crossed to the bank of elevators on the far wall, her shoes clacking on the lobby's marble floor. She stepped inside the elevator, and the doors hissed closed, her heart racing as the car began its ascent.

Mia closed her eyes and began to think through all the possible scenarios awaiting her on the seventh floor. Would her boss listen to what she had to say? Or would he tell her to "sit down and shut the hell up" before reading her the riot act?

Either way, she wasn't looking forward to the meeting.

For someone used to being in control, the uncertainty was overwhelming, and despite her outward calm, on the inside Mia was freaking out. The panic attack came out of nowhere, the surge of adrenaline and her racing mind sending her heart rate through the roof. She was sweating now, and with the brass-inlaid walls of the elevator car closing in tight around her, Mia realized she was on the verge of losing control.

You've got to get a grip.

Fighting against the rising panic, Mia closed her eyes and worked on her breathing, forcing the tension from her muscles. It wasn't easy, but by the time the car settled and the doors slid open, she was back in control. Wiping the sweat from her forehead, Mia stepped out of the elevator a picture of confidence and strode toward the door at the end of the hall.

The blond woman sitting at the secretary's desk saw her coming and leaped to her feet. "Ms. Webb, he's not ready for you yet," she said. "If you'll have a seat, I will let him know that you're here."

"Don't bother," Mia said, continuing toward the door.

"Ms. Webb, please . . ."

But she was already knocking with her left hand, her right closing around the knob as she pushed the door open.

"Sorry to disturb you, Mike, but I've got something you need to see," Mia said, holding up the photos.

Usually such an abrupt entrance would have earned her a profanity-laced tirade from the gray-haired man behind the large oak desk, but this time Mike Duncan didn't even bother to look up from his computer.

"You're early, and I've got to finish this memo for State," he said. "So you're going to have to wait."

"I would," Mia said, crossing over to his desk and slapping the photos down in front of him, "but I think you'll want to see this."

Mike glared at her for a moment, then shook his head slightly and sat back, his eyes dropping to the glossy eight-by-tens before him. "You want to tell me what I'm looking at?" he growled.

"It's an illegal mining operation in the DRC," she replied. "See anyone you recognize?"

"Holy shit, is that . . . ?"

"Gavin Roos," Mia finished. "The same piece of shit I was after in Nairobi."

"The one you *missed* in Nairobi," he corrected her. "Which is why you are here in the States pending a formal investigation and *not* back in Africa doing your job."

"Mike, that's not fair," she said.

"Maybe not," he said, shrugging, "but unless there is something you aren't telling me, I will see you at eleven for your initial hearing."

"It's Angelo Garza," Mia blurted.

"The UN investigator you used to date?" he asked. "What about him?"

"He's the one who took the pictures," Mia said, pulling the copy of the *Post* from her bag and tossing it on top of his desk, "and they killed him for it."

Mike leaned forward to read the headline, and when he looked up, his eyes had softened. "Shit, I'm sorry, Mia."

"Yeah . . . me too," she replied.

"What makes you so sure that Roos had anything to do with this?"

"Because Angelo was one of my confidential sources in the DRC," she finally managed.

"Your source?" Mike demanded.

"That's right. He was helping me create a linkage between China and a handful of transnational criminal organizations known to be working in the region," Mia said. "Companies like Crimson Ridge."

"Besides the photos and Angelo's disappearance, do you have any actual proof that Roos is involved?"

"You mean besides the photos *and* the Interpol warrants issued by the Kenyan government?"

"It's thin," he said.

"An international fugitive kills a UN investigator at an illegal mining operation in the DRC, and you call that *thin*?" she asked. "You're kidding, right?"

"I want to nail Roos just as bad as you do," he snapped, "but after that shit you pulled in Kenya, my hands are tied."

"Please, Mike, just give me a few days," she begged. "Let me fly down to Goma, ask around, and I will get you the proof you need."

"It's not only the proof I'm worried about," he said, leaning forward. "It's your judgment. This one is personal, and I think it's affecting your decision making."

The words hit like a slap to the face, and Mia stepped back, her mouth open as she stared at her boss. During her time in International Operations, she'd developed a reputation as a levelheaded and methodical investigator, but it was her ability to stay emotionally detached from her cases that marked her as a rising star.

It was a trait she worked hard to cultivate, and while Mia knew some in the office considered her coldhearted, there was no arguing with her results. But this time it was different, and as much as Mia wished she could tell Mike he was off base, she knew he was right. However, that didn't mean she was going to give up without a fight.

"Mike, please . . . just give me a chance to make the case," she pleaded. "Grant me the authorization, and I will be on the next flight to the DRC. If there's nothing there, it's on me."

He ignored her as he tapped a finger on one of the photos. "What's this star spray-painted on the conex?"

"I don't know," she said.

"Hmm."

Mia was losing him, and her gaze dropped to the floor, her mind spinning for something—anything—that she could use to regain the momentum. *Think, dammit.* Feeling her boss's eyes on her, Mia looked up and braced herself for what she knew was to come.

"There's a guy I know at Quantico," Mike said. "A mining expert named Dr. Ben Greene who *might* be able to help you ID this spray-painted star."

"What about the hearing with IA?" she asked.

"I've banked a few favors with the guys in internal affairs and think I can get it pushed back," he said, flipping through his old-fashioned Rolodex and then scrawling a number on a piece of paper.

"How long?" she asked, taking the paper.

"Two, maybe three days," he replied. "So whatever you're going to do, you better do it fast."

Mia looked at him, not sure what to say. Coming into the meeting, she'd been confident her boss was going to throw the book at her. Relieve her of duty or at the very *least* park her behind a desk and let IA determine her fate, but instead, he was putting his neck on the line. Giving her a chance to find out what had happened to Angelo.

"Why are you doing this for me?" she asked.

"Because like it or not, Angelo was working for us when he got killed, and eventually that's going to come out," he said. "The only way to get ahead of it is by going after Roos, showing the world that the FBI will do whatever it takes to protect its sources."

She nodded. "I won't let you down," she said, turning to the door.

"Make sure you don't," Mike said, "because I can't guarantee you a second chance."

CHAPTER 13

Travis Lane ran through the woods that surrounded the Broadside obstacle course with a forty-pound rucksack strapped to his back. The trail doglegged hard to the right, and he followed it, thinking this *had* to be the end, but instead of the finish line, he found a twenty-foot tower with a brown cargo net hanging from the front.

He attacked the net, any form that he'd used at the beginning of the course gone as he clawed his way to the top. His muscles shook, and his breath fogged the Avon mask strapped to his face, but he kept climbing—eager to put an end to the pain-filled morning.

The tryouts had begun at 5:30 a.m. Lane had been waiting inside the sawdust pit where the PT test would take place when the rest of the candidates came filing in. There were five of them: two Marine Raiders, one bulky Ranger, and a lanky Green Beret who reeked of booze. They'd come swaggering into the pits, cocky despite the early hour.

Lane introduced himself and then moved to the low brick wall near the front of the pit. Taking a seat, he dug a roll of pink Kinesio tape from his pocket and went to work on his knee while the rest of the operators fell into the obligatory shit talking that came with their chosen profession.

As the only Air Force representative, he knew that he was their natural target, so he wasn't surprised when they began cracking jokes at his expense.

"Are you sure you're up for this, old man?" one of the Marines asked. "I mean, that's *a lot* of tape."

"Nice color too," his blond buddy chimed in. "I mean, where do you even find *pink* tape?"

"I got it from your mom's house," Lane said, affixing the last strip to his knee.

"You got jokes, huh," the Marine said. "We'll see who's laughing when this is all over."

"Just try to keep up, OK, Junior?" Lane said, getting to his feet.

The PT test was the same required for every military school the men had ever attended, and the push-ups, sit-ups, and two-mile run that followed were more of a warm-up than anything else. After tallying the scores, they ran to the range for pistol and rifle qualification, then took another one-mile jog to the pool.

By the time they arrived, the bulky Ranger and the hungover Green Beret were sucking wind. Lane, on the other hand, was feeling nice and relaxed when he slipped into the pool. The first iteration was a fifty-meter swim followed by thirty minutes of treading water.

Lane conserved his energy while scanning the faces of his competition. If there was anything he'd learned during the pipeline, it was that the water was the great equalizer, and by the time they were told to get out of the pool, the bulky Ranger and the hungover Green Beret had tapped out.

Now on the net, Lane was almost to the top when a sudden onslaught of wind came dancing through the clearing, the shake of the net threatening to send him tumbling to the ground. With his biceps nearing failure, all he could do was hold on and wait for it to blow itself out.

Grabbing ahold of the netting, he hazarded a look over his shoulder. From his position Lane had a clear view of the entire course, and he found himself searching for the shit-talking Marines. He scanned the trees, and not seeing them, he kicked a leg over the beam, grabbed the rope, and slid down to the ground.

Lane pushed himself into a run and continued down the path. He was hurting now, the lactic acid in his muscles burning hot, but at least his knee was holding up. With no sign of his competition, the temptation was to slow down. Catch his breath. But before he had a chance, he was out of the trees, the black pickup that marked the finish sitting a hundred yards to his front.

"Let's fucking go," shouted a bored-looking cadre leaning against the truck.

Lane thundered across the finish line and pulled off his gas mask. He took a greedy breath and dropped the ruck into the grass, thinking he was finally done, but the sadistic smile that spread across the cadre's face was quick to correct him.

"You ready?"

"F-for what?" Lane gasped.

"The Bad Dream?"

"I thought the obstacle course was the—"

"That was just to get your heart rate up. *This* is the actual event," the man said, nodding toward the squat metal structure to his rear.

At the sight of the kill house, the empty holster on Lane's waist and the mag pouches on his kit began to make sense.

"Technically it's a *team* event," the cadre continued, "so you can either wait to see who shows up or go at it alone. Either way, the time starts when you step inside."

"Yeah . . . well, I don't think they're coming."

"Then it looks like you're going solo." The man grinned. "Grab your gas mask and follow me."

Lane followed the man to the table a few yards away, the blue barrels of the Glock 21 and the M4 telling him that the weapons were set up to sims—the paint-filled bullets used for force-on-force training inside the kill house.

That explains the gas mask.

With the ease born of thousands of repetitions, Lane got the weapons locked and loaded, then stuffed the extra magazines and a trio of flash-bangs into their respective pouches. Once everything was in place, he pulled on his sweaty gas mask and grabbed the high-cut ballistic helmet with the pair of PVS-23 night vision goggles already attached.

"Any questions?" the cadre asked, handing him a set of headphones.

"Yeah, what's the course record?"

"How about you just worry about finishing."

"Fair enough," Lane said, pulling the headphones over his ears.

The cadre led him just inside the building and motioned for Lane to stand on the white *X* spray-painted on the floor. "Last chance to check your gear before the lights go out," he said over the radio. Lane nodded and flipped down his night vision goggles while the other man ascended the metal stairs that led to the catwalk overhead.

"Going hot," the kill house safety officer shouted.

A second voice confirmed the command, and then the house went dark and silent. But neither was to last, because a second later the opening guitar riff of Metallica's "Creeping Death" came blasting from the speakers mounted to the ceiling, the wall of noise followed by the frantic pulse of the strobe lights mounted to the wall.

Lane knew from experience that the music and the strobing lights weren't there for the ambience but to ramp up the pressure, make it harder for teams to communicate. But since he was going at it alone, it didn't matter.

Besides, he liked the song.

Bobbing his head in time with the beat, Lane turned to the cadre, who was staring at him from the corner. "Are we going to do this or what?" he shouted over the music.

"It's on you, tough guy," the man shouted back. "Time starts when you step off the *X*."

Then let's get this party started.

Lane shouldered his rifle and stepped through an open doorway into a short hall with an open door to his right and a wall to his front. The first room was a gimme, and from the threshold he easily picked off a single shooter hiding in the far corner. With the target down, he stepped inside, and after clearing the hard corner, he headed back to the door, pausing to put a final round into the center of the man's mask.

"Dick," the shooter said.

Lane smiled and inched his head out into the hall, careful to keep as much of his body as possible behind the doorjamb. It was the right call, because a second later there were muzzle flashes from the opposite room. He jerked his head back a second before a line of sim rounds came hissing past his face.

I've got something for your ass.

Stepping behind cover, Lane pulled a flash-bang from his kit with his left hand and yanked the pin free. Still holding the spoon, he stepped back to the doorway and sent a five-round burst snapping across the hall to force the other shooter away from the door. Then, without waiting, he stepped out and flipped the flash-bang into the opposite room.

Usually he would have stayed outside the room and waited for the bang to blow before entering, but caught out in the open with an unknown number of shooters hunting for his head, Lane had no choice but to crash the bang.

Looks like it's time to ride the lightning.

He stepped into the room just as the bang went off, the rolling thunder from the mix of potassium perchlorate and aluminum hitting him like a Mack truck. Punch-drunk from the concussion and half-blind from the flash, Lane staggered left and brought his rifle onto target. Blinking away the blurred vision, he thumbed the safety to fire and dropped the shooter in the corner with a sloppy double tap to the chest.

Good enough for government work.

With the threat neutralized, Lane moved to the door on the room's far side, pausing to shake the stars from his eyes before stepping into yet another hallway. Choking on the flash powder that stuck to the back of his throat, Lane conducted a quick mag change, wondering how many more threats remained.

The answer to his question came in the next room, when he stepped inside and immediately came under fire from two opposing corners. Still woozy from the flash-bang, Lane thumbed the selector to full auto and sprayed a burst toward the shooter on his right before diving behind the couch sitting in the center of the space.

He landed on his stomach, the beesting of pain in his right leg telling him that he'd been hit. Cursing under his breath, Lane snugged up to the back of the couch and listened to the pop of the sim rounds slapping against the fabric. With no target in sight, all he could do was stick the barrel of his rifle around the couch and hammer through the rest of the magazine, trying to keep the shooters from maneuvering into position to take him out.

A muffled yelp told him that he'd hit one of the men, and Lane was working on an exit plan when he heard the safety officer yelling at him from the catwalk.

"Candidate, this is a real-world exercise."

"What the hell does that mean?"

"It means that if you don't treat that bullet to the leg in the next thirty seconds, you are out."

"Are you serious?"

"Now you've got twenty-five seconds until you bleed out."

Lane's first thought was that the Broadside safety officer was simply serious about realistic training, and he dutifully yanked a tourniquet from the front of his kit. He was wrapping it around his thigh when a voice came booming down the hall.

"Where is he?"

"I've got him pinned down in room four," the shooter on the other side of the couch yelled.

In an instant Lane realized that the tourniquet had nothing to do with training and everything to do with letting the enemy catch him in a crossfire. "This is bullshit," he shouted at the man on the catwalk.

"Hey, that's combat." The man shrugged.

"OK, if that's how you want to play it."

Lane tugged the tourniquet tight and dropped the half-empty magazine, a hint of a plan forming in his mind. He shoved a fresh magazine home and, rifle reloaded, tugged another flash-bang from his kit.

Sure hope this works.

He pulled the pin and flipped the bang over the couch, hearing the "oh shit" from the shooter as the bang skittered across the floor and detonated.

With the couch shielding him from the blast, all Lane got was a slight tickle in his throat. He leaped to his feet and engaged the stumbling shooter with a double tap to the face shield, then moved to the door and looked up at the cadre glaring down at him from the catwalk.

"Hey," he shouted. "If you want me to keep killing your guys, I'm going to need some more ammo."

Then he was moving into the hall.

CHAPTER 14

Mako Jones stepped into his office, his knees still hurting from the three-mile run he'd gone on before work. He dropped into the chair and was reaching for the bottle of tramadol he kept in his top drawer when Jake Hunter, the assistant team leader for Guardian 7, stuck his head in.

"Looking a little rough this morning, Chief."

"Yeah, might have overdone the run."

"Man, getting old is a bitch."

As one of the first operators to be recruited by Broadside Solutions back in 2012, Mako Jones was not only the most experienced team leader; he was also the oldest. And while his mind still told him that he could out-PT anyone in the room, his body disagreed, and six months after his second knee replacement, Jones knew it was about time to hang up his spikes.

For a man who'd spent the last thirty years kicking in doors and cracking skulls, the understanding that this was his last rotation as Broadside's senior team leader had been a hard pill to swallow.

"What are you, thirty-six?" Jones asked.

"Thirty-five next month." Hunter grinned.

"That's what I thought," Jones scoffed. "Come talk to me when you hit forty-six."

"Damn, Chief, I didn't know you were that old."

"Is there something you wanted?" Jones demanded. "Or are you just trying to piss me off?"

"My bad," Hunter said. "One of the guys from the range called wondering why you aren't at the tryout."

"Tryout?" Jones asked, his eyes shifting to the calendar on the wall. "We don't have any tryouts scheduled this month."

"Well, according to the guys at the range, we do."

"They say who authorized it?" Jones asked.

"You know what? Maybe it's best if we just forget I said anything," Hunter replied, taking a step back.

"If you know something, you'd better spit it out," Jones growled.

"It was West . . ."

At the mention of the man's name, Jones forgot all about his aching knees and leaped to his feet, snatching his keys off the desk. "That son of a bitch," he said, turning for the door.

"Take it easy, Chief," Hunter said, moving to block his path. "I'm sure there's a reason he didn't mention it."

As the head of recruitment, West's job was to make sure each team had the required bodies to remain operational, and since Jones's team was currently short, the only reason West *wouldn't* want him at the tryout was if there was a problem with the candidate.

Not on my watch.

Jones stomped out of the team room and climbed into his truck. He started the engine and threw the vehicle into gear, tires squealing off the asphalt when he stomped the gas. Out of all the Broadside employees, no one could get under Jones's skin faster than Carson West. The man was a dilettante. A narcissistic pain in the ass who cared more about the company's stock price than about the safety of its operators.

Jones parked his truck in front of the kill house and climbed out, taking a breath to calm his rising irritation before heading for the stairs to the control room. Inside he found West standing in front of one of the monitors, the look of surprise on his face when Jones walked in telling him everything he needed to know.

"Sorry I'm late."

"Mako . . . I, uh . . . wasn't expecting to see you here."

"This guy's going to be on my team, right?" he asked. "Why *wouldn't* I be here?"

"Yeah, of course," West said, quick to regain his composure.

"So, who is he?"

"His name is Travis Lane," West said, turning back to the monitor. "He's a former PJ with the 24th."

"The grinder is coming up," the tech said. "Twenty bucks he gets smoked in the first room."

"A hundred says he makes it through on the first pass," West said, digging a wad of cash from his pocket. "What do you say, Jones?"

The "grinder" was the culmination of the kill house, a lose-lose scenario designed to push the trainee to their limits, and Jones had never seen anyone make it through on the first pass. "I'll take your money," he said, tugging his wallet from his back pocket and slapping a hundred-dollar bill on the table.

"Anyone else?" West asked.

The two techs added their cash to the pile, and then all eyes turned to the large monitor just as Lane entered the room.

"Here we go," West said.

Lane was in trouble the minute he stepped inside, and Jones thought it was game over the moment he began taking fire from both role-players. But somehow, he made it to cover behind the couch.

"Looks like he took a sim round to the leg," the tech said.

"Advise the candidate that he will expire from the wound if not treated," Jones said.

The man behind the keyboard did as he was told, and while Lane worked to apply a tourniquet to the simulated wound, the tech looked to Jones for additional guidance. "Anything else?"

"Yeah, respawn all the role-players and have them converge on the grinder."

"That's bullshit," West said.

"Sink or swim." Jones shrugged.

Silence fell over the room, and they watched as Lane locked down the tourniquet and got back into the fight by stripping another flash-bang off his kit. He jerked the pin free and flipped it over the couch. The flash of the explosion whited out the camera, and by the time the feed came back, Lane was standing at the door, jawing at the safety officer on the catwalk.

A moment later he stepped out into the hall, rifle flashing as he emptied the rest of the magazine into the two role-players running toward him, and then, without missing a beat, dropped the empty rifle to the ground and ripped the Glock 17 from its holster.

In one smooth motion, he brought the pistol up and leveled it at the final target. He pulled the trigger, and the pistol bucked in his hand, the single shot hitting the man in the center of the face mask.

And then it was over.

"Holy shit . . ." the man at the keyboard said. "Did you just see that?"

"He got lucky," Jones said.

"Lucky my ass," West replied, scooping the cash from the table. "The kid's an animal. Hell, if you sign off on him, I bet the boss would bump him right to a retrieval team."

"That's not the way things work around here."

"No, that's not the way they *used* to work," West snapped back. "Times are changing, which means you are going to have to adapt or retire."

"We'll see what Taran has to say about that."

"Be reasonable, man," West pleaded. "If you sign off on this kid, we can get your team back in the fight. Do you have any idea how valuable that would be to the company?"

"I'm the one who decides who's ready, not you," Jones snapped before turning to the man at the computer. "I'm going back to my office. Get the wonder boy cleaned up and then send him to see me."

———

Carson West walked out of the kill house and was heading to his car when he got a call on his encrypted cell phone. Considering that only one man had this number, he knew ignoring it wasn't an option. He climbed inside his vehicle, started the engine, and put the car into drive before answering.

"Hello?"

"It took you long enough, didn't it, Carson?"

The voice on the other end of the line put him instantly on edge. "I'm sorry, Mr. Sterling. I was . . ."

"I don't care what you were doing," the man said. "I've got a problem. Correction—*we* have a problem."

"A problem?" he asked. "What kind of a problem?"

"There was a security breach at the mine in Ubili," Sterling said. "I won't bore you with the gory details, but an email was sent to a woman named Mia Webb, and I need you to find out who she is."

"That shouldn't be a problem," West said. "What kind of email account are we talking about?"

"It's a UN account, one belonging to the late Angelo Garza."

Ah shit.

"Are you there?"

"Mr. Sterling, I thought I was very clear the last time we talked about—"

"Carson, did I ask you to speak?"

"No sir . . . you, uh . . ."

"Then shut the fuck up and listen, or I will let your boss know about all the naughty things you've been helping me get away with," Sterling instructed. "Starting with that mess in Mexico you helped me clean up. I wonder what that sanctimonious prick and the rest of those knuckle draggers you work with would think about that?"

The reminder of that disaster made West feel ill. Sweating now, he tried to keep his attention on the road as the memories of that bloody day spread across his mind like spilled ink.

According to the original intel Sterling had sent him, the mission to Mexico was a routine extraction, and all that was required was a team of operatives driving to a secure location, picking up the asset, and then hauling ass back to the airfield.

A piece of cake.

In fact, after reading the intel packet, West's biggest concern had been how he was going to retask the team required to pick up Sterling's men without Taran Carter noticing. But that problem seemed to solve itself when the boss was called away to DC to help determine whether Broadside could assist US forces with the impending withdrawal from Afghanistan.

Sensing that his luck had finally changed, West did what any gambler would do. He went all in.

With the boss gone and West now the de facto head of operations, it had been easy enough to spoof the tracking signal and dispatch Guardian 7 to retrieve the package. Unfortunately, instead of the secluded stretch of Sonoran desertscape Sterling had promised, the team was forced to extract the package from a cartel hideout.

In the ensuing gunfight, two of Jones's men were hit, and by the time the team returned home, the two men were dead. That they'd managed to get back over the border was a testament to Jones's leadership, but on returning to Broadside's compound, the former SEAL had lost his mind.

Before joining the CIA, West had served as a Marine infantry officer in the Al Anbar province and, as such, had seen some shit. Had his fair share of close calls. Still, none of the death or violence he'd seen on the streets of Ramadi had prepared him for the moment when Jones burst into the TOC.

All it took was one look in the man's eyes and a glance at his gore-spattered kit to know he was out for blood. West had tried to run, but before he could move, Jones grabbed him, and in the next instant West was on the ground, a pistol reeking of gun smoke pressed to his forehead.

"What the fuck did you do?" Jones snarled.

In the end West had managed to talk his way out of it, blame the entire fiasco on a recent server upgrade that had scrambled the tracking codes, but the memory sent his guts twisting into knots. Tasting the bile at the back of his throat and realizing he was about to vomit, West pulled over and slammed the car into park. He was fumbling with his seat belt when Sterling's voice came snapping over the line.

"Carson, are you listening to me?"

"Y-yes . . . Mr. Sterling," he said, throwing open the door. "I-I'll look into this Mia Webb and let you know what I find out."

"Good," Sterling said, ending the call just before West leaned over and puked on the side of the expressway.

CHAPTER 15

Mia Webb guided the government-issued Impala south on I-395, the snarling mess of flashing brake lights and angry honks that was DC traffic causing her blood pressure to rise. A glance at the clock on the dash showed that she was dangerously close to missing her appointment with Dr. Ben Greene.

The hell with this.

Spinning the wheel to the right, Mia reached down, flipped the switch that activated the car's blue lights, and nosed the Impala into the next lane. Ignoring the angry glare from the driver of the delivery van she'd just cut off, Mia bumped the siren to stop traffic.

When a hole finally opened, she stomped on the gas, the Impala lunging through the gap, its tires vibrating from the drunk bumps that protected the emergency lane. Glad that the Agency's cars had yet to be equipped with dash cameras, she raced past the stalled traffic, engine spooling up as she sped across the Potomac.

Once on the other side, Mia cut her lights but kept her foot on the gas until the endless sprawl of the cityscape was a distant graphite smudge in her rearview. As she drove south, her mood began to change with the landscape, the rolling hills and dense oaks that marked Virginia countryside somehow calming her as she drove toward Quantico.

Mia kept up her speed, but by the time she'd made it through the security gate and found a parking spot outside the FBI Academy, she was fifteen minutes late for her thirty-minute meeting.

Slamming the car door behind her, she jogged up the steps and beneath the long portico that led to the main entrance. Where FBI Headquarters was dull and drab, the interior of the academy was bright and open, the sunlight filtering in through the high windows giving it a natural warmth. Squinting against the glare, Mia followed the signage to the second floor and, after spending the next few minutes wandering the warren of classrooms and offices, finally found the room number she'd been given over the phone.

Mia knocked, and a moment later the door swung open and a gray-haired man with thick black glasses stepped into view. "Dr. Greene?" she asked.

"You must be Mia," he said, extending a hand. "I wasn't sure if you were going to show up."

"Traffic." She shrugged.

"Yeah, they are always tearing up something," he said, motioning her to a chair in front of his cluttered desk. "In fact, I was surprised you didn't want to set up a Zoom call instead of making that drive. You were a bit circumspect on the phone as to the reason for this meeting."

"I like doing things face-to-face," she said, pulling the photos she'd brought with her out of her bag and setting them on the table. "Since I'm late, I'll get right to it. These are from an illegal mining operation in the DRC," she continued. "My boss said you might be able to identify the symbol spray-painted on that conex."

"It's not a symbol," he replied. "It's a logo."

"A logo?" Mia asked. "Why would an illegal mining company tag their equipment with their own logo? I mean, isn't that a good way to get caught?"

"Well, yes, but NorthStar isn't a mining company. They're prospectors."

"Meaning what?"

"They're prospectors, or exploration geologists, as they prefer to be called," Greene explained, leaning back in his chair. "You see, most of these big mining corporations have shareholders, and before they agree to start shelling out millions of dollars to bring in the equipment and personnel required to set up a mine, they want to make damn sure there is something there worth mining."

"And that's what a prospector does? Goes in and determines whether a mine will be productive or not?"

"That's right," Greene replied. "There are two basic types of mineral exploration: a brownfield and a greenfield project."

"What's the difference?"

"A brownfield exploration is when a company sends their geologists to one of their existing mines to look for any additional deposits. On the other side of the house, you've got the greenfield guys, crazy bastards like Winston Sawyer who actually go out and explore, looking for brand-new mines."

"And Winston Sawyer is . . . ?"

"The owner and chief exploration geologist of NorthStar," Greene said, looking at her like she was slow.

"So Sawyer is the one who found this mine?" Mia clarified.

"Well, that's his logo in all these photos, isn't it?" Greene asked.

The revelation that she'd finally found a tangible connection to Roos hit Mia like a ton of bricks, and she sat there, mouth open, her heart hammering loud in her ears. "Please tell me that you know him," she begged.

"Winston? Oh yeah, we're old friends. Though truth be told, I haven't seen him much since he took the job in Africa."

"Is there any way you could put me in touch with Mr. Sawyer?" she asked, digging a card from her bag and handing it over. "He could call or email—"

"I doubt that."

"Why not?"

"Well, Sawyer's become a bit paranoid since moving to Kinshasa," Greene said, taking the card. "Especially when it comes to meeting people he doesn't know."

"But you could talk to him," she said. "Vouch for me."

"I just met you, Agent Webb," Greene said, leaning back in his chair, "and unlike you and me, Sawyer is a civilian, so unless you want to tell me what this is all about, this is as far as I am willing to go."

If this had been an active investigation, Mia would have simply told the man that Sawyer was part of an ongoing investigation. Unfortunately, there was no investigation, and with Greene and her boss being old friends, Mia couldn't risk lying to the man and having it come back to bite her.

"Well, Ms. Webb?" he asked.

Realizing that she was going to have to tell him something or risk losing any chance of meeting with the only person who might know what had happened to Angelo, she took a deep breath.

"A friend of mine was in the DRC investigating an illegal mining oper-ation," Mia said. "Those pictures were taken before he was killed, and I—"

"And you think *Sawyer* had something to do with it?" Greene asked. "No way, not in a million years."

"No . . . I mean . . . I don't know," Mia replied. "Those pictures are all I have, and I'm just hoping that Sawyer could point me in the right direction so I can figure out what did happen."

He studied her for a moment, then leaned forward and looked down at the pictures. "Sawyer's a good man."

"I'm not denying that, but that *is* his logo in the picture," she said, leaning forward as well and tapping the photo on the desk.

"That doesn't prove anything," Greene replied.

"You're right, it doesn't," Mia agreed. "But it does indicate that Win-ston Sawyer has been there, and that makes him the only lead I've got."

For a split second, she thought Greene was going to refuse her, tell her to get the hell out of his office, but finally he nodded, his face soft-ening when he sat back in his chair.

"OK, I'll help you," he said. "On one condition."

Mia breathed out a sigh of relief and felt the tension flow from her body. "Name it."

"You fly out to Kinshasa and bring him back."

"Wait . . . what?" Mia asked.

"Like I said before, Sawyer's a good man, but he's obviously gotten himself mixed up in something that is way over his head. So if you want to find out who killed your friend, you are going to have to save mine."

"Dr. Greene, I can't just fly to Kinshasa and—"

"Mike said you were one of his smartest agents," Greene said. "I'm sure you'll figure something out."

Realizing she had no choice but to agree to the man's terms, Mia nodded her head and said, "OK. I'll go to Kinshasa and bring Sawyer back to the States, *but* this is a time-sensitive operation."

"Meaning what?" Greene asked.

"Meaning I've got seventy-two hours to make this happen, which leaves me *zero* time for Sawyer's cloak-and-dagger crap," she said. "If you want me to get him out, I need you to call him right now and set up the meet."

"And if I can't reach him?"

"Then it looks like we are both shit out of luck."

It was a bluff, and for an instant Mia thought Greene was going to call her on it, but to her surprise he nodded.

"Fine, I will give him a call and let him know that you want to meet in the next twenty-four hours. I'll text you the details when I have them."

"Thank you," she said.

Ten minutes later, Mia was sitting in her car, fingers flying as she typed out a quick text to her boss.

I need a flight to Kinshasa ASAP.

While she waited for Mike to reply, she began checking for commercial flights from DC to Kinshasa. Not only were the fares outrageously overpriced, but they wouldn't get her to the DRC in time to make the meeting she'd requested with Sawyer.

Discouraged, she placed her phone onto the center console and started the engine, her mind whirring through the available options.

What the hell am I going to do?

Then it hit her.

Mia reached for her phone and dialed the FBI booking office.

"This is Selena," an upbeat voice answered.

"Hey, it's Mia Webb. Looks like I'm going to need to book another flight."

"Already?" the woman laughed. "Wow, they really are trying to work you to death."

"Tell me about it," she replied.

"Where to this time?"

"The Democratic Republic of the Congo," Mia answered.

There was a pause followed by the clatter of keys, and then Selena's voice came back over the line. "Well, you must be living right, because it looks like the Gulfstream you used on the last flight is still on the ground at Andrews."

"How soon can they fly?"

"All I need to put them on standby is a copy of your travel orders," Selena said. "You want to fax those over?"

The silence seemed to stretch forever as Mia sat there, the implications of what she was about to do hanging like a sword over her head. She closed her eyes, and the photos from the email and the grainy picture of Angelo's shot-to-shit Land Cruiser blasted rapid fire through her mind.

If I don't do it, then who will?

"Ms. Webb, did I lose you?"

Finally, Mia found her voice. "Sorry, I'm in the car. Must have hit a dead zone."

"That's perfectly all right," Selena said.

"Go ahead and get the crew ready to go," Mia said. "I've got Mike's verbal authorization for the travel."

While it wasn't a lie, she was stretching the truth and prayed that her boss had meant what he'd said about giving her three days to handle the problem.

"Works for me. Is there anything else I can do?"

"No, Selena, I appreciate it," she said.

Mia ended the call and pulled out of the parking lot, the realization of what she'd just done leaving her mouth bone dry. By booking that flight, she had broken half a dozen FBI rules, any one of them grounds enough to get her fired. But with Sawyer being her only link to Roos and whoever else had killed Angelo, all Mia could do was pray that Mike had her back.

CHAPTER 16

The Crimson Ridge Bell 222 settled on the mine's helo pad, the downdraft from its rotors sending a cloud of dirt and superheated exhaust typhooning across the clearing. Standing off to the side, Gavin Roos clamped a hand over his grubby bush hat to keep it from being blown off his head, the bandana pulled over his nose doing little to protect him from the bits of gravel that pelted his exposed skin.

Roos waited, expecting the pilot to cut the engine, but instead, the cabin door swung open and a rangy man in an immaculately tailored suit stepped out. Seemingly ignorant of the swirling dust, he paused to button his jacket and then started toward Roos.

"Good to see ya," the man shouted.

"Wish I could say the same, Tommy," Roos shouted back.

"Don't shoot the messenger, mate."

"What's all this?" Roos asked, nodding to the helo.

"The boss wants a word."

"He could have called," Roos said.

"Not his style," Tommy said with a mirthless grin.

Roos nodded and started for the helo, but Tommy was quick to step in front of him. "Sorry, mate, but I'm going to need your burner."

"You've got to be kidding me."

"Afraid not," he said, standing his ground.

Roos spit into the dirt and then dutifully drew his Browning Hi-Power, dropped the magazine, and ejected the round from the chamber. "Anything else?" he asked, slapping them all into the man's outstretched hand.

"Yeah—a bit of advice from an old friend."

"Just because we were in the same regiment doesn't make us friends," Roos growled.

"Either way, do yourself a favor and try not to act like a fucking hard case," Tommy said. "Do that, and there's a good chance the boss won't make me throw your ass from the helo."

"That bad?" Roos asked.

"Let's just say that he wants a pound of flesh to replace the one Mr. Sterling took from his ass this morning."

He nodded, his stomach twisting into knots as he followed Tommy to the helicopter and climbed inside. Pulling the door closed, Roos grabbed the pair of headphones that hung from a hook over his leather seat. He placed them over his ears, the thick pads muting the whine of the turbine as the pilot shoved the throttle forward.

The helo leaped skyward, and Roos turned his attention to the well-dressed man sitting across from him. "Good morning, sir."

Jan Botha stared back, his index finger tapping ominously on the neatly folded paper in his lap. "Mr. Sterling gave you explicit instructions when you took over the mine, did he not?"

"Yes sir, he did."

"And what were they?"

"Keep the shipments on schedule and—"

"And keep his name out of the bloody papers!" he snarled.

At fifty-seven, Botha wasn't the young man he'd been when he first came to work for Crimson Ridge, but despite the gray around his temples and the hint of a paunch beneath his Savile Row waistcoat, he was anything but soft. And one look into the man's soulless black eyes told Roos that Botha wouldn't hesitate to kill him.

"Yes sir, that is what he said."

"But did you listen? Of course not, because *if* you had, *this* would have never made it to the *New York Times*," Botha said, throwing the paper at him.

Roos resisted the urge to catch it out of the air and instead let it hit him in the chest, his face expressionless when he flipped it over and saw the picture of the shot-up Land Cruiser on the cover. "I don't see how this is a problem," he said. "The papers are already blaming it on the rebels."

"Just how long do you think that is going to last?"

"Sir, this is the Congo. Nobody gives a shit what happens here," Roos answered. "Besides, I have the situation under control."

"Tell me."

"I brought in another crew of workers, and in forty-eight hours the remainder of the coltan will be on its way across the border," he said. "I've also sent Pieter and a few of the lads to Kinshasa to deal with that rat Sawyer."

"I knew it was a mistake to trust him," Botha said. "The man was just too clean."

"Pieter will take care of him and then—"

"Mr. Sterling wants him alive."

"Alive?" Roos asked. "Why the bloody hell would he want that?"

"Because if he talked to anyone else besides Angelo Garza, the boss needs to know."

"Then we'll take him alive," Roos conceded.

Botha was silent, his eyes drifting to the window as he digested the information. Finally, he nodded and turned back to face Roos. "I will let Mr. Sterling know that you have the situation under control. But until the job is done, I am going to send Tommy and another team to back you up."

"Tommy, sir?" Roos asked. "No offense, but he's a bit too pretty to be out sweating in the bush."

"You let me worry about that," Botha said. "Now, is there anything else?"

"The email Angelo sent," Roos said. "I still haven't received any information from Sterling's source in the States and was hoping you might give him a nudge."

"I haven't gotten this far in life by 'nudging' men like Alexander Sterling. *Especially* when they've already got their dander up."

"I understand that, sir, but it's critical that we know who Angelo sent the email to."

"Fine, I'll ask," Botha said. "But this is the last time I go to bat for you."

"I understand, sir."

"I'm serious, Roos," he said, his voice growing cold. "No more mistakes. If you screw up again, you're a dead man."

CHAPTER 17

A freshly showered and dressed Travis Lane stood in the gallery looking down on Broadside's operations center. The platoon of analysts hunched behind their workstations and the floor-to-ceiling monitor that encompassed the far wall reminded him of something from a Jason Bourne movie.

"So . . . uh . . . what *exactly* do you guys do here?" he asked.

"Officially, Broadside Solutions is a private security company that offers evacuation and retrieval services for individuals who operate in high-risk environments," Jones said.

"What does that mean in English?"

"It means that if you're rich and get into trouble in a foreign country, we will help you get out. If you're stupid rich, we will send in a team of pipe hitters to come and literally *take* you out."

"And you do that how?" Lane asked.

"With one of these," Jones said, picking up a black cylinder with a tapered nose and a red button on the end from the desk in front of him.

"What is that, an EpiPen?" Lane asked.

"Yeah, but instead of epinephrine it has a subdermal transponder that goes live once it's injected into the skin."

"And then what happens?"

"The satellite picks up the signal and sends it back to one of the tracking computers," Jones said, pointing to the bank of refrigerator-sized processors lining the far wall. "Once we have a lock, the battle captain launches the standby team."

"How long does an operation last?"

"Depending on the location, twelve hours from alert to pickup."

"No shit?" Lane said. "And how much does that cost?"

"About five million dollars."

Lane whistled.

"But I'm putting the cart before the horse, because new guys have to spend at *least* six months on the evac side of the house before going to an extraction team."

"Funny, that's not what Carson West said."

"Listen, man, West is just a businessman, and his job is to get guys on the team."

"And what's your job?" Lane asked.

"My job is to get the *right* guy on the team."

Before Lane could respond, Carson West marched into the operations center and, seeing the two men talking, moved swiftly across the room.

"Is there a problem, gentlemen?"

"You tell me, West," Jones said. "Are you going to give me time to train this guy up, or you going to pull another Mexico on us?"

"This seems like a conversation best had behind closed doors," West said, nodding toward one of the offices on the back wall. "Don't you think?"

"I've got nothing to hide," Jones said. "What about you, West?"

Lane felt the temperature in the room drop a good five degrees, and while he wasn't exactly sure what was going on, it was pretty clear the two men had bad blood. "Maybe I should go somewhere else," he suggested. "Give you two some privacy."

"Good idea," Jones said.

"I don't think that's necessary." West smiled as he ushered them into a nearby room.

"Really?" Jones asked. "And why is that?"

"Because *you* work for *me*, remember?"

"Oh, so you're gonna pull rank on me now?" Jones demanded.

"If I have to," West said, taking a step closer. "The way I see it, you have two options. You can continue to be a problem and be replaced, *or* you can fall in and do what you're told."

"Is that a threat?" Jones asked.

"No, it's a promise," West said.

Jones held his gaze for a second longer, then turned to Lane. "Do yourself a favor, kid, and stay the hell away from this guy."

Before Lane could reply, Mako was gone, the slam of the door knocking a frame off the wall.

"I'm sorry about that," West said, bending down to retrieve the picture. "Jones is . . . an acquired taste."

"Anything I need to know about?"

"He's a loose cannon and a pain in my ass, but that's it. At any rate, I didn't come here to talk about the past," West said, pulling an envelope from his jacket pocket. "I came to talk about your future."

"Is that right?"

"That's right," West replied, opening the envelope and pulling out two pieces of paper. "This is a letter of intent stating that you've agreed to come and work at Broadside—complete the job your brother-in-law signed up for."

"And the second?"

"Is a two-year contract."

"A contract?" Lane repeated. "You never said anything about a contract."

"As a rule, Broadside pays more than any other firm on the market," West explained, an oily smile spreading across his lips. "But that one hundred and fifty grand sitting in escrow was an advance on future earnings. Not for one job."

Lane had gone into the tryouts thinking it was a one-and-done kind of deal, and the mention of the contract had caught him off guard. "I'm going to need to talk to my sister," he said.

"Take the night and think it over," West said, handing the envelope to Lane. "But I need you to know that this is our best and *only* offer, and like all good things, it comes with an expiration date."

"Yeah, I got it," Lane replied.

"Good. I look forward to seeing you in the morning."

CHAPTER 18

Lane was sitting on the bed in his room at the Mimslyn Inn, a half-empty bottle of beer in his hand. The room, like everything else he'd experienced since boarding the private jet back in Memphis, was top-notch. But despite Broadside's impressive setup and massive signing bonus, all Lane could think about was Carson West.

That smug little bastard.

Lane had met his share of assholes during his time in the service and was well acquainted with the type A personalities that were inexorably drawn to the ranks of special operations. But there was something about how casually the other man had dismissed him that made it impossible to let go.

Draining the rest of the beer, Lane peeled off the label and set the bottle next to the rest of the empties lined up on the bedside table. He got to his feet and shuffled across the room to the minifridge.

When he'd checked in that afternoon, there had been two six-packs of Shiner, three airplane bottles of Jack Daniel's, and a thirty-dollar bottle of King Family chardonnay.

Now all that was left was the wine.

Good thing I'm not a picky drunk.

He pulled the bottle from the fridge and was looking for a corkscrew when his cell phone rang. It was Abby, and he answered the call and held the phone to his ear while continuing his search.

"How'd it go?" she asked.

"Nothing I couldn't handle," Lane said. "Have you heard from the Air Force about when they are going to release TJ's remains?"

"We can get them next week," she said, her voice sounding tired. "I figured we could drive up to North Carolina and bring him home together."

"Yeah," Lane said, "he'd like that."

"So what are you going to do about Broadside?" she asked.

"I don't know," he said. "They want me to sign a contract."

"For how long?"

"Two years," Lane replied. "There's something about signing my name to another dotted line, agreeing to fight for money, that doesn't feel right."

"Then don't do it."

"If I don't, they're going to take the house. I've spent the last four months focused on getting out and back to the farm. And now, given everything that's happened, the money we need, I—I just don't know what to do," he finally admitted.

"For TJ, being a PJ was always about the rush," Abby said.

"Yeah?"

"He was an adrenaline junkie, and he was always looking for that next fix," she said. "It's the reason he was always doing such stupid shit."

"I never thought of it that way," Lane said.

"That's because you became a PJ to save lives," she said. "You're a protector—helping people is what you do."

"I couldn't save TJ," he muttered quietly.

"Travis, don't let that guilt eat you alive. TJ made his choices. He lived his life, and if he were here, he'd expect *you* to do the same."

"Damn, sis, when did you get so smart?" Lane asked.

"I've been watching a lot of *Dr. Phil*," she laughed. "But I'm serious about what I said. If it's just about the money, we'll figure something out. If it's more than that, well, you have to decide what *you* want to do."

They chatted for a few more minutes, and then Abby ended the call, leaving Lane alone to process her words. He tossed the phone on the bed and got to his feet, his mind racing as he paced the room. The truth was if it hadn't been for the helo crash, Lane knew he'd still be with the 24th, but the knee injury had taken that from him. Robbed him of the only job he'd ever wanted to do.

Twelve months ago he would have jumped at the chance to get back in the action, but after the long rehab and the additional four months sitting around Camp Lemonnier waiting on missions, Lane wasn't even sure *if* he could still operate at the level he had with the 24th.

"Do I still have it?" he wondered aloud.

Knowing there was only one way to find out, he picked up the phone off the bed and dialed the number from memory.

———————

West sat in his office, his vision blurred from staring at the computer sitting on his desk. A glance at the clock showed it was almost 9:00 p.m., late considering that early-morning flight to Little Creek, Virginia, he still hadn't prepared for. But as much as West wanted to be home, he knew he couldn't leave until the computer finished its search.

Despite all the databases Broadside had access to, finding Mia Webb was turning into a massive undertaking, and part of him just wanted to turn the damn computer off. Roll the dice and tell Sterling that he couldn't find her. But West's survival instinct told him it was the wrong move.

Frustrated, he got to his feet and crossed to the bottle of Blanton's sitting atop the bar on the far side of the room. He poured two fingers into a glass, wishing he had some ice, but as he didn't want to make the long trip down to the cafeteria, West lowered himself onto his leather couch and took a sip.

The whiskey went down smooth with just the right amount of heat, and he let out a contented sigh, wondering how in the hell he'd gotten himself under the thumb of a man like Sterling. It had started out as a thrill. A way to satiate the inner gambler that the CIA had cultivated in each of its operatives, but somewhere along the way, West had fallen in love with the monthly deposits that arrived regardless of whether he'd done any work.

Now Sterling owned him, and West had come to the sober realization that short of killing the man, he would never be free.

You stupid, greedy bastard.

The ring of his cell pulled West from his self-loathing, and he dug the phone from his pocket, his heartbeat picking up when he saw the name.

"Travis, you had me worried. I wasn't sure you were going to call."

"That makes two of us, sir," Lane said.

The comment gave West pause, but he brushed it off and scooted to the edge of the couch. "So what's the verdict, son? Are you ready to save your farm?"

"Yes sir, I'll take the job."

It was a much-needed win, and the moment he heard the words, West was on his feet, ignoring the splash of the amber liquid over the cuff of his $200 Theory dress shirt as he pumped his fist in the air.

Fuck yes.

"I've got a few more questions I'd like to ask," Lane continued, "but I'm in."

Tamping down his excitement, West moved to the bar, where he gave himself a celebratory pour. "Typically, our team leaders handle all that, but if Jones can't answer your questions, then . . ."

The chime of the computer cut him off, and West corked the bottle and headed back to his desk, instantly forgetting what he'd been saying when he saw the picture on the screen.

"Then what, sir?"

"Travis, I—I wish we could talk more, but something's come up," West said. "But since we're shorthanded, I'm going to need you operational as soon as possible."

"What do you need me to do?"

"I'm going to have one of the support guys drop a car off at your hotel," he said, eager to get off the phone. "In the morning I need you to drive over to the compound and get your gear squared away. Can you do that?"

"Roger that, sir."

"Good. Now I've got to go," he said.

Before Lane could respond, West ended the call and turned his attention to the brown-haired woman with the "don't fuck with me" eyes staring back at him from the screen. But it wasn't Mia Webb's pretty face that made him weak in the knees; it was the blue-and-yellow FBI seal to the left of her name.

Oh my God, she's a fucking Fed.

Unsure if his legs would hold him, West lowered himself into his chair, the rush of panic that came with the discovery threatening to overwhelm him. The first thing that leaped into his mind was that he needed to call Sterling, but he held the thought captive and forced himself to wait.

Just breathe.

West closed his eyes and used the four-count breathing exercise he'd learned at the Farm to settle his frantic thoughts. It took two rounds of breath work to get over that initial shock, but with the panic gone, West felt the start of a plan begin to unspool in the back of his mind.

CHAPTER 19

Kinshasa, DRC

The pilots of the Gulfstream G700 prepared for landing, the hydraulic whine of the flaps and the weightless tickle in Mia's stomach bringing her back to the land of the living. She sat up in the oversized leather chair, the file that had been perched on her knees falling to the floor.

"Can I get you anything?" the steward inquired.

"Water, please," she said, rubbing her eyes.

She bent to retrieve the papers and, after returning them to her bag, took the bottle of water from the steward. "What time is it?" she asked.

"Twelve p.m. local," he said, nodding to the digital clock mounted to the bulkhead.

"Thank you," Mia replied.

She thumbed the button on the armrest that opened the window shade and twisted the top off the bottle of water. Squinting against the rush of sunlight that came blasting into the cabin, Mia took a long pull from the bottle. With her thirst quenched, she pulled her sunglasses from her bag and put them on just as the Gulfstream dropped through the clouds and Kinshasa appeared below.

First established as a trading post in 1881, what had once been a sleepy fishing village had rapidly been transformed into the crown jewel of the so-called Congo Free State. Now it was a megacity of fourteen million, an energetic, modern metropolis of glass-fronted skyscrapers, gallery forest, and heavily farmed savanna.

But looking down from the Gulfstream, Mia also knew that beneath its gilded exterior, Kinshasa was a city divided. A place where the rich threw lavish parties inside their gated communities, while just outside their walls children starved on the streets of the endless slums that stretched south across the cityscape. No different from any other large city but an important reminder that life wasn't fair and she had to do whatever possible to even the playing field. And in this case, that meant taking down Roos for good.

The shudder of the wheels touching down on the runway told her they'd arrived.

While the pilot guided the Gulfstream to a row of hangars on the south side of the tarmac, Mia struggled to her feet. Worn out from the eighteen-hour flight, she waited for the steward to lower the airstair, her mind running through the thousands of things that could still go wrong.

That she was pushing the envelope was obvious, but after her talk with her boss, Mia knew bringing in Roos was the only chance she had of saving her career. Now the only thing that mattered was getting Sawyer to help her prove that Roos had killed Angelo and then bringing the slimy South African back to the States in chains.

Grabbing her bag, she stepped off the aircraft and down the stairs, the African sun hot against her skin. She crossed to the hangar, guzzling what was left of her water. Once inside, she tossed the bottle into the trash can on her way to the immigration desk at the far end of the cavernous space.

Mia pulled out the diplomatic passport she'd been issued for a trip to Cuba from her back pocket and handed it to the customs officer with a tired smile. Typically reserved for foreign service officers, consuls, or other high-ranking government officials, the black-jacketed passport was proof that the holder was traveling under "special status." Usually, the sight of the black cover was enough to get her waved through security, but to Mia's surprise the customs officer took his time examining the document.

"How long are you staying in Kinshasa, Ms. Webb?" the man asked in accented English.

"A few days."

"And the hotel where you will be staying?"

"Excuse me?"

"The name of the hotel?"

"I don't see how that is any of your business," she said.

"It is a simple question."

"Either stamp it or go get your supervisor," Mia responded.

The man glared at her for a moment longer, then took the stamp and punched it down on the page. "Have a *safe* trip, Ms. Webb," he said.

"I will," she replied.

Mia took the passport and shoved it back into her pocket before crossing to the door that led out to the street. The exchange with the customs agent had put her on alert, and when she stepped outside, all she could think of was getting out of the area as quickly as possible. She moved to the curb and scanned the cars parked on the street, searching for her ride.

"Hey . . . Jane Bond," a familiar voice called out.

She followed the voice to its source and found a bearded man in a Hawaiian shirt and wraparound sunglasses sitting behind the wheel of a Nissan Pathfinder. Mia crossed the street and opened the passenger door, shrugging out of her backpack before climbing inside.

"You're hilarious, John," she told him.

"I know," he said, grinning and throwing the truck into gear.

While he waited for a break in the traffic, Mia glanced back at the hangar to see the customs agent standing at the door, a cell phone pressed to his ear. Mia had the uneasy feeling that the man was looking right at her, but before she could think anything more about it, John punched the gas, and they drove away.

"Nice tradecraft," he said, nodding to her khaki 5.11 pants and blue polo.

"What do you mean?" she asked.

"You look like a Fed who's trying not to look like a Fed." He smirked. "All you need is a blue windbreaker with *FBI* stenciled across the back."

"It's not *that* bad, is it?"

"Yeah, it is, but don't worry. I brought you some clothes," he said, nodding to the bag in the back seat. "Vest too."

Given the meeting with Sawyer was set for 1:00 p.m., Mia knew she didn't have time to stop and change, so she climbed into the back seat and opened the bag, half expecting it to be full of oversized T-shirts or whatever it was that men thought a woman might wear. But she was pleasantly surprised by the jeans, gray tank top, and olive-drab button-down she found inside.

"Not bad," she said, pulling off her polo.

"I had help from the wife," John said, glancing at her in the rear-view mirror. "Figured you two were about the same size."

"You mean Tanya hasn't kicked you out yet?"

"Kicked me out?" John demanded. "Please, that woman would be lost without me."

"Is that a fact?" Mia asked as she shimmied into the jeans.

"Oh yeah," he said. "You tell me where she'd find a man who cooks, cleans, and knows how to fold the laundry."

"You do laundry?" she asked skeptically.

When Mia first met John five years ago in Bucharest, he was a dedicated bachelor who didn't own, much less know how to operate, a washing machine. But then he'd met Tanya during an embassy party. The former prima ballerina was a knockout with a reputation not to suffer fools lightly, and the first time Mia met her, she'd been sure their burgeoning relationship wouldn't last the week.

But smelling the floral scent of the clothes as she pulled them on, Mia realized that she'd been wrong. "Wow, what is this smell?"

"Lilac and lavender," John said, grinning. "I told you, my laundry game is on point."

"Well, you were right about the shirt," she said, strapping the Kevlar vest over the tank top and then pulling on the button-down, "but not the pants."

"Can't win all the time." He shrugged.

Mia climbed back into the passenger seat. "How do I look?"

"Like a local," John said. "Now, you want to tell me what's going on?"

"It's Angelo," she said.

"What about him?"

Mia tried to answer, but a surge of emotion killed the words on her lips. Unable to speak, she turned to the window, tears scalding the corners of her eyes.

"Mia, what is it?" John asked. "What happened to Angelo?"

"He was in that ambush outside of Ubili," she said. "They haven't recovered a body, but . . ."

"That was him? Oh Jesus, Mia . . . I'm so sorry."

"Yeah," she said, wiping the tears from her cheeks. "Me too."

In the ensuing silence, Mia watched the cityscape scroll past the window. The maggot sellers and jewelry merchants hawking their wares beneath drooping power lines were blurred by the shimmer of tears. She took a deep breath, pushing the sadness away, and then, when she trusted herself to speak, turned back to John.

"The guy we are going to meet is Winston Sawyer," she said.

While John maneuvered the truck through traffic, Mia filled him in on the sequence of events that had brought her to the DRC. She told him about the email from Angelo and how it was tied to the investigations she'd been running in Nairobi. By the time she finished bringing him up to speed, they were arriving at the Jardin Botanique de Kinshasa, where Sawyer had arranged to meet her.

"What does Mike think about all this?" John asked as he searched for a parking spot.

"It's complicated."

"Does he even know you're here?" John asked, the alarm in his voice impossible to ignore.

"Well, I sent him a text," she replied.

John backed the truck into a parking space close to the main entrance and cut the engine before turning to her. "You sent him a text? Mia, what the hell is wrong with you?" he demanded. "I mean, the FBI has rules for a reason."

"Look, he knows what I'm doing, OK," she said. "We're just trying to keep it under the radar."

The answer seemed to pacify him, and he offered a curt nod. "So what's the plan?"

"You watch my back while I talk to Sawyer," she answered, handing him one of the radios she'd taken from her pack. "If he tells me what I need to know, we'll take him back to the airport."

"And if he *doesn't*?"

"You let me worry about that," she said, shoving the Glock back into its holster and then stepping out of the truck.

CHAPTER 20

It had been a shitty day, and thanks to a pair of canceled flights, it was 5:00 a.m. by the time Carson West walked out of the terminal at Shenandoah Valley, and all he could think about was getting home. He crossed to the slate-gray BMW M5 waiting for him in the parking lot and climbed inside, the contoured leather seats a welcome relief from the cramped confines of the Embraer 145 that had shuttled him from DC.

He started the engine and pulled out of the lot, the BMW's high-intensity xenon headlights easily cutting through the darkness. He followed the road north and merged onto Interstate 81, his mind drifting over his wasted trip to Joint Expeditionary Base Little Creek.

Located on the northwest corner of Virginia Beach near the mouth of the Chesapeake Bay, Little Creek was home to Naval Special Warfare Group Two and three active-duty SEAL teams. West had spent a previous trip courting a handful of operators who were set to retire, selling them on the competitive pay and benefits they'd receive *if* they decided to come work for Broadside. It was a productive meeting, and he'd left with a stack of personnel files from the interested applicants.

If it had been up to him, West would have taken them all right there, but thanks to the recent spate of movies, TV shows, and books speaking to America's craving for everything SEAL related, the men knew they had options.

"We'd like to see what else is out there," they'd told him. "Can you come back in a couple of weeks?"

Knowing that it was a tough sell, West had spent the next flight there refining his pitch, honing his talking points until they were sharp as a razor, and by the time he landed at Norfolk International, he was confident he had a good chance of finally solving Broadside's staffing problem.

But instead of giving him the warm welcome they had on his last visit, the men waiting for him inside the team room were distant, almost cold. Each interview was set for thirty minutes, but instead of questions about pay, insurance, and retirement, West was met with silence, each man offering little more than his name, rank, and date of retirement.

Halfway through the morning he finally asked a grizzled senior chief with double-digit deployments what was going on. "Last time I was here, you guys were pumped about coming to work for Broadside," he said.

"We *were*," the man said, "but then we got a call from Jones."

"Jones?" West asked. "As in Mako Jones?"

"That's right," the man replied. "He's not a big fan of yours."

The realization that the team leader had sabotaged his mission had nearly sent West over the edge, but he was a professional and managed to keep his anger in check. Now alone in his car, West finally vented the rage that had been building inside of him for the previous nine hours. "That slimy, backstabbing son of a bitch," he snarled, slapping his hand hard on the leather-wrapped steering wheel.

Before the trip Jones had been a minor irritant, an itch that wouldn't stop no matter how much it was scratched. But after this stunt, he was now at the top of West's hit list. If he'd been any other operator, getting rid of the man wouldn't have been a problem. But Jones wasn't just another operator.

No, he was the *first* operator Taran Carter had hired, and to a man who valued loyalty above everything else in the world, that made Jones more than an institution. It made him untouchable. Still, West had been in the game long enough to know that there were exceptions to every rule, and while he couldn't force the man off the team, he could damn sure make him miserable.

Starting with taking his team away from him.

For a man like Jones, being out of the fight was a fate worse than death, and the thought of him sitting alone in his office while the rest of the team was out running and gunning sent a smile spreading across West's lips. The man wouldn't go quietly, of that West was certain, but he knew something about Jones that his boss did not—mainly the black-market bottles of painkillers and opioids the aging operator kept in his desk.

The pills alone wouldn't get him kicked out, but they'd be a start, and the idea was enough to dampen the residual anger West felt from his failed mission. Feeling the tension seep from his body, he turned on the radio and toggled through his presets before settling on a classical station. As he leaned back in his seat, his thoughts turned to a hot shower and the few hours of sleep he might get before having to head back to work, until the trill of his phone through the speakers alerted him to an incoming call.

Who the hell is calling me now?

Then he saw the +243 country code on the information display, the number reminding him of the email he'd sent to the network of sources he'd carried over from his days at the CIA. Per Sterling's orders, his only job was to ID Mia Webb and pass that info up the chain, and while he'd already done *more* than his part, West had figured it wouldn't hurt to forward her name and picture to his sources.

Could they have found something?

Curiosity getting the better of him, West answered the call, and the rapid-fire French that came blasting through the speaker caught his sleep-deprived mind off guard. He tried to understand what the man was saying, but despite the four years of French he'd taken in college, all he could make out was *la femme.*

The woman? What woman?

"Joseph . . . Joseph, you've got to slow down," he insisted.

But the other man kept jabbering away until West finally lost his temper. "Joseph, take a fucking breath," he shouted. "And for God's sake, speak English."

There was a moment of silence, and when the man began speaking again, his voice was still excited, but at least West understood what the hell he was saying.

"The woman in the email . . . Mia Webb . . . she is here."

"In Kinshasa?" West demanded, his fingers white on the wheel.

"She just left the airport. I have one of my men following—"

"Joseph, shut up and listen to me," West interrupted. "Whatever happens, he cannot lose her. Do you understand?"

"Yes, of course."

"Good, now hang up and text me his number," West instructed.

The line went dead, and for the second time in as many days, West pulled off onto the side of the road, his heart hammering in his chest. As soon as he received the text, he dialed the number Sterling had given him.

C'mon . . . Pick up.

The phone rang three times, and then a man with a thick South African accent answered.

"Yes?"

"We've got her," West said.

CHAPTER 21

MIMSLYN INN

Luray, Virginia

Lane was up before the sun, and after brushing his teeth and pulling on some clothes, he headed downstairs for breakfast. He followed the smell of fresh bacon across the entryway, his stomach growling, and was almost to the dining room when the woman behind the desk called his name.

"Mr. Lane?"

"Yes ma'am," he said, moving to the counter.

"Someone left this for you last night," she said, handing him a temporary ID and a set of keys.

He thanked her, shoved both the keys and ID card into his pocket, and continued into the dining room. With most of the guests still in bed, he had the space to himself, and he wasted no time filling up a plate with bacon, eggs, and a heaping portion of grits. After pouring himself a cup of coffee, he carried everything to a table by the window.

He ate in silence and watched the shadows retreat across the lawn as the purpled horizon announced the coming of the sun. Finishing his food, he searched for a place to put his dirty plates but, not finding anything, left them on the table.

After filling a Styrofoam cup with coffee for the road, Lane went outside and double-clicked the key fob. The flash of brake lights led him to a red Ford Explorer parked in the second row.

Careful not to spill his coffee, he climbed inside and started the engine, and the green button on the SUV's navigation screen told him that the route to Broadside had already been programmed in. Impressed by the thoroughness of his new employer, Lane threw the Explorer into drive and followed the arrow to the highway.

He drove east, the coming dawn illuminating a dappled sky and a blanket of fog that stretched north over the undulating hills of the countryside. Lane had the road to himself, and he settled back in his seat, the Explorer tires humming contentedly over the asphalt. It was a short drive to his destination, and five minutes later, Lane pulled up to the gate and handed his temporary ID card to the guard who stepped out of the shack.

The man studied it for a second before leaning in to give Lane the once-over. "You know where you're going?"

"Yes sir," he said, nodding to the GPS.

"You look awful young for this kind of work."

"Must be all the healthy living," Lane said.

"Uh-huh."

The guard studied him for another second, and Lane was beginning to wonder if he was going to let him through, but he finally handed back Lane's ID. "Well, good luck then."

"Thanks, Pops," he said, taking the ID.

"Smart-ass."

Lane grinned and pulled through the gate, the GPS guiding him around the main building to a row of prefab hangars on the far side of the runway. He slowed, wondering which one was his, but seeing the signs staked in front of each hangar, he continued until he found the one that said *Guardian 7.*

The parking spots at the front of the building were vacant, but Lane knew better than to park near the door and chose one near the end. He exited the car and had started up the sidewalk when a thick-chested man with blond hair stepped out of the side door to meet him.

"Lane?" the man asked.

"That's right."

"Jake Hunter," he said, sticking out his hand. "I'm the assistant team leader for Guardian 7."

They shook hands, and Lane followed Hunter inside.

The layout of the building was similar to what he'd had at the 24th, with an open squad bay full of desks near the front followed by a pair of offices for the team leaders. Down a short hall was the locker room and showers, followed by the team room with its ubiquitous rumpled couches and fully stocked bar.

At the end of the hall, Hunter punched a code into the door lock and led Lane into an expansive bay full of ATVs, dirt bikes, and a row of gear cages.

"This is you," Jake said, stopping next to a cage and handing him a key. "Any questions?"

"Yeah, what are those for?" Lane asked, pointing to red lights mounted to the far wall.

"That's the red ball—the mission light." Hunter grinned. "But don't worry, cherry, Jones isn't going to let you go anywhere until you're trained up."

"Good to know."

"If you need anything that's not in your cage, let me know and we'll order it," Hunter said. "Otherwise, I'll be in my office."

As Hunter left the bay, Lane unlocked the padlock securing the door and stepped into the cage, his eyes drifting over the weapons hanging carefully from their pegboards and the gear packed neatly into the wall lockers. He'd been measured by the quartermaster the day prior but was still surprised to find that everything from the olive-drab undershirts to the Salomon hiking boots was in his size.

Again impressed by Broadside's efficiency, Lane turned his attention to the steel locker bolted to the ground on the far side of the cage and pressed his index finger to the reader. He waited for the magnetic lock to disengage and then pulled the door open. The contents of the locker caught him off guard, and for a moment all he could do was stand there and stare at the weapons, optics, and suppressors arranged neatly on their racks.

"Ho-ly shit," he said.

As much as he wanted to take the guns to the range and get some lead therapy, the real reason he'd come in early was to square away his most important weapon—his med ruck. And with that thought in mind, Lane shut the weapons vault and turned his attention to the medical gear arranged neatly in the far corner.

Besides their rescue and recovery skills, PJs were certified paramedics capable of performing emergency surgeries in the field. In fact, on most operations, Lane's only limitation was whether he had the required equipment to perform said surgery—which made a well-stocked medical ruck more valuable than his rifle.

As a younger PJ, Lane had been so afraid that he *wouldn't* have the equipment he'd need that he would routinely carry a med ruck the size of a refrigerator. Back then he'd weighed 150 pounds, but add body armor, water, food, weapons, and the various other lethal tools required, and by the time he strapped on his med ruck, he weighed well over 250 pounds.

Humping that kind of weight around an objective was a different kind of hell, and it didn't take Lane long to figure out that ounces made pounds. At the 24th everything was about traveling light and fast, and after a few missions and clever packing of his med ruck, he got things down to a science.

Broadside, however, was an unknown, and sitting there in his cage, looking at the empty pack, Lane figured the best course of action was to split the difference. He started with the basics: combat gauze, pressure dressings, chest seals, two 500 ml bags of sodium chloride, and two of hetastarch.

Slowly the bag began to fill. Lane was thinking about what pharmaceuticals and painkillers he might be called upon to administer when there was a polite cough from his rear. Caught off guard, he leaped to his feet and whirled to find Mako Jones standing at the open door.

"Damn, Chief, you scared the hell out of me."

Jones cracked a smile. "Mind if I come in?"

"Not at all," Lane replied.

Jones stepped inside, his eyes drifting to the med ruck.

"You going to carry all that shit?"

"Can't do my job if I don't."

"Yeah, I guess not," Jones said. Shifting gears, he turned his gaze to

Lane. "Yesterday, that thing between me and West . . . you didn't need to see that."

"Chief, you don't have to—"

"I'm not apologizing," Jones snapped. "I'm just telling you what happened."

"Roger that."

"Look, I might not like the way you got on the team, but there is no denying that you have the skills to be an asset," Jones went on. "That said, this isn't the Air Force, and sometimes we are forced to do things on a mission that are borderline unsafe."

"What do you mean?" Lane asked.

"From the moment that light goes on, the only thing that matters is recovering the principal," Jones explained. "We go in outgunned, with little to no intel on the objective and knowing that if we screw it up, no one is coming to save us. That's the job."

"I know how to do my job."

"I know you do," Jones said. "But out there it's what you *don't* know that will get you killed."

CHAPTER 22

JARDIN BOTANIQUE DE KINSHASA
Kinshasa, DRC

Mia followed the sidewalk to the park entrance and pressed the push-to-talk clipped to the cuff of her shirt. "Radio check." There was a hiss of static, followed a second later by John's voice in her ear.

"Loud and clear."

"Give me a thirty-second lead, then follow," Mia said. With that, she walked through the gate.

According to research Mia had done on the plane, the Jardin Botanique de Kinshasa had been created in 1933, when the Congo was still a Belgian colony. After the freedom movement of the early 1960s, the seventeen-acre park had spent the next couple of decades in a state of neglect before finally being rehabilitated in the early 2000s. Following the cobblestone path originating beneath the gate, Mia paused in the shade of a cacao tree to get her bearings before continuing toward the row of concrete benches where she and Sawyer were supposed to meet.

Having arrived ten minutes early, she was hoping to have a chance to map the ingress and egress routes in case there was trouble, but the sight of the man in a sweat-stained fedora told her that Sawyer had beaten her there.

"He's here," she advised over the radio as she crossed to the bench.

Seeing her coming, Sawyer rose to his feet, his face nervous beneath the wide brim. "Ms. Webb?" he asked as she drew near.

"Thank you for meeting me," she said.

"Of course," he said, hoisting a worn leather pack over his shoulder. "I think it's best if we talk during the ride to the airport."

"First, you tell me what you know about the mine in Ubili."

"That wasn't the deal." He frowned.

"The deal was that I would take you back to the States *after* you told me what you know about the mine."

"And if I refuse?"

"That would not be in your best interest, Mr. Sawyer."

"No," he said shaking his head. "I'm not telling you anything until you get me out of here. I just can't risk it."

"Well, good luck then," she said, turning to leave.

"Wait," he said. "What do you want to know?"

That's what I thought.

"Let's take a walk," she said.

"Fine."

They followed the promenade east, the shouts from the street vendors and the putter of the tap-taps whizzing past spoiling the oasis feel of the garden. Even in the shade there was no escaping the heat, and as they walked, she found herself inexorably drawn to the shimmering spray of water rising from the fountain that served as the park's centerpiece.

God, it's hot.

Shoving away her discomfort, Mia focused on the task at hand. She needed answers, and she needed them now.

"Tell me about the mine," she said.

"What do you want to know?"

"What are they mining that is valuable enough they were willing to kill a UN investigator to protect it? Is it gold? Diamonds?"

"No, something much more precious," Sawyer said. "Much more dangerous."

"Tell me."

"What do you know about columbite-tantalite—or coltan, as it is more commonly known?"

"Not much."

"It's a conflict mineral, and along with tin, tantalum, and tungsten, it is one of the most prized substances on earth."

"Why?" Mia asked.

"Because without it you can't produce tantalum capacitors—a vital component in just about every consumer electronic on the market."

"So it's valuable and rare?"

"Valuable, yes; rare, no," Sawyer answered.

"I don't understand," she said.

"There are plenty of coltan mines here in Africa, but due to its status as a conflict mineral, it's heavily regulated."

"You're talking about the Dodd-Frank Act?"

"That's right. Originally, the US thought that if they could regulate companies buying and selling conflict minerals, they would be able to cut the flow of money to the militias," Sawyer said.

While he spoke, Mia scanned the scene around them, her eyes constantly moving, studying the faces of the passersby before shifting to the figures milling around the fountain.

Finding it clear, she turned back to Sawyer, her instincts telling her it was time to get to the point. "Listen," she said, "I don't give a shit about the money. All *I* care about is finding the men responsible for Angelo's death."

As expected, the sudden shift in her demeanor caught Sawyer off guard, and his face went bone white. "Y-you knew Angelo?" he asked.

"That's right," she said, edging closer. "I came here for one reason: for answers, names."

Sawyer stopped and licked a nervous tongue over his lips. "Names?" he asked.

"Yeah, like who hired you and why."

"I—I was hired by Alexander Sterling."

Now it was Mia's turn to be caught off guard.

"Alexander Sterling?" she asked. "*The* billionaire philanthropist who has pledged ten million dollars to end hunger in Africa hired you?"

"That's correct," Sawyer said, continuing forward.

"Why would a guy with that much money risk dealing with conflict minerals?" she asked, walking next to him.

"Because he's a bottom-feeder," Sawyer said. "A lowlife with a terrible reputation who spends millions of dollars a year making sure none of his jet-setting cronies ever figure out what he's really about."

Mia was processing Sawyer's response when she noticed the wide-shouldered man standing at the far edge of the fountain. At first glance there was nothing untoward about him, but on closer inspection, there was something about his close-cropped hair and forced slouch that just wasn't right.

On instinct, Mia grabbed Sawyer by the back of the arm and steered him away from the fountain and toward an adjacent path.

"Are we leaving now?"

Mia ignored him and doubled down on her questions. "Tell me about Sterling. Why did he hire you?"

"He wanted me to find an untapped deposit of coltan."

"An untraceable source of coltan," Mia corrected him.

"Well, obviously he didn't come right out and tell me the plan when he hired me," Sawyer snapped back, suddenly defensive. "And by the time I finally figured out what he was really after, I'd already signed enough documents to make me legally complicit."

"Then what happened."

"He revoked my access and made me turn over every shred of documentation I had before he would pay me," Sawyer said. "Then he had me escorted off the property."

"So he blackmailed you?"

"Yes, and that is when I reported the mine to the UN investigators at Goma."

"Names. I need names," Mia said.

"To Angelo Garza, but I never thought they would kill him."

Mia was about to ask Sawyer what the hell he'd *thought* was going to happen when she heard the crunch of gravel beneath boots coming up from behind. She turned to see the man from the fountain jogging toward them, the black automatic in his right hand sending a shot of adrenaline coursing through her.

Mia's training kicked in, and she shoved Sawyer behind the wide trunk of a baobab tree, her right hand dropping to the grip of the Glock. She yanked it free and was bringing it up onto target when the man fired.

The first bullet cracked wide overhead, and before he could adjust his aim, Mia had the Glock up in a two-handed grip, sights centered on the man's chest. She fired twice, the boom of the gunshot echoing loud as a cannon beneath the trees.

The pair of 9 mm hollow points to the chest dropped the man in his tracks, and Mia made sure he stayed down before keying up on the radio. "We're blown," she shouted to John over the screams of the pass-ersby. "Get back to the truck."

"On my way."

Grabbing Sawyer by the arm, she pulled him from behind the tree and shoved him onto the path. "We've got to go."

Then they were running, the distant wail of sirens following them out onto the promenade and into the sunlight. Squinting against the glare, Mia shoved Sawyer into the crowd rushing for the exit.

Mia could see the parking lot and John running for the truck. *We're going to make it.* But no sooner had the thought crossed her mind than a blacked-out Suburban came bouncing over the curb and onto the grass. The driver brought the truck to a sudden halt, and the armed men that came spilling out sent the crowd stampeding in all directions.

Still holding Sawyer by the arm, Mia tried to tear free, but the press of the frantic bodies around them held them fast, and like driftwood on the sea, they were carried through the gate and out into the open.

Finally, they managed to get out of the crowd, and seeing a low wall to her left, Mia shoved Sawyer into cover.

Holding him down with one hand, she turned to see two men advancing toward her, their submachine guns up and ready. But before they could close the distance, John appeared behind them and opened fire.

He dropped the closest shooter with three rounds to the chest, then hit the second man with a bullet to the leg. But before he could do any more damage, a third shooter dropped John with a single bullet to the center of the forehead. Mia screamed and fired as fast as her finger would pull the trigger.

Her first shots were low, and the bullets sparked off the bumper, but she was quick to readjust and put two rounds through the shooter's throat before the Glock's slide locked back. Mia dropped the empty magazine and ripped the spare from her belt, but before she could reload, a burst of rifle fire sent her diving for cover.

She landed flat behind the wall and, after getting the pistol back into action, crawled to the left edge. Braving the snap of the bullets and shards of concrete whipping overhead, she inched out in time to see two men break away from the main group. Realizing they were trying to flank them, Mia opened fire.

The Glock bucked in her hand, and Mia saw one of the men stumble, but before she had a chance for a follow-up shot, a hail of return fire from the men at the truck sent her scrambling back to cover.

"We can't stay here," she shouted to Sawyer.

"You're crazy if you think I'm going out there," he said.

"If we stay here, it's game over," she said.

"It's not happening," he replied, pulling a black cylinder from his backpack and popping the cap.

Mia had no idea what was in the cylinder, and she didn't care. All she knew was that they were running out of time, and she was done screwing around with Sawyer.

The hell with this, she thought, moving in behind him and grabbing his arm. "You're coming with me." She pulled harder than she'd intended, and he spilled backward, the black cylinder in his hand stabbing down at her leg.

There was a metallic snap followed by a stinging in her thigh. Mia looked down to see blood pooling around the hole that he'd punched in her jeans.

"You have about two seconds to tell me what that was, and then I'm going to shoot you," she said.

"It's a tracker," he replied, tossing the now-empty injector into the tall grass that lined the walk. "They will come and get you. Until then, do—"

Before he could finish, a flash-bang came cartwheeling over the low wall and hit the ground between them. Seeing it lying there, Mia had just enough time to open her mouth and close her eyes before the open-handed smack of the concussion knocked her unconscious.

CHAPTER 23

Mount Jackson, Virginia

Ron Granger pulled into the Broadside compound at exactly 7:45 a.m. and, after being waved through by the security guard at the gate, followed the drive to the front of the building. He swung the F-250 into his parking spot, cut the engine, and grabbed his briefcase before climbing out.

Granger stepped through the front door and crossed the lobby, his shoes squeaking on the freshly buffed tile. He walked down the hallway past the line of empty admin offices before finally coming to a metal security door with a bloodred *Restricted Entry* sign stuck to the middle.

Swiping his card across the reader mounted to the wall, he waited for the *click* of the magnetic lock before pulling open the door and stepping inside. Compared to the brightly lit hallway, the operations center was dim, with most of the ambient light coming from the bluish glow of the monitors that dotted the techs' workstations. Granger was forced to wait for his eyes to adjust to the gloom before starting across the room.

Mindful not to disturb the bleary-eyed techs who'd been on watch for the previous twelve hours, he stopped at the single desk in the back of the room, where the night-shift battle captain was finishing up his log.

"You guys have a good night?"

"Nice and quiet," the man said, clipping a stack of papers to the thick logbook before handing it over.

"Good to hear."

Granger took the log and carried it into his office, closing the door behind him before turning on the lights. He dropped his briefcase onto the chair by the door, took a seat at his desk, and then opened the log. Before coming to Broadside, Major Ron Granger had spent five years with the 3rd Special Forces Group before being recruited by the CIA.

Using a process known as *sheep dipping*, the Agency quietly removed his official records from the DOD and replaced them with a set that said he'd retired from the service. With this bureaucratic sleight of hand now complete, Granger was assigned to the clandestine services and, after completing training at the Farm, was sent overseas. It was during his second tour in Iraq that he met Taran Carter and forged the bond that would bring him to Broadside.

As the executive officer, or XO, Granger's job wasn't much different than it had been when he was in SF. In fact, when he'd first started at Broadside, once he'd caught up on the training and equipment logs, most of his time had been spent making sure he had at least two teams ready to deploy at a moment's notice.

But it wasn't long before word of their services got out and they began gaining more clients. The operation tempo began to grow, and within eighteen months they'd expanded from three teams to seven. The increase in contracts required an equally large expansion in both logistics and the manpower required to service them. Broadside was already struggling to keep up with demand when Guardian 7 lost an operator during an operation in Mexico two months prior.

Despite their best efforts to find a replacement, the search had proved difficult, and with Guardian 7 on the sidelines, the operations center was stretched to the max. Granger was keeping things going for now, but he hoped they'd find a solution to the problem soon.

He opened the logbook and flipped through the pages until he found the section that listed the clients slated for upcoming travel. Grabbing a dry-erase marker from his desk, Granger stepped to the whiteboard on the wall and began jotting names and dates into the corresponding blocks.

That Granger still used a whiteboard to keep tabs on their clients, despite Broadside's massive computer database and state-of-the-art tracking software designed specifically for the company, seemed archaic to most of the command staff, and Taran Carter especially never missed a chance to bust his balls.

"Why do I give you these great computers if all you want to do is play with an eraser and markers?" he wanted to know.

"Because my whiteboard isn't going to get a virus and dump all my data," he'd respond.

Technically, having unencrypted data in an office was against Broadside policy, and while the boss wouldn't hesitate to chew someone else's ass, he let Granger do what he wanted mainly because while he'd been the XO, they hadn't lost a single client. Most men in his position would have let that go to their heads, but Granger knew that all it would take was a single misstep or planning failure for everything to collapse around him, leaving men injured or, even worse, dead. Even with that thought at the forefront of his mind, he'd been unable to stop what happened to Guardian 7 in Mexico.

This singular failure was what kept Granger up at night and the reason he came in early every day. Pushed his staff to the limits to make sure they'd covered every contingency. But with five of Broadside's seven teams currently on active operation or forward deployed to support clients in high-risk countries such as Ukraine, it was never enough.

Back at home he had one evac team and the recently plussed-up Guardian 7. Granger had nothing but respect for Mako Jones and the rest of Guardian 7, but until their new guy was fully trained, he was more of a liability than an asset. Knowing this, Granger had come in early to see if he could recall any of the forward-deployed teams, but before he had a chance to work through his options, a high-pitched alarm from outside his office had him on his feet.

Shit.

Granger flung open the door, the wash of lights now blaring down from the ceiling confirming his worst fear. "Do we have a lock?" he demanded of the tech at the desk nearest him.

"Working on it, sir."

"Well, work faster," he said, "and someone turn off that damn alarm."

A less disciplined man would have rushed into the fray and started barking orders, but Granger knew his team was the best in the business, so he stayed back, waiting to be briefed.

One of the techs killed the alarm, and the room went silent, the only sounds the clatter of fingers across keyboards and the low-pitched cross talk between the staff as they worked at their respective tasks.

"Location is coming up on the board," someone said.

A second later a satellite map appeared on the large monitor at the front of the room, the targeting crosshairs centered over a blinking red dot in Kinshasa. "We've got a solid lock," the operator said. "Target is currently moving east at forty miles an hour."

"Who does the tracker belong to?"

"It's assigned to Sterling Mines," the tech answered a second later.

Sterling Mines?

As the founder and CEO of Sterling Mines, Alexander Sterling was one of the wealthiest men on the planet. He was also a savvy venture capitalist who'd been quick to see the potential in Broadside Solutions when it first opened shop. They'd been cash strapped in those early years, and it was no secret that if it hadn't been for Sterling's sizable investments in the company, Broadside would have never gotten off the ground. In fact, Taran Carter had been so appreciative that he'd given the man a seat on the board without bothering to consult the rest of the directors.

Eighteen months later, Carter had received a call from his lawyers that the SEC was opening an investigation into Sterling and his holdings. At first, they thought it was yet another federal witch hunt and were determined to weather the storm. But soon after the news broke, Carter received an unexpected visit from the SEC.

Granger hadn't attended the meeting, but it was his understanding that whatever the enforcement agents told the men in the room, it was enough that they agreed to immediately terminate all of Sterling's contracts, which was why the beacon on the screen made no sense.

"That can't be right," he said. "Bring up the information box and check the serial number on that tracker."

The tech nodded, and after a few keystrokes the data appeared on the screen. "It's one of the older models, a Mark II."

What the fuck?

"Vic, go ahead and alert the pilots that we've got a mission package to launch," Granger said.

"What about Guardian 7?" Vic asked. "Shouldn't we alert them too?"

"No, they're not ready."

"But West just cleared them," Vic replied, pointing to the active board.

"I know he did, but it's too soon," Granger responded, pulling out his cell phone. "I'll call the boss and let him know. While I'm doing that, I need you to find out how long it will take to get Archangel Five to respond from Poland."

"Yes sir."

Granger stepped into his office, closed the door, and took a deep breath before dialing Carter. The line connected on the second ring, and Carter's tired voice came hissing through the speaker.

"What's going on, Ron?"

"We've got a problem. We just had a Mark II go active in Kinshasa."

"That can't be right. West told me they were all deactivated."

"Yes sir, but I verified the serial number myself," Granger said. "And it gets worse. The tracker is assigned to Alexander Sterling."

"Dammit. How is that possible?"

"Sir, I have no idea, but considering the circumstances and the fact that we *don't* have a positive ID on the principal, I think our best option is to recall one of the other teams," Granger said. "Give Guardian 7 time to train up their new guy before we send them out."

There was a silence on the other end of the line, and when Taran finally spoke, his voice was resigned. "Ron, I understand your concern. Unfortunately, we don't have the time to recall another team."

"Are you sure?" Granger said.

"No, but we're on the clock here. And as pissed off as I am about what's going on here, we have an obligation to meet and a client to save."

"Roger that, sir," Granger said. "I'm launching Guardian 7 now."

"Good, keep me posted," Taran said.

"Yes sir."

Granger hung up the phone and took a deep breath. He was confident that he'd done everything in his power to express his concerns about both the mission and the team, but there was no escaping the guilt that came with having to send an unready Guardian 7 into harm's way. Still, he had his orders; now it was time to carry them out.

CHAPTER 24

Lane had finished packing his gear and was taking a break in the team room when the red ball went off. The flash of amber light was followed by the howl of a distant alarm that echoed like a banshee throughout the building.

His first thought was that they were screwing with him, pranking the new guy. But then Hunter came barreling into the team room. "Lane, get your shit together. We've got a mission."

"What . . . now?"

But he was talking to himself, because Hunter was already racing through the door and out into the bay. Lane scrambled to his feet and followed him out.

"Hunter," he shouted. "Are you serious?"

"Hell yeah, I'm serious. Some big-shot mining executive just got himself snatched in the Congo," Hunter answered. "The team's been called in, and I need you kitted up and ready to move in fifteen mikes—can you handle that?"

"Sure, but ready for what?"

"No idea, but seeing how fast things are moving, it has to be big," Hunter said. "So move your ass."

Flustered, Lane hustled back to the cage and, for the second time that morning, unlocked the padlock and stepped inside. But instead of staring at all the equipment, he grabbed a large kit bag from the shelf and got to work filling it with what he might need. Since all he knew was that they were going to the jungle, Lane first grabbed a set of Crye Precision's G3 tiger-stripe BDUs.

He stripped out of his civilian clothes, pulled on a set of the utilities, and laced up his boots before tossing two extra pairs of cammies into his kit bag. Now properly dressed, he threw in a chest rig, a helmet, and a boonie cap and then turned his attention back to the gun locker.

Working fast, Lane pulled an HK416 with an attached 40 mm grenade launcher from the shelf. He checked the Nightforce ATACR 1-8x24 scope mounted to the rail, twisted on the Surefire RC2 suppressor, and then added the rifle and a pair of Harris ENVG-Bs, or enhanced night vision goggle-binoculars, to the bag.

With his primary weapon taken care of, Lane turned back to the locker in search of a pistol. He opened the drawer inside the weapons case, expecting to find the usual suspects. But instead of the pimped-out Glocks and SIGs so common to the world of special operations, he found a single pistol sitting inside—a Staccato V3 with a Leupold DeltaPoint Pro reflex sight mounted to the top.

"Whoa," Lane said, taking the gun from its foam insert and racking the slide.

When it came to 2011s, the Staccato was an innovator in the field, and the V3 was its flagship model. A pistol built from the ground up and torture tested to provide the user with the most reliable and accurate handgun on the market.

It was a work of art. A masterpiece of lethal precision.

Lane shoved the pistol into its holster, clipped it to his belt, then tossed a Ka-Bar into his bag and zipped everything up. Now properly equipped, he slung his medical ruck and was dragging his gear bag from the cage when Jones came sweeping into the bay.

"Looks like it's time to see what you're all about," he said.

"I won't let you down," Lane responded.

Jones was about to reply when a mountain of a man with a

six-barreled minigun stepped out of the office. "Hey, Chief," he said, his Swedish accent on full display.

"What is it, Magnus?" Jones demanded, his eyes never leaving Lane's.

"The plane is loaded, and the crew needs to weigh our gear before we can take off."

"You and the boys head out to the flight line. We'll be there in a second."

"Yes, boss," the man replied.

Jones waited until Magnus was gone and took a step forward. "When I first joined the team, we didn't have any of this," he said, holding out his arms in a gesture that encompassed the entire building. "Back then we used whatever gear we could get our hands on. Now each member of the team gets a two-thousand-dollar Staccato just for showing up."

"It's a nice pistol," Lane said.

"Yes, it is," Jones said. "But it takes a hell of a lot more than a flashy pistol and some new gear to make it on *this* team. Are you sure you're ready for this, kid?"

"I won't let you down, Chief."

"I hope you're right," Jones said, "because Carson West isn't going to be out there to protect you if you screw up."

It was the second time he had insinuated that Lane was in West's pocket, and it was beginning to piss him off. "Whatever drama you and West have, it's got nothing to do with me," Lane said. "I'm just here to do a job."

Jones studied him for another long second, then nodded and stepped out of his way. "Good, now load up."

Lane slung his rifle over his shoulder and carried his gear out to the Bombardier 7500 idling on the tarmac. After handing his kit bag off to one of the crew, he started up the airstair, where the big Swede he'd seen earlier was waiting.

"Don't take it personal," the big man said, nodding back to the tarmac, where Jones stood consulting with the pilots. "He's a prick to all the new guys."

"Good to know," Lane said. "I thought it was just me."

"Just do your job, and you'll be fine," Magnus said, slapping him hard across the back. "Now come—let's get you settled in."

Magnus steered him past the galley and through the first cabin, nodding to the three men who were busy setting up their computers on the walnut table. "That's our support crew," he said. "They handle our communications and the other high-tech gear the boss doesn't trust us with."

"Thanks to you," a swarthy man said as they entered the next cabin.

"And that glowering little shit is Felix," Magnus said. "He's a Corsican, so make sure you lock up your stuff when he's around."

"Keep it up, you stupid Swede," Felix said.

"Don't listen to those two," Hunter said from where he sat. "They were in the Legion together, spent too much time out in the sun, and now they're crazy as a pair of shithouse rats."

"Says the man who almost got us killed in Brazil," Felix said.

"Hey, that was an accident and—"

Before he could finish, Mako appeared in the doorway, his dark eyes playing over the team. At the sight of their team leader, the four went silent, and all eyes shifted to Hunter.

"Are we ready to roll?" Jones asked.

"Roger that, boss."

Five minutes later, the Bombardier was sitting at the end of the runway, its twin turbofans screaming as the pilots advanced the throttles. The plane tried to surge forward, but the pilot kept his foot on the brakes and increased the power until the aircraft was shaking like a greyhound in the starting box. Then he released the brake, and they were racing down the runway, the sun glinting off the paint as they lifted off and up into the sky.

Once they reached altitude, Jones gathered the team in the rear cabin and briefed them on what he knew.

"A tracker just went live in Kinshasa," he said. "It's an old unit, so we are still waiting on the details."

"How old?" Hunter asked.

"A Mark II."

"We still use those?" Magnus asked. "I thought West said they were all pulled out of service."

"Well, that's what we get for listening to West," Mako said. "Either way, the tracker is live, and since the contract is still valid, it's business as usual. We're going to have to be flexible on this one, so everyone make sure you're ready to roll when we touch down in the DRC."

Lane waited for Mako to leave and then leaned over to Magnus. "Can you translate all of that into English?"

"Broadside has gone through three versions of trackers since I've been here," the big Swede said. "The Mark I was a piece of shit. It wouldn't sync with the satellites, had terrible battery life and a bunch of other problems. They got most of that fixed with the Mark IIs, but it wasn't until the Mark IIIs that they figured out how to verify the target."

"And how do they do that?" Lane asked.

"They use DNA. Don't ask me how it works. All I know is that according to the geeks at the lab, if the blood of the host doesn't match the genetic profile stored on the computer, the tracker won't go live."

"Holy shit, that's some serious Big Brother stuff."

"Tell me about it."

"So just to make sure I'm clear, we are going into an unknown hostile environment to pick up a target who may or may not be the person we're supposed to recover?"

"Welcome to Broadside, mate." Magnus grinned.

This just keeps getting better and better.

CHAPTER 25

Ubili, DRC

Mia lay facedown in the back of the vehicle, the black hood they'd pulled over her head tickling the end of her nose. She was desperate to scratch it, but with the zip ties securing her hands behind her back, there was nothing she could do. Not knowing where she was in the vehicle or, more importantly, where exactly her captors were, Mia knew it was best to lie still. Stay down until she had a better sense of her surroundings.

She focused on the whine of the tires on the street and the muted conversation from the front of the truck, but the more she ignored the tickling sensation, the more it grew, until she couldn't take it any longer.

The hell with this.

Throwing caution to the wind, Mia rolled onto her back and pulled her knees to her chest until her tailbone was off the ground and then looped the cuffs past her feet. With her hands now in front, she ripped the bag from her head and finally scratched at her face.

Oh my God, that felt good.

She'd no sooner returned her hands to her sides than the Suburban was veering left, the smooth sound of the tires over the blacktop giving way to the stuttering crush of gravel. Looking around her, Mia realized she was in the cargo space of a Suburban SUV. Crawling onto her knees, Mia hazarded a quick look over the seat back in front of her. A scan of the interior showed four armed men and a badly beaten Sawyer slumped against the window.

Her eyes snapped from the bleeding man in the back seat to the windshield, and the sight of the idling Huey in the center of the field a quarter mile ahead caused her stomach to twist into knots.

Up front, one of the men shifted in his seat, his hand reaching out for the satellite phone on the center console. Mia immediately threw herself flat, her head banging hard off the wheel well. The impact starred her vision, and she stifled a groan, the pain transforming to fear when one of the men asked, "What was that?"

"Viktor's shit driving is slinging around our precious cargo," another one laughed.

"Either that or she's awake," the first man said.

"Lemme check."

Mia scrambled to pull the bag over her head, praying the man didn't notice that her hands were now in front. She forced herself to go limp and lie still, eyes staring through the porous fibers of the material surrounding her face.

A shadow stretched over her, and then she felt fingers fumbling around the top of her shoulder. For a moment Mia was confused; then she realized that he was searching for her subclavian pressure point and braced herself for what she knew was coming.

On cue, the man gripped down hard, his fingers digging deep into the underlying tissue. The pinch of the nerve unleashed a kaleidoscope of agony, and it took everything Mia had not to tense up. Or cry out.

The pain seemed to last forever. Then just when she was ready to admit defeat, it was over.

"Well?" the first voice asked.

"Nah, she's out like a light," the man said, returning to his seat.

With the threat minimized, Mia turned her attention to what she was going to do next, how the hell she was going to get out of this. Her mind slipped back to the two-day countercustody course her father had made her attend in Elgin, Texas. It had been a brutally hot summer, and like any sixteen-year-old girl, Mia would have much rather spent the weekend hanging out with her friends at the pool than sweating through a class on learning how to survive a kidnapping.

She'd told her father as much. Tried to explain that not everyone they met on the street was trying to hurt them, but the man wasn't listening.

"Mia, there's a good chance you will *never* need any of this stuff I've been teaching you," he'd said. "But it's better to have it and *not* need it than the other way around."

They were not the words Mia had wanted to hear, and like a petulant child, she'd lashed out. "You're just paranoid because of what happened to your sister," she snapped.

Her words hit like a fist, and her father stepped back, the flash of pain Mia saw in his eyes inducing instant regret. "Dad . . . I'm so—"

"No, you're right . . . I am paranoid," he'd said with a soft voice. "Because I know that if Polly had half the training you do, she'd still be alive. And that's *exactly* why you're going."

The class wasn't as bad as Mia had thought. In fact, she'd actually enjoyed the real-world scenarios the instructors had used to teach them threat detection and situational awareness. They'd preached *avoidance* of high-risk situations as the best strategy for not becoming a victim of a kidnapping.

"Stay away, stay alive."

Unfortunately, while Aunt Polly had been minding her own business when she was snatched off the street in Brownsville, Texas, Mia had gone looking for the trouble. Still, as she lay hooded and zip-tied in the back of the truck, it wasn't fear but the knowledge of what the news of her abduction would do to her father that had Mia's full attention.

Losing his sister had aged the man, sent him stumbling down into a black hole of depression that he was just now beginning to emerge from, and the thought of what he would do when he found out about *her* abduction was simply too terrible to bear.

I've got to get out of here.

Mia focused on remembering everything she could from the class so many years ago, trying to recall what the instructors had told them to do *after* they'd been taken. There had been three rules: manage the initial shock, control the fear . . . Damn, what was the last one?

She could feel the answer lingering at the edge of her mind, like a splinter lodged just out of sight. *What is it? Think, dammit, think.*

Before she could summon the correct response, the truck was pulling up to the clearing, the rhythmic beat of the Huey's rotors washing loud overhead. Her mind screamed at her to fight, and as the doors were flung open and the men climbed out, she was desperate to get out of the flex cuffs.

Bending herself double, she went for the Station IX Scorpion tucked into her boot, but just as her fingers found the handle, the final tenet appeared out of thin air.

Prepare the escape.

And with that she lay back and waited to see what would come next.

CHAPTER 26

REBEL CAMP
Ubili, DRC

Twenty miles northwest of the mine, the convoy of six Ural-4320s trundled through the jungle, their springs creaking under the full loads of ore. Near the back of the line, Gavin Roos studied the fragmentation grenades bobbing on the length of paracord stretched across the cab of the truck.

Mineral smuggling in the DRC was a dangerous game, and even with the network of government agents, crooked cops, and trigger-happy rebels Sterling paid off each month to let Roos and his men through, he could never be sure if his allies were going to wave him along the way or put a bullet in his head. Roos did what he could to minimize the risks, but no matter how many times he changed the routes or how well armed they traveled, there were only so many ways through the jungle.

So he kept his head on a swivel and double-checked the Vektor R4 assault rifle slung across his chest. Then, needing a nicotine hit, Roos lit a cigarette, his eyes drifting over the landscape scrolling past the window.

Hostile or not, it was still beautiful country, and despite the constant threat of death, many called it home. Roos envied them for that. He liked to imagine that at one time there might have been a place for him among the thatched huts and ferrous red dirt, but just as quickly as the thought had occurred, reality came rushing back.

The truth was, Roos had been living on borrowed time ever since he'd killed Angelo, and if Pieter and the men he'd sent to find Sawyer came back empty handed, he knew that the next time he saw Botha, the other man would have orders to put a bullet in Roos's head.

Which was why he and Pieter had come up with an escape plan.

Stealing from a man like Alexander Sterling was a death warrant—a surefire way to earn a bullet and a shallow grave in the middle of the bush. But since that was where Roos and his men were already headed, they might as well enjoy the ride.

Siphoning from the loads had been as easy as recalibrating the scales so no one would notice, but unlike Sterling, who had the processing facilities and connections to sell his ore directly to his customers, Roos had to sell his stolen shares at the *comptoirs*—the markets where the black-market mineral merchants would buy the illegal ore for pennies on the dollar.

He had sold a few smaller shipments that way but been quick to realize that the paltry sums he and Pieter were making were not worth the risk. No, to make the kind of cash necessary to retire, Roos needed a single client with deep pockets. He'd found exactly what he was looking for in the Chinese.

The only problem was he'd been forced to cut Major Rambo—one of the local rebel leaders—in on the score, pay him to keep the roads clear and the rebels off his ass. It wasn't the optimal relationship, but so far the man had kept up his end of the bargain by providing safe passage for the first two loads. Now all Roos had to do was figure out how to deal with Tommy and the rest of the men who were set to arrive later that afternoon.

The slowing of the truck brought him back to the present, and he looked up to see the turnoff ahead. Switching the radio channel to his team's secure net, he instructed the lead driver, "Our turn is coming up—you guys are on your own."

"Copy, boss."

While the first four vehicles continued straight, Roos's driver tapped the brakes and worked the gears, trying to slow the overloaded vehicle before making the turn.

"Hold on, boss."

Roos took an anxious drag of his cigarette and braced an arm against the A-pillar, praying the vehicle didn't flip. With four tons of ore in the back, the truck handled like a barge with a stuck rudder, its springs squealing in protest as they reached the apex of the turn. Branches smacked against the hood, slapping the passenger-side mirror off the truck, but then they were through, the road straightening out before them.

"I owe you a case of beer for that one," Roos said, releasing the breath he hadn't realized he'd been holding.

The man grinned and shoved the truck back into a higher gear, exhaust billowing from the stacks as it accelerated. Now in the lead of his own two-vehicle convoy, Roos turned his attention to the map and the tiny *X* he'd scratched on the surface.

"Almost there. Everybody stay frosty," he said over the radio.

They continued down the road for another five miles until he motioned for his driver to slow down as they neared the spot where they were supposed to meet Major Rambo. The driver brought the truck to a grinding halt, and Roos grabbed the binos from the dash as he scanned the jungle, searching for any sign of the rebel commander.

The seconds ticked by, and with no sign of the man they'd come to meet, Roos was beginning to get that itchy feeling that had saved his life countless times before.

We need to move.

Roos was about to tell his driver as much when a spray-painted jeep with a Russian-made PKM machine gun mounted to the back came bouncing out of the bush.

"All right, boys, here we go," Roos said over the radio.

The driver of the jeep cranked the wheel hard over, its tires kicking up a rooster tail of dirt as he pulled a U-turn in the middle of the road. Then he was heading back the way he'd come, the gunner hanging onto the belt-fed machine gun motioning for Roos to follow.

Half a mile down the rutted path, the rebels' encampment was in a clearing that had been hacked out of the jungle. It was a chaotic, undisciplined scene, the collection of half-dressed armed men lounging around some equally bedraggled tents looking more like a traveling circus than a military operation.

"You sure about this, boss?" Roos's driver asked as he brought the truck to a stop.

Roos wasn't, but he was out of options, and before he could answer, a gangly man in a black beret and leather vest stepped out of one of the tents.

"Too late to back out now," Roos said, climbing down from the cab.

"Welcome, my bruddah," Rambo said, holding his arms wide, "to my humble abode."

"Humble, my ass," Roos said, nodding to the weapons cases with fresh Cyrillic writing stamped on their sides sitting next to the tent. "Where did you steal these?"

"They fell off a truck," Rambo said with a grin.

"Speaking of trucks, I need to get this stuff off-loaded as soon as possible."

"Not a problem, my friend," he said, nodding to a clump of gaunt-looking men huddled in the tall grass. "We have many hands to take care of such work."

Roos immediately recognized them as refugees, but before he could ask where Rambo had gotten them, an Asian man in a sweat-soaked linen shirt stepped out of the tent, his bodyguard tight on his hip as he crossed toward them.

"Fell off a truck, huh?" Roos asked under his breath.

"What can I say." The rebel commander shrugged. "Mr. Chin and his people are *very* determined to get their hands on this coltan."

Great.

Roos had first met Mr. Chin, or Colonel Lin Yu as he was known in the People's Liberation Army, in Kenya, and while they'd always had a cordial relationship, Roos had seen the man's brutality firsthand as he cleared villages outside Nairobi.

Yes, Chin was a coldhearted bastard who wouldn't hesitate to kill him and his men if they didn't keep their end of the bargain. But he was also the only man Roos knew who had the cash and the contacts to ensure that they kept breathing once Sterling found out about the theft.

With that thought at the forefront of his mind, Roos turned to greet the man.

"Good afternoon, Mr. Chi—"

"How much ore did you bring?" he snapped.

"Eight tons."

"And the final load?"

"It will be ready in twenty-four hours," Roos replied.

"There can be *no* delay," Chin said.

"And there won't be—you have my word."

"Good, then we have a deal."

"What about the money?" Roos asked.

Chin snapped his fingers, and his bodyguard stepped forward, handing him a ruggedized tablet with Roos's account already pulled up. "In your account as agreed."

At that, Rambo turned and began barking orders to his men. "Up on your feet and get these lazy bastards to work." His men jumped up, their batons hissing through the air as they rounded up the refugees and drove them toward the trucks.

With the human chain unloading the ore, Roos stepped away to light a celebratory cigarette. He was just turning his mind to what he was going to do about Tommy when the Iridium sat phone in his vest pocket came to life. He pulled the phone from his pocket and, seeing Pieter's number on the screen, answered the call. "How did it go?"

"That bitch Mia Webb spotted our snatch team in the gardens and tried to get Sawyer out," his lieutenant said. "Things got messy."

"How messy?"

"We killed her partner but lost Vickers in the park and two more during the takedown," Pieter said.

"And Mia?" Roos asked.

"She's alive—for now."

Dammit.

Getting into a gunfight in downtown Kinshasa was exactly the attention Roos had been warned *not* to attract. However, with Sawyer now firmly in their hands, he was confident that they could deal with any heat from Sterling if they tied everything up nice and neat. Still, with the date for the final shipment closing in, now he had a new problem: mainly what in the hell he was going to do with Mia Webb.

When it came to killing, Roos had never hesitated to pull the trigger—do what needed to be done. Yet there was something about killing an American federal agent that gave him pause.

But why?

He wasn't sure, and instead of giving the order he knew Pieter was waiting for, Roos decided to play it safe.

"You did a good job," he told him. "Take them back to the mine, and make sure you keep them separated until I get there."

"Roger that, boss."

Roos ended the call, wondering if he'd made a mistake, but before he had a chance to explore the question, Rambo stepped out of the tent with a bottle of palm wine.

"Stop moping around. It's time to celebrate."

CHAPTER 27

Atlantic Ocean

The Bombardier Global 7500 sliced across the Atlantic at 45,000 feet, its pair of GE Passport engines running wide open. While the pilots were hard at work searching for the optimal balance between speed and fuel efficiency, in the main cabin Travis Lane was double-checking his med ruck, and the rest of the team was finishing up a late lunch.

Compared to the nylon seats and bone-chilling interiors of the military transports he was used to, the $90 million Global 7500 was like something from another planet. From the fully stocked kitchen to the designated sleeping berths and fully adjustable chairs, everything about the aircraft was designed to make sure the Broadside operators arrived at their destination rested, fed, and ready to rock and roll.

But despite all its features, there was one thing the aircraft could *not* do, and that was tell the men of Guardian 7 what was waiting for them on the ground. A fact highlighted by the tension lines etched across the team's faces when a ding from the laptop sitting on the walnut table pulled Magnus to his feet.

"Well, it's about damn time," the big Swede said, moving to the table.

"What's going on?" Jones asked.

"Looks like the tracker has finally stopped moving."

"Put it on the screen," Jones said.

The Swede typed another command, and the flat screen mounted to the bulkhead blinked to life, the thick carpet of trees and rugged terrain eliciting a collective groan from the team.

"How the fuck are we supposed to get a Mi-17 into that shit?" Hunter demanded.

"You start by stowing the chitchat," Jones snapped. "Then you find me an LZ."

After taking off from Virginia, the team had walked Lane through the standard operating procedures, or SOPs, they had developed during their time together. Trying to take in that much knowledge in a short time was like drinking from a fire hose, but the one thing Lane had quickly grasped was that almost every operation Guardian 7 had conducted in the past revolved around their ability to use a helicopter to get the team in and out without being compromised.

Looks like that's not going to happen, he thought, looking up at the screen.

While it was obvious to Lane they weren't going to be able to find a landing zone that would accommodate the hulking Russian-built helo waiting for them in Goma, the other men spent the next ten minutes trying to do exactly that.

"I think I found one," Hunter said, pointing to a clearing ten klicks east of where the tracking icon was blinking. "Yeah, that looks like it'll work."

"There is no way," Magnus replied. "Those trees have got to be at least thirty meters tall."

"How many times do I have to tell your dumb ass to give me shit like that in American?" the former Marine demanded.

"A hundred feet," Lane answered.

"A hundred *feet*." Hunter nodded. "You see, I can work with that shit."

"No, you can't," Magnus said, "because the longest ropes we brought are sixty feet."

"Dammit!"

"I could rappel in," Felix said, looking at Jones. "Wrap the trees with det cord and blow them to create a landing zone."

"The idea is to get in and out *without* being noticed," Jones said. "Besides, that's a hell of a lot of det cord."

"So then how are we supposed to get in there?" Magnus demanded.

The cabin went silent, but while the rest of the team's attention stayed on the monitor, Lane could feel his team leader eyeing him.

"What about it, Lane?" Jones asked.

Lane looked up from his gear, not sure if the man wanted another fight or was legitimately interested in his opinion. "What do you mean, Chief?"

"You were a PJ, right?"

"Roger that."

"Well, since getting into tight places is what you do, I'm asking for your feedback," Jones said. "How would *you* get a team in there?"

"I'd jump," Lane replied.

There was a moment of silence as the four men tried to figure out if he was joking or not, and then Hunter burst into laughter. "Jump? Like with a parachute? That's the dumbest shit I've ever heard."

While the rest of the team was quick to discard his suggestion, Jones was obviously intrigued and silenced the men with a scowl before turning back to Lane.

"How?"

"When I was at Fort Bragg, we trained with the 57th Engineers," he said. "They were sappers, guys who used special equipment to jump into rough terrain."

"What kind of *special* equipment?"

"They used Kevlar suits and helmets with cages welded to the front so they could jump into the trees."

"And how the hell did they get down from there?" Jones asked.

"They tied ropes to their risers and rappelled down," Lane said.

"Sounds like a great way to break a leg," Hunter commented.

"Not if you keep your feet together."

"Where in the hell are we going to get that type of equipment?"

"There's a wildland firefighting team in South Africa that has it," Lane said. "If we have one of the supply guys back at Broadside reach out, maybe the South African team will meet us halfway with a couple of suits."

"Do you think they'll have one big enough to fit the giant?" Felix asked, nodding toward the Swede.

"I guess there's only one way to find out," Jones said, digging his sat phone from his pack.

———————

The Broadside jet touched down at Goma International Airport a little after 3:00 a.m. and followed the Russian-made Tigr SPM-2 to the lone hangar at the far end of the cargo terminal. While the pilots turned the aircraft around, Mako Jones stood up and slung his rifle over his chest rig.

"Lane, get your shit on and follow me," he called out.

"Roger that," Lane replied, blinking sleep out of his eyes. Giving his head a shake to wake himself up, Lane strapped his plate carrier over his chest, shoved a magazine into his HK416, and followed his team leader toward the front of the aircraft.

"What's going on?" he asked.

Jones ignored him and continued to the cockpit, where one of the men from the support team stood waiting with a black duffel bag.

"I already advised the pilot to keep the engines running," the man said, handing the bag to Jones.

"What about the helo and the gear we requested?" Jones asked.

"Cost us a fortune, but it's here," the man said, nodding to the Mi-17 visible through the hangar's clamshell doors.

"Good, now what about the guy I'm about to meet?"

"His name is Inspector Laurent, and so far, he seems to be playing ball."

"Heard that one before," Jones said with a slight shake of his head.

While they talked, Lane glanced out the window, the sight of the Russian-made armored car catching him off guard. "You're not seriously thinking about going out there, are you? I mean, they've got a tank."

"First of all, it's not a tank. It's an infantry mobility vehicle," Jones said. "And second, if we don't go out there and hand *this* bag of cash to *that* customs official, this is going to be a very short trip."

"I think this is a terrible idea," Lane said, chambering a round.

"Well, good thing nobody asked you. Now shut up and open the door."

Lane disengaged the lock and opened the cabin door, the wet smack of the humid Congolese night catching him off guard. "Shit, it's hot," he said.

"Wait until the sun comes up," Jones said, before descending the airstair.

Lane followed him down to the tarmac, his eyes shifting from the tall man in the starched uniform to the three soldiers standing around the Russian armored car.

"Mr. Jones?" the man asked.

"That's right."

"I am Inspector Laurent," he said, extending a hand. "I understand that you need to buy some discretion?"

"That's right," Jones said. "I'm also going to need some fuel and a bogus flight plan for the Mi-17 that landed early this evening."

"A *bogus* flight plan?" Laurent repeated.

"Is that a problem?" Jones asked, unzipping the bag.

"Mr. Jones, I'm afraid that even in Africa things are not quite that simple," he replied. "There are protocols that have to be followed . . . forms that need to be filled out."

"Yeah, well, we don't have time for all that," Jones said, tossing the duffel at the man's feet, the impact sending banded stacks of crisp hundred-dollar bills spilling out to the ground.

At the sight of the cash, Laurent's eyes went wide as dinner plates, and for a moment Lane thought the man was going to pass out. But he was quick to recover, and after shooting a guilty glance back toward the soldiers at the armored car, he dropped to a knee and scooped the fallen cash back into the duffel.

"Well, Inspector," Jones asked, "do we have a deal?"

"Y-yes . . . yes," Laurent said, zipping the duffel and standing.

"Good," Jones said. "Now, if you would excuse us, we've got work to do."

"*Libaku malamu*—good luck," the inspector said before turning on his heel.

The soldiers standing around the Tigr SPM-2 mounted up, and after the inspector climbed back inside, the armored car roared off in a cloud of diesel. As the brake lights faded, Lane wiped the sweat from his brow and turned toward his team leader.

"That dude just made more money in five minutes than he has in the last five years," he said as they walked back to the Bombardier.

"Yep." Jones nodded. "And the worst part is, if we aren't out of here by the time he comes back to work tomorrow, the slippery little shit is going to want even more."

CHAPTER 28

Goma, DRC

An hour later, all the gear had been unloaded and the support crew had launched the drone they'd unpacked from one of the shipping crates. While the rest of the team was huddled around the laptop, watching as the tech guided the UAV to the target area, Lane stood at a long table, his olive-drab undershirt soaked with sweat as he looked over one of the parachutes the crew of the Mi-17 had brought with them.

As they'd already provided the pilots with the coordinates for the drop zone and the approach heading, all that was left to do was check the chutes. The rigger tags attached to each parachute showed that they'd been recently packed, and at a glance, the buckles and straps that made up the harness all appeared to be in good condition. But Lane wasn't in the habit of putting his life in the hands of strangers, and knowing the team was counting on him to keep them safe, he dutifully repacked each one himself.

It was tedious work, but he gave it his full attention and was just finishing up the final parachute when Jones stepped to the table. "How much longer?" he asked, pulling a can of Copenhagen Long Cut from his pocket.

"Just finishing up the last chute," Lane said, wiping the sweat from his eyes.

"What's the altitude?"

"Right now, we've got a full moon and a clear sky. If that doesn't change, we will drop at seven hundred feet."

"And if it changes?" Jones asked, returning the can of dip to his pocket.

"We jump lower." Lane shrugged.

Jones grunted and turned his attention to the Kevlar jumpsuits and caged helmets that had come with the parachutes. The equipment looked like something out of a *Mad Max* movie, and while Lane's team leader was doing his best to hide it, his nervousness was palpable. Not that Lane blamed him.

There was nothing normal about jumping out of a perfectly good aircraft, especially in the middle of the night, and considering the low altitude, there were literally hundreds of things that could go wrong. Still, they had a job to do, and if Lane had learned anything during his time with the 24th, it was that fear was contagious, and the *last* thing he needed was for Jones's uncertainty to spread to the rest of the team.

"Tell you what, Chief," he said, handing over his chute. "Why don't you take my chute. I set it for a nice, *easy* opening."

"You can do that?"

"Hell yeah," Lane lied. "Don't tell me they didn't teach you that at SEAL school."

"It's called BUDS," Jones replied, "and the answer is no: they don't give a shit about our comfort in the teams."

Before Lane could respond, a shout from Hunter alerted them that the drone was finally over the target area.

"Time for the brief," Jones said.

Lane grabbed his rifle and followed his team leader over to the table. At $20,000, the Latvian-made Penguin C was the most sophisticated UAV on the market, and despite weighing less than fifty-five pounds, it could carry enough fuel to stay aloft for twenty hours. But more impressive than its range was the 60 mm infrared camera mounted below the nose, and thanks to the clarity of the video feed being beamed back to the hangar, the team had a clear view of the mine below.

Usually, Lane would have taken comfort in having real-time intel on a target, but one look at the treacherous terrain waiting for them, and he found himself wishing they'd gone in blind. After a second pass around the target, Jones moved to the map taped to the side of the equipment boxes and walked them through the mission brief.

"We are going to drop here," he said, pointing at the red X on the map, "and head east to rally point one. Once we are in position, the drone is going to mark the target building with its IR laser, and once we have confirmation, Felix and Magnus will set up a support-by-fire position. When they're set, the rest of us will move to the target building and grab the principal. Any questions?"

"Yeah," Hunter said. "That's a nine-kilometer movement. How in the hell are we going to make it through that and get into position before the sun comes up?"

"If we don't, you'll miss the extraction bird," Jones said, "and I promise you, the *last* thing you want is to be stuck out in that jungle alone. Anyone else?"

"Yeah," Lane said. "Do you want me inside?"

"Negative. You stay on the exterior in case Hunter gets another one of his nosebleeds."

"Nice try, rookie." Magnus winked.

"*After* we rescue the principal, we will move to the primary extraction site, which is this ridge on the southwest corner of the mine," Jones said, pointing to the map. "Then we board the helo and return to base."

"And the secondary extraction?" Lane asked.

"Secondary extraction?" Hunter asked.

"Yeah, like if something happens to the helo," Lane added. "I mean, you do have a secondary extraction site, right?"

"Negative, we've got one way in and one way out," Jones said.

Now it was *Lane's* turn to be nervous, and he stared at his team leader, not sure if he was messing with him or if they were serious about not having an alternate way out. "You're screwing with me, right? I mean, there's no way we are going in without an alternate extraction point or at least a contingency plan."

"It's not an ideal situation, but it's up to us to make it work," Jones said.

"But what if—"

"This isn't the Air Force," Jones snapped. "We work with what we have. Now, get your shit and let's get ready to roll."

Knowing there was nothing else he could say, Lane snapped to and headed over to his gear, fighting the growing apprehension as he kitted up.

CHAPTER 29

Carson West sat inside the Spring House Tavern, the remains of his Jack and Coke leaving rings on the bar. He'd been waiting for a refill, but the bushy-haired bartender was too busy flirting with the tanned coeds perched at the edge of the bar to pay him any attention, and West was running out of patience.

With its wood-paneled walls and rough-hewn tables, the Spring House was trendier than the dive bars West had favored during his time with the CIA. But the ambience notwithstanding, the booze was cheap, and as West was looking to get tanked, that was all that mattered.

Now, if he could only get that drink.

"Hey, buddy," he said, shaking his glass at the bartender.

"I'll be right there," the man replied.

Patience had never been one of West's virtues; still, waiting a few extra minutes for a drink wasn't usually an issue. But his nerves were stretched thin, and sitting there at the bar, he was beginning to feel like a jar of nitroglycerin—ready to blow at the slightest provocation.

The day had started off well enough, and after a solid nine hours of sleep and a double espresso, West had headed into the office feeling reborn. Despite the humidity, summer in Virginia was beautiful, and with the BMW feeling like it was driving on rails, he'd opened the sunroof, cranked up the stereo, and let himself forget about Jones,

Sterling, and all the other bullshit that had his stress level at an all-time high.

But the euphoria was quick to fade when he walked into his office and the anxious buzz of voices drew his attention to the window that overlooked the TOC. Unnerved by the sound, West opened the blinds and looked down. The frenzied activity and the satellite feed being displayed on the mission monitor quickly sent him to his computer to find out what in the hell was going on.

Tugging his ID card from his pocket, West shoved it into the reader and typed his password at the prompt. The hard drive hummed as it worked through the start-up programs, and when the home screen finally came up, he accessed the mission log, and the name he found at *Active File* made his heart skip in his chest.

Alexander Sterling. No, this is not fucking happening.

West stepped back, his knees suddenly weak. He took a seat and began tugging at his tie, desperate to figure out how Sterling had gotten ahold of one of their trackers. Then he remembered the Mark IIs that he'd been ordered to deactivate.

Oh shit.

His first thought was to reach for the phone and call Sterling's office, demand to know what in the hell he was thinking, putting him at such risk. But before he had a chance, the door swung open, and a tight-faced Taran Carter came stomping into his office.

"You want to tell me why in the *fuck* we've got a tracker that isn't supposed to exist going live in Kinshasa?"

West studied his boss for a moment, not sure what to say. Then his training came rushing back, and he remembered his hollow-eyed counter-interrogation instructor back at Harvey Point lecturing on what they should do if they were ever scooped up in a nonpermissive environment.

"Everyone breaks," he'd said. "But until you do, your *only* chance to make it out alive is to lie, deny, and make counteraccusations."

It was a skill West had mastered and one he was quick to put to use. "Sir, it has to be a software error," West said, forcing a calm he didn't feel. "Have you talked to the engineers?"

"No, Carson," his boss snapped. "I haven't talked to the engineers—do you know why?"

"No sir, I don—"

"Because you are the one I told to handle this bullshit."

"And I handled it, sir. *You* signed off on the paperwork," West countered.

"Then why do I have an extraction team on its way to pick up a client we don't have?"

"I have no idea."

"Then get your ass up and go find out," his boss barked.

West was on his feet and moving around his desk in an instant, but before he reached the door, Taran grabbed him by the arm and pulled him in close.

"There have been too many odd coincidences around here lately," he said, his voice cold as a blade. "Too many things happening in the shadows."

"What do you mean?" West asked, praying his voice sounded more confident aloud than it did in his head.

"First Jones's team gets hit in Mexico, and now this tracker in the DRC," he hissed. "It's Sterling—I know it is. That narcissistic fuck is trying to ruin me because I kicked him off the board."

West had never seen his boss this paranoid, but he took it for what it was. A gift. "There's only *one* person on Broadside who's been there for both of those operations," he said, matching the man's conspiratorial tone. "And that's Jones."

"Mako?" Taran responded. "Why would he—"

West pressed his advantage, his mind racing as he worked to shift the blame onto the aging SEAL. "Think about it, sir; he is the only one who has never talked about what *really* happened in Mexico."

"What about the rest of the team, and more importantly, why would Mako do something like that?"

"Maybe he needs the money, or maybe it's his ego"—West shrugged—"or maybe he sees it as a way to bring *me* down."

"You?"

"Yes sir. Since I was the one technically in charge of the mission, he blames me for what happened."

It was all bullshit, of course, and West knew that once the paranoia wore off, his boss would realize that Jones didn't have the brains or the ability to manipulate Broadside's systems. Which left West with two solutions: fabricate the proof to pin it all on Mako, *or* alert Sterling to the ongoing mission in the DRC and let him and his mercs take care of the issue.

The bartender setting down a fresh drink before him brought West back to the present, and he looked up to see the man offer an apologetic smile. "Sorry about the delay," he said.

"No problem," West replied. He sipped on the drink and studied himself in the mirror, his mind circling back to Jones. Ruining a man's career was one thing, but killing him was something else. Something the civilized world said was to be avoided at all costs. Still, at the end of the day, West knew that someone had to take the fall.

Fuck it, he thought, gulping the rest of the drink. *Better him than me.*

CHAPTER 30

Goma, DRC

The pilot of the Mi-17 twisted the throttle, and the Russian-made helicopter shuddered. The static electricity building up on the tip of the big helicopter's blades looked yellow through Lane's night vision as they lifted off.

"Big Top, Archangel One is airborne."

"Archangel One, Big Top copies," the commo tech back at the hangar said.

The pilot banked west and dropped the nose, while the men in the cargo hold double-checked their weapons and gear.

They flew west over the Virunga National Park at fifteen thousand feet, the dense cloud bank below them an impenetrable gray shroud. While the pilot fought the crosswinds that threatened to slap the helo out of the sky, the copilot kept his eyes glued to the terrain-avoidance radar and the digital *X* that marked the drop zone.

Back in the cargo hold, Lane sat on the nylon bench, the unyielding collar of the Kevlar jumpsuit he wore digging into his throat. He was trying to adjust it when the amber jump light flashed to life and the copilot advised that they were ten minutes out.

Lane pulled the carbon fiber jump helmet onto his head and was securing the chin strap when the radio hissed in his ear. "This better work," Jones said.

"It will," Lane replied, feigning a confidence he didn't feel.

"Good, 'cause you're going out first."

"Wait . . . what?"

Before Jones could say anything else, the aircraft began its descent and the ramp cracked open, the wind rushing into the cargo hold loud as a freight train. Lane got to his feet and waddled toward the rear of the aircraft, the scarred metal cage welded to the front of the jump helmet distorting his vision.

By the time he made it to the ramp, he was sweating, the parachute and the kit bag full of guns and gear strapped to his body threatening to bend him double. He clipped his static line onto the cable that ran the length of the cargo hold, shuffled to the edge of the ramp, grabbed the metal support beam, and leaned out as far as he could, searching for a terrain feature that would tell them where in the hell they were. But with the Mi-17 still in the clouds, for all intents and purposes, he was blind.

Lane checked the GPS strapped to his wrist and, seeing they were still at a thousand feet, came up on the radio and ordered the pilot to descend to eight hundred feet. The helo bucked like a bronco as it dropped, the turbulence threatening to throw Lane from the ramp when he leaned out to check again.

"Still negative visibility," he said over the radio. "Take us down to five hundred."

"Five hundred?" the pilot demanded. "Are you serious?"

"Just do it," Lane replied.

At seven hundred feet, the gray haze began to clear, and by the time they reached six hundred feet, Lane got his first clear look at the ground. But instead of giving him a warm and fuzzy feeling, the endless stretch of green that marked the triple-canopy jungle sent his stomach twisting into knots.

"Hold it here," he said.

As a former PJ, Lane was no stranger to jumping out of airplanes, and during his career, he'd jumped into some of the most austere and dangerous environments in the world. But whether it was the basic static line jumps he'd first learned at Airborne School or the more advanced HALO jumps that he'd conducted in the mountains of Afghanistan, there was one rule that had never changed—stay the hell out of the trees. That was clearly going to be a problem here.

Man, I hope this works.

"Drop zone five minutes out," the pilot advised.

Again, Lane leaned out of the aircraft, the slipstream threatening to slap the night vision goggles off his face as he searched for the tiny clearing they'd identified on the map. But traveling at over a hundred miles an hour, he found it hard to see anything but the dizzying blur of trees.

Where the hell is it?

He was about to pull himself back in and tell the pilot that they were going to have to make another loop when he saw it, the slight scar of bare earth cut into the jungle. Leaning back inside the aircraft, Lane blinked the tears from his eyes and held up his left index finger.

"One minute," he yelled.

His team nodded back and tightened up, each man going over his last-minute check.

"Thirty seconds."

Lane watched the jump light, his lower back tight from all the gear strapped to his body. That plus the pressure in his bladder from all the water they'd been guzzling to stay hydrated, and all he could think of was getting to the ground.

Finally, the light flashed green. Lane stepped forward and threw himself off the ramp, the prop blast slapping him in the face like an invisible hand, the slipstream catching his legs and threatening to flip him over. Jamming his chin to his chest to protect his neck from the riser, he grabbed the rip cord and yanked it free.

The spring-loaded canopy shot from the pack tray and caught air, jerking him to a sudden halt. Immediately, Lane looked up to inspect the canopy for holes and then grabbed the toggles and steered into the wind. On a normal jump this would have been the time to settle in and enjoy the ride, but jumping this low, all Lane had a chance to do was clamp his legs together, and then he was crashing through the canopy like a meteorite.

The limbs slapped his body, and the rake of the scrubby branches tore at his face shield like wooden talons. He kept his core flexed and his feet and knees together, waiting for one of the branches to catch the canopy.

But instead of being jerked to a halt, he kept falling, his body bouncing around like a human pinball. Thankful for the face guard, Lane hazarded a look between his boots, searching desperately for the ground, but all he saw was another large limb rushing up to meet him.

This is going to hurt.

He hit hard, the impact buckling his legs and blasting the air from his lungs, but worse than the spine-jarring pain that came with the collision was the fact that he was now tumbling forward, the risers of his parachute wrapping around his right leg.

By the time he'd fallen through the first layer and into the understory, Lane felt as if he had just gone a full round with Mike Tyson, but with the sight of the ground rushing up to meet him, he knew that was the least of his problems.

Desperate to stop his fall, Lane reached forward and was fumbling with the handle of his reserve when the chute finally snagged on a branch, the risers wrapped around his leg snapping tight. Dazed by the impact and now hanging upside down, Lane was unable to protect himself when his gear bag swung down and into his face. The weight of the bag was enough to dent the protective mesh of his jump helmet and smash his night vision against the bridge of his nose. There was a muted pop followed by blinding pain and the taste of blood in his mouth, but at least he was alive.

However, the relief was short lived, as he heard the unmistakable sound of ripping fabric.

Before he could deploy his reserve chute and climb down, his main tore free of the branch. He pitched forward and fell another five feet before the chute once again snagged a limb. With his suspension lines wrapped around his ankle, Lane was unable to do anything but watch as gravity took hold of his rifle and pulled it off his back.

It fell free and clattered through the lower branches before hitting the ground. Desperate to get down before Jones or anyone else on the team found him hanging there like a piñata, he deployed his reserve and then carefully unhooked his riser straps. Free of the harness, he crunched himself into an inverted sit-up, determined to get to the knife strapped to his boot.

He could hear Jones taking a head count below him as the rest of the team shrugged out of their chutes. "Felix, Hunter, Magnus . . . where the fuck is Lane?"

Fueled by the impending embarrassment and his head pounding from the blood rushing to his brain, he lunged for the handle.

Ripping the blade free, Lane grabbed onto the reserve chute with his left hand and sawed at the riser with his right. It was harder than he'd imagined, but somehow he made it happen without cutting his leg off, and as the last strand of 550 cord snapped free, he tossed the knife and grabbed the reserve with both hands, and then he was on a fast ride to the ground.

He landed on his shoulder but quickly rolled to his feet and grabbed the rifle lying beside him just as Jones came stomping toward him.

"Where the hell have you been?"

"Pulling security, Chief," Lane lied, leaving his helmet on so the man couldn't see his face.

"Well, get out of that stupid suit," Jones said. "We're moving out in five mikes."

Lane didn't need to be told twice, and after checking his rifle for damage, he unhooked his med ruck from around his waist and pulled off the helmet and Kevlar suit. He wiped the blood from his face and then pulled out a tube of camo greasepaint from the pouch on his kit. Careful to avoid his damaged nose, Lane smeared it across his face and then pulled on his boonie cap.

When he moved to rejoin the team, Jones checked his wrist-mounted computer to make sure they still had a lock on the beacon and then pressed the transmit button on the L3Harris tactical satellite radio.

"Davy Jones, this is Guardian 7."

There was a moment of silence as the transmission was collected by a communications satellite and bounced back to the States, and then came the reply. "Guardian 7—this is Davy Jones; go ahead."

"Davy Jones, Guardian 7 is on the ground and moving out, time now," Jones said.

"Davy Jones copies all—good hunting."

With that, Jones switched back to the team's internal net. "All right, let's move out. Lane, you're on point."

CHAPTER 31

Ubili, DRC

Lane was fully aware that the GPS strapped to his wrist was all but useless in the triple-canopy jungle. Knowing it would sync when it got a clear view of the sky, he tugged his lensatic compass from the breast pocket of his tiger-stripe BDUs, and after shooting an azimuth, he began making his way west.

Land navigation, the military's name for orienteering, was a perishable skill, a task that once learned must be honed until it was second nature, but Lane knew that wasn't the reason he was taking the lead. No, Lane was on point because he was the new guy, and until he was accepted by the team, he was expendable.

Fuck it. He could do this.

By the time he'd made it two hundred meters, he was sweating profusely from the humidity, and the camo paint smeared across his face was already starting to run. The terrain was a nightmare, an uphill slog through wait-a-minute vines and thorn-studded liana and around tree trunks the size of Buicks.

Lane wiped his face with the back of his glove, the caustic scent of mosquito dope stinging his nostrils. With the trees blocking the moon, his night vision was worthless, and he switched the toggle, turning night vision to thermal. The jungle was alive with heat signatures, and it took Lane a second of working the knob on the side to find the right spectrum. Finally, he got it dialed in and picked up the pace.

The heavily overgrown area they were marching through was prime real estate for an ambush. The intel reports said there hadn't been any rebel activity in the area for the last few days, which was good, because with the men behind him sounding like a herd of drunk elephants, anyone in the bush was sure to hear them coming.

Jones must have been thinking the same thing, because a moment later he came up on the radio. "Lane, you keep moving. The rest of you loud-ass motherfuckers, hold here."

"Five copies."

Now alone, Lane pushed his pace harder, his eyes locked on the distant light shimmering through the trees. He stopped four hundred meters short of the target and keyed his throat mike twice to tell Mako that he'd arrived. Dropping to a knee, he tugged the tube of his hydration bladder free and put the valve in his mouth. He took a deep pull, the water warm and tasting of plastic, but it was wet, and after spending the last two and a half hours battling the heat and the terrain, that was all that mattered.

"We've got thirty minutes till hit time," Jones whispered over the radio. "I need you to move up and get eyes on the target."

Lane double tapped his push-to-talk to let the man know that he was moving and rose to a crouch.

The sun was coming up in the east, and day's first light filtered through the trees. Lane flipped up his NODs and scanned the area before him, searching for the path of least resistance so he could make his way forward.

He found a break in the undergrowth fifty feet from the edge of the tree line and dropped to his stomach. Careful to keep his rifle out of the mud, Lane slithered through the tall grass and was almost to the edge when the voice of the drone operator came over the radio.

"Hold. You've got a hostile to your right."

Shit.

Lane froze and slowly turned his head, nearly stroking out when he saw a man leaning against a tree five feet to his right, his rifle slung casually across his chest.

"Can we get past him?" Jones asked over the radio.

"Negative," Lane replied, his voice barely a whisper.

"Roger. Take him out."

Slinging the rifle, Lane drew the Ka-Bar from its sheath, got up slowly, and stepped forward, the outsides of his feet making contact with the ground first as he crept toward the man, blade at the ready. He slipped in behind him, left hand clamping down tight over the other man's mouth, his right driving the blade through the top of the guard's shoulder and down into his heart.

It was a killing blow, but the man's brain didn't know that, and his reaction was one of pure survival. He arched his back and kicked his leg, using the last of his life's blood to try to get away, but then he went silent.

Lane pulled the knife from the man's chest and wiped the blade across his shirt before lowering the body to the ground. He returned the weapon to its sheath and then keyed up on the radio.

"Clear."

The rest of the team materialized from the shadows, Jones looking down at the dead guard at his feet and giving Lane a thumbs-up. "Let's go," he said, pointing to the machine gunners.

The two men moved up with their machine guns, Magnus pausing to give Lane a congratulatory clap on the shoulder while Felix continued toward the break in the trees. Just as Lane turned to follow, there was a *tink* of metal, followed by the guttural roar of a Claymore mine.

Lane threw himself to the ground, his ears ringing from the explosion as the seven hundred ball bearings packed into the antipersonnel device came tearing through the undergrowth. Choking on the caustic burn of the expended C-4, he quickly rose to his feet, drawn to Felix's pained cries.

"We've got a man down," Magnus shouted.

"I'm coming," Lane yelled back. But before he'd taken a step, he heard the distinctive whoosh of a flare rushing skyward.

Shit.

He managed to duck behind a banana tree a second before the flare burst with a pop, the glaring burn of its magnesium light slicing through the gloaming like a searchlight. Two more flares followed the first, and then an unseen machine gun chugged to life, the bullets slicing toward him like a buzz saw.

CHAPTER 32

NORTHSTAR MINE

Ubili, DRC

Mia sat alone in the center of the room, her only companion the distant clang of sledgehammers. It was hot inside the makeshift prison, and her head pounded from whatever they'd dosed her with back in Kinshasa.

Still, she was alive, and right now that was all that mattered.

Mia wiped her face against the sleeve of her shirt to clear the sweat from her eyes, the metal chain that ran from the handcuff on her left wrist down to the eyebolt mounted to the floor rattling as she moved. Removing the slack from the chain, she grabbed it with both hands and pulled until her biceps began to burn.

But the anchor held fast.

Worth a shot.

Dropping the chain to the floor, Mia settled back in the chair, the pain in her thigh reminding her of the tracker lodged beneath the skin. If Sawyer was to be trusted and the tracker actually worked, then someone was coming to get her. Which meant Mia wasn't completely alone. But whatever solace she might have found in the impending rescue was soon eclipsed by the bitter realization that John was dead.

While Mia hadn't pulled the trigger, there was no escaping the fact that she'd gotten her friend killed. No way to rationalize the pain or assuage the soul-crushing guilt that followed. But Mia had been in the game long enough to know that this was *not* the time to grieve.

"In combat you let the dead bury the dead," her father used to say. "Your job is to stay alive long enough to mourn them."

At the time it hadn't made any sense, but as she sat there in the room, the meaning was crystal clear. Shoving the emotions back into their box, Mia closed her eyes and forced herself to focus on what she'd seen when they'd landed at the mine.

Obviously assuming she was no threat, her captors had taken the bag off before marching her into the building, and she'd managed to get a quick look at her surroundings. It was a primitive place, the living conditions and technology here on par with the mining techniques used during the California gold rush. In fact, despite the diesel-powered excavators she'd seen, the place didn't look anything like a mine. There were just a collection of corrugated-steel buildings and a patchwork of hand-dug pits filled with brackish brown water. But the worst part of it all was the workers she'd seen panting at the edges of the pits, their hollowed eyes void of any hope.

Mia wasn't a doctor, but she'd worked long enough on the border to recognize malnutrition. How these men were even moving was beyond her, and the suffering she'd seen in their eyes rekindled her determination to make Sterling and whoever else was responsible for this human suffering pay for what they'd done.

But first she had to get free.

On cue, there was a rattle of keys, followed by the *thunk* of the lock retracting. The door swung open, and the man who'd pulled her from the back of the truck stepped inside with a military-issued mess tin. The smell of whatever was in it caused her stomach to rumble.

"I brought you some food," he said, handing her the tin.

It was simple fare, beans and a piece of boiled chicken, but Mia couldn't remember anything tasting that good. She tore into the food, her mind slipping seamlessly back to her training as she studied him.

The fresh tread on his jungle boots and the state of his uniform told her that he was new. The fact that his shooting hand never strayed from the grip of the AK-74 slung to his front told her that he was dangerous.

"You work for Crimson Ridge?" she asked between bites.

"That's right," he said, shaking a cigarette from the pack he took from his front pocket.

"For Gavin Roos?"

He nodded, then lit the cigarette and took a drag.

"What's your name?"

"Liam," he said. "What's with all the questions, lady?"

"Force of habit," she replied. "So what happens now?"

"All they told me was to bring you something to eat," he said. "I just do what I'm told."

Mia nodded, a plan slowly unfolding in her mind. Keeping him talking was the best way she knew to keep him loose, but with Liam being brand new to the unit, there was a chance that continued questions might put him on guard.

"You didn't happen to bring any water, did you?"

"I forgot."

Mia shrugged and finished the rest of the food in two large bites. Then, when she was done, she set the tin on the ground near her left foot and wiped a hand across her lips. "That was good," she said.

Liam nodded, and while he continued to smoke, Mia flexed her right foot until she felt the reassuring heft of the Station IX Scorpion in her boot. Knowing she had one chance to make this work, she waited for him to come and retrieve the tin.

Time seemed to slow to a crawl, but finally Liam crushed the cigarette beneath his boot and started over. "Tell you what," he said. "I'll get you some water on my way back."

Mia shot him a smile and turned her attention to the far wall, pretending to take stock of her makeshift prison as he walked over to retrieve the tin. She drew her right leg in close and shifted in her chair, her muscles quivering as she watched him out of the corner of her eye.

Mia could feel the tension rising as Liam drew near. She focused on her breathing, forcing herself to stay calm and praying he couldn't hear her heart hammering in her chest.

Liam stopped right where she'd hoped, and holding the AK against his body with his right hand, he bent over to retrieve the tin with his left.

Wait for it . . . Wait for it. Now.

Mia turned her body to the left and was preparing to kick him in the head when an explosion came echoing through the night. The rumble of the concussion against the side of the building and the roar of the machine gun fire that followed stopped Liam just out of her reach.

"What was that?" he asked, looking up.

Giving up on the kick, Mia lunged forward and grabbed him by the front of the shirt. She pulled him in and at the same time snapped her upper body forward, driving her forehead into the bridge of Liam's nose.

The cartilage gave with a wet snap, and Liam pitched backward, the back of his skull bouncing off the floor. He lay there, eyes unfocused, blood and snot streaming from his flattened nose, while Mia fumbled to retrieve the ceramic cuff key she'd sewn into her belt before her first overseas assignment.

She found the seam and tore at it with her fingernails, the already difficult task made much harder by the fact that she only had one hand to work with.

C'mon, c'mon.

Liam groaned, and seeing that he was coming to, Mia redoubled her efforts, her fingers bleeding as she pulled at the final threads that held the small pocket shut. The last knot finally gave, and she pinched the key from its pocket, careful not to drop it when she brought it around to her front.

Her hands shook as she shoved the key into the keyhole, and then with a twist of her wrist, Mia was free and running for the door.

CHAPTER 33

The sun was just coming up when Gavin Roos stumbled out of the tent, his head pounding from the copious amount of palm consumed the night before. Staying the night had not been in the plan, but eight tons of ore was still eight tons of ore, and even with the rebels beating on them, the bedraggled refugees could only move so fast.

Fumbling his dark aviators down over his eyes, Roos went in search of his driver. He found the man passed out beneath a scrub tree, a pile of empty beer cans scattered around the mosquito net he'd pulled over his face.

"Get up," Roos said, kicking the man's boot.

The man grunted and sat up, his eyes bloodshot in the early-morning sun. "What's going on, boss?"

"Did you load that weapons case into the back of the truck?" he asked.

"Yes, boss."

"Good, we're getting the hell out of here," Roos said. "Go fetch the rest of our men and meet me back at the trucks."

The man scrambled to his feet, pulled on his plate carrier, and slung his rifle before trotting off to complete his mission. Roos watched him go, the spring in the man's step reminding him of his younger days in the army, when he and the lads would drink until three in the morning, get two hours of sleep, and then wake up and knock out a seven-kilometer run.

Hard to believe I was ever that young.

Pushing the thought out of his mind, Roos made his way over to the truck and the bottle of aspirin he prayed was waiting for him in the glove box. Rummaging around inside, Roos found what he was looking for. He unscrewed the cap and shook the remaining three pills into his mouth before chasing them with a long drink from a bottle of water.

Ten minutes later they were back on the main road, the sway of the now-empty trucks and the gentle seep of the early-morning sun through the trees easing his mood. There was no denying that the trip had exceeded his expectations, and with Sawyer and the girl now in custody, Roos could feel his luck beginning to change.

Still, he needed to know who Sawyer had been talking to and what he'd said. Then he could kill the man and tie up yet another loose end. The girl was a different story, and his thoughts immediately turned to the dinner he'd had with Rambo and the Chinese agent the night before. Looking back on it now, Roos wasn't sure if it had been the alcohol talking or if the wily Chinese colonel had been toying with him, but halfway through the first bottle of palm wine, the man had leaned in close and said, "My people in Kinshasa are talking about an American agent who went missing in the city."

The statement had caught Roos off guard, and he'd almost choked on his wine. Luckily Chin was too deep in his cups to notice and had continued without breaking stride.

"They are only rumors at this point," the man said ruefully, "but if they prove to be true, I can't imagine a more powerful commodity."

"Commodity?" Roos asked. "More like a death sentence if you ask me."

"If she was kidnapped by a jihadist, perhaps," the man agreed. "But if she was taken by someone who *knows* how to play the game, I can't think of a better form of insurance."

Insurance.

The word had gone off like a bottle rocket in Roos's head, and he'd cursed himself for not seeing Mia's value before. But how was he going to capitalize on it?

By the time they'd reached the halfway point of the drive, Roos had revived enough to try his first cigarette of the day. He lit it and took a cautious drag, waiting to see how his stomach would react, and when it didn't protest, he settled back into his seat—the answer to his question still hovering just out of reach.

And what am I going to do about Tommy?

That his old friend had been sent to spy on him was obvious. The question was, should Roos try to bring him into his confidence, buy his silence until the last load of ore could be delivered, or should he put a bullet in the back of Tommy's head and be done with it?

For most people in his position, the fact that the two men had a friendship that went back to their days together in the army would have been enough to ensure the man's life. But for Roos it wasn't loyalty but the man's utility that mattered to him now. He had to take the ore to the Chinese so he and his men could get out of this shit life once and for all, and Roos wasn't going to let anyone—not Tommy, not Sterling, and certainly not some nosy Fed from the United States—stand in his way.

Roos weighed his options, his mind spinning as he worked the angles, trying to figure out who, if any of them, was of value. But in the end, none of them mattered.

No, Tommy had to die. The question now became a matter of logistics, how and when to do it so as not to draw undue attention to himself. By the time they neared the mine, Roos had made a decision. He would kill Tommy before handing off the final load to the Chinese, and then he and Pieter would pay Rambo what they owed before slipping off to a nonextradition country. Someplace like Indonesia or Vietnam, where the girls were hot and the booze was cheap.

It was a good plan, nice and simple, and Roos lit a victory cigarette off the butt of the first as he leaned back in his seat. He closed his eyes, a contented smile spreading across his lips, until the distant boom of an explosion came echoing through the trees.

What the hell was that?

"Boss, look," his driver said, pointing to a break in the jungle ahead and a column of black smoke rising from the area where the mine was located.

Roos snatched the radio mike from the hook on the dash and spun the dial to the mine's security channel. "Pieter—what the hell is going on?"

Instead of an answer, he got a distorted hiss of static that told him they were out of range.

"Faster, dammit," Roos said, slapping the dashboard with the palm of his hand.

"I'm trying, boss," his driver replied.

The Russian-made cargo trucks were many things, but fast wasn't one of them, and even without the load of ore, the speedometer remained pinned at fifty miles an hour. Cursing himself for not thinking to bring one of the faster Land Rovers, Roos sat there, listening to the distant hammering of machine gun fire.

It was another five minutes before he finally was able to make radio contact, but even then it was hard for him to understand Pieter over the roar of gunfire.

"We're taking heavy fire from the south," the man said, his voice calm despite the battle raging around him.

"Is it the rebels?" Roos asked.

"Negative. They've already killed two of ours and taken out the tower," Pieter replied. "They're definitely pros."

Thinking they were after the ore, Roos was about to tell Pieter to send men to protect the mineral-processing building when Pieter said, "They're going for the prisoner."

Shit.

"I need you to send the helicopter to Rambo, tell him to load up as many fighters as will fit."

"You really think he will help us out?"

"Oh, he'll help us out, all right, for no other reason than he knows that if he doesn't, that Chinese bastard will kill him and everyone he's ever cared about," Roos said. "Now go."

CHAPTER 34

Lane threw himself to the ground, the bullets kicking dirt into his face and shredding the bark of the banana tree. He pulled a 40 mm HE round from his kit, shoved it into the grenade launcher mounted below the rifle, and snapped the breech closed. Rolling to his right, Lane prepared to send the grenade sailing toward the enemy.

But before he could fire, the big Swede leaped to his feet. "You motherfuckers," he yelled, spooling up the electric motor that powered the six-barreled minigun strapped across his chest.

Lane shouted at him to get down, but the man's only response was to mash his thumb down on the trigger. The minigun buzzed to life, the flame from its rotating barrel licking the tree line like a fire serpent as Magnus sent a burst of five hundred rounds rushing downrange in the blink of an eye.

Immediately all return fire ceased, but the big Swede worked the weapon deliberately from right to left, the hail of 5.56 tearing through trees. When he finally let off the trigger and the cloud of gun smoke passed, it was as if someone had run a bush hog through their position.

No way anyone survived that, Lane thought.

But no sooner had Magnus dropped to a knee beside his screaming comrade than Lane saw three men burst from one of the aluminum buildings and sprint for the tree line to their left. Realizing they were trying to flank them, Lane snapped the grenade launcher onto target and pulled the trigger, sending the first HE round arcing through the newly shorn trees.

"Contact left," he yelled.

The grenade hit the ground in front of the men and detonated in a wash of smoke and flame, the explosion flinging the men through the air. Lane ejected the casing and shoved a fresh grenade into the breech, then moved up to help Felix.

Jones was right behind him, and as Lane dropped his med ruck and went to work on the injured Corsican, his team leader began barking orders.

"Magnus, get that fucking machine gun up," he shouted at the vapor-locked Swede. "Hunter, watch our flank."

While the men moved to carry out his orders, Lane focused on Felix.

The blast had caught him in the left leg, the hail of 3.2 mm ball bearings amputating it below the knee. Lane yanked a tourniquet from his bag and looped it around the man's mangled limb. Ignoring the bullets snapping all around him, he tightened the windlass, desperate to stop the blood loss.

It took two tourniquets and a pressure dressing to get the bleeding under control. Once he got it stopped, Lane bundled Felix onto the collapsible litter and was just starting an IV when Jones dropped to a knee next to him.

"How bad is he?" Jones yelled over the gunfire.

It was a question Lane had been asked hundreds of times in the past, and one he'd learned had to be answered with absolute honesty.

"If we don't get him to a hospital in thirty minutes, he's going to die."

"The helicopter is on its way," Jones said. "ETA ten minutes."

With the helo en route and Felix packaged and ready to move, there was nothing else Lane could do for the man. He scooped up his rifle and turned his attention to the gunfight unfolding fifteen feet to his front.

It didn't take a tactical genius to realize they were in a bad spot, and with Hunter and Magnus playing dueling machine guns with the PKM firing from the guard tower at his eleven o'clock, their left flank was wide open. Realizing the threat, Lane took the initiative and hooked around Magnus to take up position behind a dry-rotted stump.

He brought the rifle to his shoulder and scanned the edge of the clearing through the Nightforce 1-8x24 scope mounted to the rail. A flutter of movement drew his attention to a depression in the terrain, and he snapped onto target just as three men broke cover. Lane thumbed the selector to fire, but before he could take the shot, the men disappeared from his field of view.

"We've got three men working around the left flank," the drone operator advised. "Another group is heading for the target building. You guys need to move."

Staying low, Lane crawled over to where Jones was trying to direct Hunter onto target. "You're too low. Adjust your fire," Jones instructed.

The former Marine lifted the barrel an inch and reengaged, but the string of profanity that followed told Lane that he'd missed his mark. "I can't get an angle on that fucker."

"Hey, Chief, the eye in the sky says—" Lane started.

"I heard what they said," Jones snapped. "What the hell do you want me to do about it?"

With the men from the east threatening to cut off their access to the LZ and the tower keeping the team pinned down, Lane realized that waiting for Hunter to get on target was not an option. He scanned his surroundings, a plan forming in his mind as he noted the small creek to his right that led to an open area on the west side of the target building. Crawling over to Felix's fallen rucksack, he retrieved the M72 light anti-tank weapon, or LAW, strapped to the side and slung it over his back.

Before he could key up on the radio and inform Jones of his plan, the man beat him to it. "What the hell are you going to do with that?" he asked over the radio, nodding toward the olive-green launcher.

"I can get a shot on the machine gun from that target building," Lane replied.

"This ain't the time to play hero," Jones said.

"Well, unless you want to walk back to Goma, I don't see another way."

Jones cursed under his breath and shook his head, the expression on his face telling Lane everything he needed to know.

"Chief, I can do this," he said.

Suddenly they both heard the sound of a Huey lifting off from the helo pad and turning east.

"We've got a bird in the air," the drone operator advised.

"Right now we've got the element of surprise, but in about thirty seconds, those assholes are going to get their shit together, and we're all going to be dead. So unless you've got a better idea, this is the only way," Lane insisted.

Jones glared at him, the twitch of his jaw muscles telling Lane that his words had hit home.

Come on, you hardheaded bastard, let me do my job.

"Whatever he's going to do, he better do it fast, because I'm running low on ammo," Hunter said.

"Fine!" Jones said, unbuckling the wrist-top computer. "But take this and grab the principal while you're at it. Hell, maybe we'll make it out of here alive."

"You just keep those assholes off my back," Lane said, strapping the computer to his arm.

Then he was gone.

CHAPTER 35

NORTHSTAR MINE
Ubili, DRC

Lane stayed low and moved to the edge of the tree line, where he took up a position behind a gnarled tree stump. Ripping the pin from the smoke grenade, Lane rose to a knee and hurled it toward the tower. It bounced across the broken ground and hissed to life, but before the cloud of smoke could build, the gunner transferred his PKM toward Lane's position and opened fire.

Fucker.

He threw himself flat, the dirt and grass kicked up by the round slapping him in the face. He rolled to the right, just as the flash of the tracers raced past him, close enough that he could smell the magnesium as he scrambled for the creek bed.

He dove over the edge and into the fetid water and dank mud below. The smell was overpowering and his stomach heaved, but Lane kept moving. He low crawled through the all-consuming muck, fighting the urge to vomit. The bile scalded the back of his throat, but he choked it down and slithered forward, his eyes locked on the roof of the target building.

Finally, Magnus opened up with the minigun, and when the gunner shifted his fire back to the trees, Lane pushed to his feet and scrambled up the muddy bank and out into the light, the sludge that had filled his boots squishing as he sprinted for the back side of the aluminum building. He slid into cover and unslung the launcher. At its most basic, the

M72 LAW was a tube within a tube, and to get it into action, Lane had to remove the arming pin and the muzzle cover. With a sharp tug, he extended the tube, and when it snapped into place, he flipped up the front sight. Moving the trigger handle to the armed position, he shouldered the rocket and inched forward until he could see the orange strobe of the PKM's muzzle flash through the smoke. He sighted in on the flash, made a small adjustment for the range, and then depressed the trigger.

Compared to the guttural bark of the PKM, the thump of the launcher seemed laughably puny, but while the sound was anemic, the bite of its 66 mm rocket was anything but. It slammed into the side of the tower and detonated into a ball of flame, the resounding boom that followed echoing loudly over the mine.

Dumping the empty launcher, Lane wiped a gloved hand across the face of the wrist computer and used the device to navigate the warren of aluminum-sided structures until he reached the edge of the target building. With the blinking dot telling him that the target was less than five feet away on the other side of the wall, Lane hefted his rifle and moved to the corner of the building.

Edging out from cover, he started for the metal stairs that led up to the front door and was almost there when two men came sprinting from the space between the two buildings to his left. Seeing him standing there, the men stopped, their training kicking in as they tried to determine if he was friend or foe.

Lane, on the other hand, was quick to engage, and after dropping the first man, he transitioned to the second. He centered the reticle on the man's chest and pulled the trigger, but instead of the muffled *thwack* of the bullet leaving the suppressor, he got the sickening *click* of a misfire.

Shit.

Lane dropped to a knee behind the stairs and canted the rifle to the left. His actions to clear the jam were automatic, a direct result of the thousands of hours spent on the flat range when their instructors had used every devious trick in the book to replicate the myriad ways a weapon could malfunction in combat. But the moment he saw the glint of the brass casing sticking awkwardly from the ejection port, he dumped the rifle and was yanking the Staccato from its holster when the second man opened fire.

The bullets slammed into the stairs, the rounds sparking off the metal. Lane managed to get off a single shot and then threw himself flat, the shards of steel from the impacting bullets slicing across his cheek. He wiggled behind the stairs, the coppery taste of blood seeping between his lips.

The man continued to hammer the stairs, the bullets keeping Lane's head down as his attacker maneuvered into position to try to deliver the kill shot. Lane counted the rounds, hoping to catch the man when he reloaded, but then he remembered the words the tactical instructors used to yell. "*Hope is* not *a viable strategy.*"

Lane had seen enough death during his time overseas to have developed a healthy immunity to the fear that ruled the lives of most of those who inhabited the planet. He knew that when it was your time to go, all you could do was try to leave in a pile of empty brass.

With that thought in mind, he shoved the pistol between the gaps in the stairs and opened fire, the muzzle rise barely noticeable even in a one-handed grip. The first shot broke clean as glass, and the man was down, a clover leaf of neat holes where the front of his kneecap should have been.

Damn, this Staccato rocks.

Not one for letting an enemy suffer, Lane aimed the final round through the man's forehead and then rolled from cover. A quick scan showed the area clear. He shoved a fresh mag into the pistol, then turned his attention back to the target building.

Leaving the useless HK behind, he bounded up the stairs and was reaching for the knob when the door came flying open.

CHAPTER 36

Mia made it to the door and grabbed the knob, her hands shaking as she tried to twist it open, but the door refused to budge. Realizing that it was locked, she fumbled with the clasp and almost had it undone when Liam grunted and got to his feet.

"I'll kill you for that," he said, spitting a glob of blood onto the floor as he dug a silver balisong from his back pocket and deployed the blade with a flick of his wrist. The sight of the knife sent a double shot of alarm racing through Mia's veins, and she redoubled her efforts, her palm beginning to bleed as she hammered at the clasp.

Finally, the lock snapped free and she shoved the door open, rushing out onto the landing only to find her way blocked by a man in tiger-stripe BDUs. He froze and opened his mouth to speak. "It's OK, I'm here to—"

But all Mia saw was the pistol in his hand, and she lowered her shoulder and slammed into him.

It was a hard collision, and the impact sent them both tumbling down the stairs to the ground, the pistol in the man's hand bouncing away into the dirt. Mia lay there for a second, trying to regain her breath, until she looked up and saw Liam appear at the doorway, the AK-74 swinging up to fire.

Oh shit.

The first bullet cracked over her head, the sound freezing her in

place. She stared at Liam, the realization that she was going to die crashing over her like a tidal wave. Before that moment Mia had thought
that she was strong—unbreakable even—but looking into the yawning
barrel, she knew it was a lie.

Mia understood that she needed to move, but her brain was locked
by the bullet's close call, and her legs felt as if they were full of sand. She
closed her eyes, waiting for the burn of the bullet, but before he could
fire, the man she'd knocked off the landing grabbed her by the shoulder
and pulled her out of the way.

Mia rolled over just as the soldier in the tiger stripes pulled a
flash-bang from his chest and tossed it at Liam.

It landed at the man's feet and exploded—the flash of the magnesium
powder bright as a lightning bolt. The concussion sent Liam staggering
back through the doorway, the man who'd just saved her life running
up the steps after him.

Run, dammit.

But instead of taking her own advice, Mia started up the stairs as well.

She stepped through the door and into the room just in time to
see Liam body-slam the soldier onto the table, balisong glinting in the
light as he slashed at the other man's throat. Mia was expecting to see
blood, but the stranger parried the blow, and instead of finding flesh,
the knife sliced through the small computer strapped to the man's wrist.

Liam elbowed him in the face and then brought up the knife, intent
on ramming it through his chest, but before he had a chance, Mia sprang
into action. She crossed to the table in two quick steps and kicked Liam
hard in the back of his leg. The joint folded and he went down to one
knee, but before she could capitalize on her success, he slashed at her leg.

Mia jumped back, and the man on the table sat up, his right hand
grabbing Liam by the wrist, his left closing around the barrel of the man's
AK. "Shoot him," he said, flinging the rifle across the table.

The AK clattered to the ground, and she picked it up.

The rifle was much heavier than the AR-15s she'd trained with at
the Federal Law Enforcement Training Center at Glynco, Georgia, and
her arms shook as she lifted it to her shoulder. Mia dropped her eye to

the sight and tracked the two men across the room, the voice of her firearms instructor echoing in her head.

"Aim small, miss small."

She was a good shot who'd scored expert on every weapon they'd had. But those targets were made of paper, a far cry from the man she had in her sights. Mia needed to think, but there was no time for that. No time to do anything but pull the trigger.

I'm sorry.

Mia squeezed the trigger, expecting a single shot, but sometime during the fight the selector had been knocked to full auto, and instead of one she got three. The rapid-fire recoil of the heavy 7.62 × 39 mm cartridges kicked like a mule. She stumbled backward, the burn of the gun smoke clouding her vision. Mia blinked away the fog, a hollow thump drawing her attention back to Liam, and she found him sitting against the wall, his eyes curious as he looked down at the crimson stain spreading across his shirt like spilled wine.

The stranger in the tiger-stripe fatigues stepped forward, and she instinctively swung the muzzle of the rifle to cover him.

"Easy," he said.

"Who the hell are you?"

"My name is Travis Lane, and I'm here to get you out."

"You're with Broadside?"

"That's right," he said, taking a step forward. "Now, would you mind not pointing that thing at me?"

"Oh, sorry."

Mia let the muzzle drop to the floor, and Lane stepped outside to retrieve his own rifle. "It's clear. We're getting ready to move," he said, coming back inside and slapping a fresh magazine into his HK. "You ready?"

"Yeah."

"Then let's get the hell out of here."

CHAPTER 37

TARGET BUILDING
Ubili, DRC

Lane looked at the woman in front of him to make sure she understood what he had said. Shock left some people confused, but Mia looked switched on, her hands steady on the AK.

"Are you good?"

"Yeah," she said.

Lane nodded and moved to the door, where he keyed up on the radio. "I've got the package, but I think we might have a problem."

"What kind of a problem?"

"Best if I show ya," Lane said.

"Roger that. The helo is two minutes out—move your ass."

"We're en route," he replied. Then, turning to the woman, he said, "Ma'am, we've got to go—now."

"It's Mia," she said.

"OK, Mia. I need you to stay on my ass and shoot anything that tries to stop us. Can you do that?"

"Yeah." She nodded.

"Good, then let's roll."

Lane moved to the door and looked outside. Finding it clear, he stepped out of the building, Mia tight on his heels when he started across the landing. They were almost to the stairs when the drone operator came up on the radio.

"Be advised, we've got three trucks entering the main gate. They appear to be—"

"Who gives a shit what kind they are," Lane said, grabbing Mia's hand and pulling her down the stairs and toward the trees. "Where are they headed?"

"Lead vehicle just made a left turn . . . Looks like he's coming your way."

Shit.

Lane spun around just as the truck rounded the corner, and thumbed the selector to full auto. Centering the reticle on the driver's-side windshield, he fired two quick bursts. The bullets punched through the glass, and there was a flash of blood, but before Lane could get a follow-up shot, the man in the passenger seat reached across and shoved the wheel hard over.

The sudden turn sent the truck crashing through the side of the closest building. The moment it was out of sight, Lane grabbed Mia and pulled her into the brush.

He kept his hand on her back and guided her through the trees to where the rest of the team was getting ready to move. Magnus and Hunter bent down to retrieve Felix's litter while Jones turned to face them.

"Who the hell is this?"

"Her name is Mia," Lane said. "She was inside the target building."

"Anyone else in there?" Jones asked.

"No one who's alive."

"You're sure about that?" Jones asked.

"I think I would have noticed," Lane said. "But if you want to go check it out, then be my guest."

"No, we've got to move," Jones said.

"Roger that."

Jones took point, and they fast marched toward the landing zone, the drone operator guiding them in.

"We've got hostiles to your two o'clock."

"You didn't smoke those dudes?" Lane asked Jones.

"We've been a little busy," he responded. "Now, why don't you make yourself useful and find some cover."

While Jones pushed out to try to get eyes on their attackers, Lane moved Mia to a tree stump between a pair of man-sized boulders. He dropped to a knee beside her, eyes searching for the impending threat.

"When the shooting starts, I need you to stay down," Lane said, shoving a HE round into the breech of the grenade launcher.

"That's not happening," Mia said, lifting the AK.

Before he could respond, the rattle of gunfire through the jungle cut him off. Turning toward the sound, Lane brought his rifle up just as Jones came racing through the trees.

"They're right behind me."

Usually, Lane would wait for a target to come to him, but wanting to keep the men at a distance, he fired the grenade back the way Jones had come. It sailed through the air and detonated, the rumbling explosion followed by a scream of pain.

"Two more men coming in from the—" the drone operator began. But before he could finish the transmission, a man stepped through the smoke, the machine gun on his hip already spitting flame.

Lane shouted for Magnus and Hunter to bring the litter and provided the necessary covering fire, one of his shots hitting the machine gunner in the shoulder. The man spun behind a tree, but a second shooter was quick to take his place. Lane hit the man with a double tap to the chest and then ducked down as the machine gunner poked his barrel out and squeezed the trigger to the rear.

The fire wasn't accurate, but it was enough to keep their heads down, and Lane hammered through the rest of his magazine before he dropped behind cover.

"Frag out," Jones yelled.

While he flipped a grenade toward the machine gunner, Lane shucked the empty magazine from his rifle and slapped in a fresh one, the incoming rounds snapping around his position like angry hornets.

Where the hell is that helo?

The thought had no sooner crossed his mind than the radio came to life, the pilot's disembodied voice distant but readable through the Peltors over his ears.

"Guardian 7, this is Archangel coming in from the west."

"Archangel, Guardian 7," Jones said. "We are taking accurate heavy fire from the tree line to our south. Request immediate suppression—danger close."

While Jones talked to the pilot, Lane ripped a smoke canister from the front of his plate carrier and held it up to his team leader.

"We are marking our position with yellow smoke—I say again, yellow smoke," Jones said.

"Roger that—Archangel is two mikes out."

Lane waited until he could hear the rotors in the distance before pulling the pin and then, after judging the wind, flipped the canister into the grass off to his right. It hit the ground and hissed to life, the smoke billowing around them.

Thinking the team was about to make a run for it, the fighters opened up with everything they had, and Lane could feel the tree trunk he was using for cover vibrate as it absorbed the rounds. The volume of fire was intense, but knowing that all the fusillade was going to do was give the door gunner something to shoot at, Lane calmly shoved a fresh HE round into the breech of his 203 and waited.

The Mi-17 wheeled into view, the door gunner already spooling up the electric motor that powered the minigun. Just as Lane had suspected, the man zeroed in on the mercs' muzzle flashes and mashed down the thumb trigger.

The six-barreled GAU-17 burped to life, and the gunner raked the lance of flame back and forth across the tree line, the five hundred rounds of 7.62×51 mm bullets shredding the bush like the finger of God.

"We're peeling left," Jones said. "Lane, you've got the principal—"

"What about Felix?" Hunter broke in.

"I've got him," Magnus barked.

While the helo made another pass, Lane told Mia, "Once the helicopter finishes its gun run, it's going to land on that flat spot behind us—it can't stay on the ground long, so we are going to have to haul ass."

"OK," she said. "I'll be right behind you."

A second later the pilot of the Mi-17 pulled the helicopter out of its orbit over the camp and twisted it toward the LZ. The moment it clattered overhead, Jones yelled, "Peel left."

While the rest of the team laid down a wall of lead, Lane sent his last 203 round sailing through the trees and then pulled Mia to her feet. "Let's go," he said. They turned and headed up the hill just as the helo reared like a stallion over the LZ. It was less than two hundred yards to the top of the rise, but with the steep terrain and bullets flying around them, it might as well have been a mile.

Almost there.

"Keep your head down," he yelled.

They ducked under the rotors and ran up the ramp, the rest of the team tight on their heels. Jones was the last to climb aboard and, after a quick head count, ordered the pilot, "Get us the hell out of here."

The man twisted the throttle, and the turbine screamed, the helicopter shuddering from the sudden increase in power. Eyeing the gauges, the pilot waited for the RPM needle to creep higher and then yanked back on the stick. The helicopter leaped skyward, and while the pilot turned to the right and dove for the valley, his copilot keyed up on the radio and advised, "Archangel One is airborne."

CHAPTER 38

The Ural's heavy bumper tore through the exterior wall and plowed halfway into the building before slamming into one of the concrete-reinforced support pillars. The sudden stop whipped Roos forward, and his head ricocheted off the dashboard, but other than a trickle of blood down his face, he was unharmed.

Reaching over to cut the engine, he grabbed his rifle and climbed out of the truck, his legs unsteady as he clambered over the upturned shelves and boxes of spare parts surrounding him. Once on the ground, Roos was heading for the gaping hole where the wall had been when Pieter came rushing into view.

"Boss, are you OK?"

Roos ignored him and pushed outside, his head spinning from the impact. "What the fuck is going on?"

"They took the girl."

"Where did they go?" Roos demanded.

Before Pieter could answer, an olive-drab Mi-17 came thundering overhead, the miniguns mounted to the doors buzzing to life. While one of the gunners directed his fire onto the tree line to the south, the other engaged the remaining cargo trucks parked near the fuel dump.

The five-hundred-round burst cut through the vehicles like a buzz saw. As the helicopter rocketed toward the far end of the mine, the gunner kept his finger down on the trigger, and Roos watched in horror as the puffs of dirt from the impacting rounds marched steadily toward the fifty-gallon drums of fuel oil stacked near the maintenance shed.

Realizing what was about to happen, he yelled at the remaining men, "Get down." But before they could comply, a line of magnesium-tipped tracers found their target. The blast lifted him off his feet and flung him backward, slamming him hard into the side of the toolshed.

Coughing against the acid smell of the diesel smoke, Roos slowly got to his feet. He scanned the sky, fully expecting to see the helicopter whirling around for another gun run, but to his surprise the Mi-17 continued south, its nose tipped skyward as it flared for landing.

Determined not to let his unknown attackers get away, Roos yanked Pieter to his feet, ordering him to retrieve one of their Polaris RZRs. The man nodded and went staggering through the smoke, freeing Roos to head back into the mangled building behind him.

He climbed up on the Ural's bumper, unlatched the tailgate, and reached in for the ruggedized weapons container he'd gotten from Colonel Yu. Roos pulled the case to the edge and eased it onto his shoulder. The case wasn't as heavy as it was awkward, and he paused to get it balanced before heading back the way he'd come.

Once outside, Roos eased the case to the ground and opened the lid, revealing a Russian-made SA-18 surface-to-air missile. He pulled the self-contained launcher from the packing foam and gave it a once-over. Not finding any damage, Roos was snapping the grip stick into the tube when Pieter came racing around the corner in the Polaris.

Unlike the plodding six-wheeled ATVs the mechanics used for hauling parts and people around the mine, the RZR Pro R looked like a bullet with wheels. With its 225 hp engine, selectable throttle control, and independently controlled suspension, it was built for speed, which was exactly what Roos needed if he was going to catch the helo before it left for good.

He strapped the SA-18 into the back seat and then climbed into the front. "Get us to the ridge."

Pieter nodded and stomped on the gas, the RZR's knobby tires kicking up a spray of gravel and loose dirt as it raced up the service trail that led to the top of the ridge.

It was a short ride to the summit, but by the time they made it, the last figure had run up the ramp of the Mi-17, and a second later the helo was lifting off, the pilot shoving down the nose and diving out of sight.

"They're getting away," Pieter shouted.

Not bloody likely.

Roos was betting heavily that the men in the helo were heading for Goma, and if that was the case, there was only one way out.

"Keep going," he ordered.

"Go where?" Pieter demanded.

"There's a game trail on the other side of the brush that will take us to the river."

"I don't see it."

Realizing what needed to be done, Roos ordered Pieter out of the RZR and slid behind the wheel. "When Rambo's men show up, I need you to bring them down to the river," he instructed. Then, without waiting for Pieter's response, he shoved the transmission into drive and eased the RZR forward.

It had been four months since Roos had last used the game trail, and when he punched through the curtain of vines and scrub, he found the area horribly overgrown. The narrow dirt track was barely visible beneath the briars and knee-high grass. If there had been a faster way to the river, he would have taken it, but there wasn't, so he tightened the racing harness over his chest and pressed down on the gas.

Roos guided the RZR south, its 2.0 L engine howling like a scalded dog as he raced beneath the lattice of low-hanging branches. He drove like the devil himself was chasing him, ignoring the scrape of the chassis against stones and the whirlwind of dust rolling thick into the open cab.

The trail hooked hard to the west, and he spun the wheel to follow. The back end began to slide, but Roos was quick to recover and had no sooner centered up than he was sailing over the top of the hill. For an instant he was weightless, and then the RZR crashed back to earth, the brush guard tearing a deep furrow through the ground below.

Up ahead Roos could see the shimmer of sunlight that marked his destination, and he sped toward it, sweat rolling down his forehead and stinging his eyes. He wiped his forearm across his face as he burst from the trees, the rocky shelf that overlooked the river rushing up fast to meet him.

Roos stomped on the brakes and brought the RZR to a sliding halt. He killed the engine, unbuckled his racing harness, and leaped out to retrieve the SA-18. Missile in hand, he moved to the edge of the cliff.

Staring down at the canyon below, he shoved a battery into the grip at the bottom of the launcher and waited for the gyros to stabilize before shouldering the weapon.

Dropping his eyes to the sight, he scanned the surrounding area, searching for the helicopter, but there was nothing. The seconds ticked by, and Roos stood there—the silence deafening. With no sign of the helo, he was beginning to think that he'd made a mistake and was about to lower the launcher when he heard the distant rumble of rotors, followed by the sight of the Mi-17 twisting into view. Realizing he was only going to get one shot, Roos brought his eye to the sight and centered the reticle on his target. A half pull of the trigger uncaged its infrared seeker head, and the missile began to hum as it searched for its target.

In less than a second it was locked onto the superheated metal around the helicopter's exhaust, and the gentle hum quickly turned into an angry growl. Like it was a dog begging to be let off its leash, the intensity of the sound continued to rise, but Roos waited until the red light in the optical sight flashed to *shoot*, and then he fired.

There was a hiss of smoke as the booster charge kicked the missile from the launch tube, and for an instant it looked as if it would fall to the ground. But then the rocket booster roared to life, and it was racing skyward, the only sign of its passing a trail of white smoke as it coiled toward its target.

CHAPTER 39

EXTRACTION

Ubili, DRC

It was silent in the rear of the Mi-17, all eyes on Lane as he worked to keep Felix alive. The tourniquet he'd secured to the man's leg had come off during their mad dash to the helo, and the metal floor was soaked with blood. Fearing that Felix was on the verge of hypovolemic shock, Lane knew he had to get the bleeding under control, and he stripped a fresh tourniquet from his kit and strapped it over the jagged wound.

He twisted the windlass until he thought it was going to snap, expecting Felix to scream in pain, but all he got was a barely audible moan. "Stay with me," Lane begged as he hooked up the heart monitor.

The screen flashed to life, the steady drop of Felix's systolic blood pressure confirming his worst fears. Knowing the only way the injured man's beleaguered heart could catch up was with a massive influx of fluids, Lane grabbed a catheter from his med ruck and went searching for a vein.

He found one on his left arm and got the needle in on the first stick, then connected the line to the bag of saline. But by the time he got it flowing, Felix's breathing had shallowed, and his pulse was feathered and weak.

He's lost too much blood.

The frantic alert from the heart monitor confirmed his suspicions, and as Felix's blood pressure continued its free fall, his breathing became even more erratic, the lack of oxygen in his blood turning his skin a pale shade of blue. Realizing that he was going into cardiac arrest, Lane began chest compressions.

But Felix was gone.

"Shit."

Having done everything he could, Lane got to his feet and moved to the box near the ramp where he'd placed the body bags. Carefully he placed his fallen comrade inside one and zipped it up, and then with a heavy heart he turned his attention to the rest of the team.

"Hunter, let me get a look at you," he shouted over the roar of the rotors.

The man nodded and got to his feet, but before he'd managed a step, the voice of the door gunner came screaming through his headset.

"Pilot, break right."

The warning sent Lane's eyes to the ramp and the streak of white smoke turning toward the helicopter. Out of all the weapon systems that America's special operations had to contend with during the war on terror, none were more dangerous than the man-portable surface-to-air missile. These shoulder-fired missiles were light, cheap, and incredibly lethal to slow-moving helicopters. A triple threat that offered an enemy combatant the ability to inflict maximum damage on America's best-trained soldiers.

Before this mission to the DRC, Lane was lucky to have never been on the receiving end of the fearsome weapon system, but as the missile closed in on the helicopter at 1,600 feet per second, he knew that was about to change.

Spinning on his heel, he opened his mouth to shout a warning to Mia, but before he had a chance, the pilot rolled the Mi-17 onto its side in a desperate attempt to dodge the incoming threat. The sudden maneuver spilled the team from their seats and sent them banging across the hold. Lane grabbed onto the cargo netting to keep from falling out of the helo, unable to do anything but watch as Mia crashed into the bulkhead.

The impact knocked her out cold, and she dropped to the floor just as the pilot hauled back on the stick. The move sent her sliding toward the open ramp, and Jones yelled for someone to grab her. Magnus stepped forward and was reaching for her arm when the missile slammed into the bottom of the helo.

The warhead detonated on impact, the rush of superheated gases tearing through the fuselage—killing the big Swede where he stood. Choking against the noxious cloud of smoke and raw aviation fuel that poured into the ruptured helo, Lane stretched out his arm and snagged Mia's boot.

The helicopter shuddered like a wounded beast, and the pilot fought against the controls, desperate to get the nose up. Dazed by the concussion and choking on the billowing smoke, it was everything Lane could do to hold on, but having already lost Felix and now Magnus, he was determined not to lose Mia too.

But with half of her body hanging out of the jagged hole that had moments before been the floor of the aircraft, he was fighting a losing battle. He strained to pull her back in, but hanging by the cargo net with his legs off the ground, Lane didn't have the leverage needed to make it happen.

The pain radiating into his shoulder was intense, and with his arm fully extended, he could feel the grate of the bone against the socket. A lesser man would have succumbed, but Lane refused to quit.

As a PJ, Lane had been around enough stricken helicopters to know two things. The first was that the wounded Mi-17 wasn't going to make it, and the second was that he didn't want to be on board when it crashed. Knowing that Mako and Hunter would figure out what to do, he craned his neck toward the cockpit and shouted at the pilot, "Bring the helicopter back toward the river."

"What?" the pilot demanded.

"The river!" Lane shouted. "Get us over the river."

The pilot did as he was told, and while he wrestled the helicopter back to the east, Lane's eyes moved to the escape-and-evasion bag mounted to the bulkhead six inches to the left of the cargo netting. Once they were over the river, he summoned the last of his strength, and with a powerful tug, he swung his body toward the ruck. Letting go of the netting, Lane reached out and hooked his forearm through the strap, and then he was falling.

Still holding on to Mia's arm, he tumbled through the air, the slipstream slapping him hard in the face. Below him, Lane could see the churning mass of the silt-laden river and the shine of the jagged rocks breaking the surface. Praying the water would revive his still-unconscious charge, he let go of her hand and watched her splash into the river, the currents quickly sweeping her away.

Then it was his turn.

Lane slammed into the water at twenty-four miles per hour. The river swallowed him whole, its deep-water currents spinning him like loose change in a washing machine.

Having learned to swim at a young age, Lane had always felt at home in the water, a fact that had kept him calm during the drownproofing stage of dive school. But unlike in training, there were no safety officers in the Congo, and that plus the fifty pounds of combat gear strapped to his body was enough to send his heart rate spiking through the roof.

After his feet found the bottom, Lane kicked off, his lungs screaming for oxygen as he raced toward the yellow light filtering through the mud-stained water. He quickly broke the surface and took a much-needed breath, the rush of the current sending him speedballing downstream.

Where the hell is Mia?

He kicked hard to see over the brown-capped waves, his waterlogged boots trying to pull him under as he scanned his surroundings. Then he saw her, scrambling up onto a sandbank ten yards to his front.

"Over here," she shouted.

Lane tried to pull free of the current, but with the body armor and rifle still slung around his neck, he knew he wasn't going to make it. Realizing that he needed to dump some weight, he fumbled with the quick release on the front of his vest, but before he could pull the tab, the Huey they'd seen at the mine flashed low across the river.

The pilot flared for landing, and the moment the skids touched the ground, a handful of armed men came leaping out from the cargo hold and opened fire. The slap of the bullets in the water all around him immediately forced Lane to change course.

The hell with this.

Staying low, he filled his lungs and took a second to study the sandbar, noting the angular point where the river split into two separate channels. He dove for the bottom, feeling the current pulling at his legs like an invisible hand. Kicking hard, he aimed for the channel to the left of the sandbar, but before he'd reached what he assumed was the halfway point, his lungs were on fire.

His brain begged him to surface, but Lane stayed down until his vision had begun to darken at the edges. Knowing that he was dangerously close to passing out, he had no choice but to claw for the surface. He only managed a quick glance at the sandbar before the men were shooting again, but it was enough to see that the current had pulled him off course. Making a quick correction, Lane went back down into the water.

The mercs had him dialed in, and with the bullets slicing through the water all around him, he had no choice but to dive deep. Lane kicked hard for the bottom, his vision obscured by the churn of the river slamming into the sandbar, his body twisted by the sucking vortex of the rip current. He was swimming blind, and his legs burned from the lactic acid that filled his muscles. Once again, Lane could feel the inevitable creep of hypoxia, the mix of pain and euphoria that preceded a shallow-water blackout. It was a sensation he'd become well acquainted with during the Special Warfare predive course, and Lane knew he was on the verge of unconsciousness, but he was determined to make it to Mia, and considering the stakes, failure was *not* an option.

CHAPTER 40

Mia crept through the reeds, her eyes on the men massing on the opposite shore. She was alone and unarmed and knew it was only a matter of time before they crossed over to get her. Mia studied the mercenaries, the menace in their voices and the glint of the sun off their rifle barrels sending a current of fear rushing through her veins.

Her brain instructed her to find a hole to hide in until Lane came to rescue her, but no sooner had the thought crossed Mia's mind than she shoved it away.

Get your head in the game. Move, dammit.

Mia scrambled to her feet, and as the mercenaries fired at Lane, she raced for the protective cover of the water-slicked boulder on the far side of the sandbar. She was only up for a second, but it was just long enough to see more mercs leap from the cargo hold of the old Huey and open fire on her.

The bullets pelted the rock next to her and exploded, showering her with bits of broken stone. *Fucking assholes.* Burrowing deeper into the sand, Mia scanned the water, her eyes searching for any sign of Lane, but the man had disappeared. Alone and with all the men on the bank hammering the boulder, she was trying to come up with her next move when the bulbous nose of the Huey came sliding back into her field of view.

Looking up at the helicopter, Mia's first thought was that there was no way in hell they were taking her alive. Her second was that there was no way either of the men in the cockpit could see her through the typhoon of dust and sand kicked up by the helicopter's blades.

Or could they?

Holding her breath, Mia forced herself to stay still. For an instant it looked as if they were going to pass right over; then the pilot pulled the helicopter into a hover directly over her position, and a man with an AK-47 leaned out of the cargo hold.

He swung the rifle toward the boulder, and Mia watched, her heart hammering in her chest, as he brought it up to fire. The muzzle yawned wide as a tunnel, and Mia instinctively closed her eyes. But in an instant, all the things that she still wanted to accomplish came racing through her mind.

Fuck this. If this asshole is going to kill me, I want to see it coming.

Mia opened her eyes, but instead of firing, the man with the AK ducked back into the helicopter. Looking up through the acrylic chin bubbles on the bottom of the nose, she watched as the mercenary slipped into the cockpit and began shouting at the pilot. It was obvious from the dismissive shake of the pilot's head that he wasn't having it. But the man was not to be denied, and after he lifted his AK to the pilot's head, the Huey began its descent.

Unlike an airplane, there was nothing aerodynamically sound about a helicopter. It was a fact her father had stated repeatedly when he'd finally agreed to give her lessons. "Look, Mia, the first thing you need to know is that helicopters don't fly; they beat the air into submission."

The Huey pilot must have had a similarly careful instructor, because it was obvious that he wanted nothing to do with the loose stones and pieces of driftwood that littered the sandbar. Realizing that the man's finely tuned caution was the only thing keeping her from death, Mia was determined to capitalize on his hesitation. Shifting her gaze to the area around her feet, Mia sifted through the sand, searching for a rock or anything else she might be able to use as a weapon. She found what she was looking for in a softball-sized stone, and after digging it free, she spent a second contemplating her target.

The main rotor was the biggest and therefore the most tempting, but as a pilot, Mia knew that it was the smaller tail rotor that was really the helicopter's Achilles' heel. The only problem was that in order to get a clear shot, she was going to have to leave the protective confines of the boulder. Mia knew that even *if* she hit the tail rotor, it wouldn't bring the Huey down, but there was a good chance that it would make the pilot reconsider his altitude. Or better yet, head back to base to check out the damage.

It was a risky play, but she knew that she could either stay where she was and die or do something and live. For Mia it was a no-brainer, and easing onto her stomach, she crawled back to the reeds. It was barely five yards, but with her progress measured in inches rather than feet, it seemed to take forever.

Coughing from the grit, she rose to her feet, and summoning everything she'd learned during her two seasons of softball, she reared back and fired the rock at her target. Her aim was true, and the stone bouncing off the vulnerable blade was all it took to send the pilot hauling back on the stick.

CHAPTER 41

It was midnight, and Ron Granger stood in the center of the work-room, his eyes on the drone orbiting over the crash site. The Mi-17 lay at the edge of a small clearing, a tendril of black smoke coiling up from the rotor box. With its crumpled blades and shattered tail boom, the helicopter looked like a broken toy. However, it wasn't the damage but the lack of movement that had everyone on the edge of their seat.

One of the commo techs picked up the satellite hand mike and tried to make contact with the pilots. "Archangel One, this is Davy Jones." When there was no reply, he switched over to Guardian's internal chan-nel and repeated his transmission. "Any Guardian element, this is Davy Jones. How copy? Over."

The hiss of dead air that followed sucked the oxygen out of the room, and Granger slowly stepped backward, lowering himself into one of the chairs that lined the wall.

While he pondered his next move, he looked up to see the feed on the screen tilt on its axis as the drone banked east toward the river. "Where the hell is it going?" Granger demanded.

"Not sure, sir," a tech said. "We've lost our communication uplink with the support team."

"What the hell does that mean?"

"It means that until the next satellite moves into position, we can listen, but we can't talk."

"How long?"

"Five minutes, sir."

Fuck.

Now a spectator, all Granger could do was watch as the drone operator crossed the river and set the Penguin into an orbit high above the fighters gathering on the east bank.

How did things go to shit so fast?

Granger didn't know, but of one thing he was certain: if they didn't get some assets into the area fast, Guardian 7 was going to get wiped out. With that thought in mind, he was on his way to his office—determined to beg, borrow, or steal whatever he needed to try to save the seemingly cursed team—when the voice of the battlefield captain stopped him in his tracks.

"Sir, we've got movement on the sandbar," the man said. "It looks like . . . It's Lane."

"Does he have the package?" Granger demanded, whirling back to the drone feed.

"There's someone with him."

"Zoom in."

CHAPTER 42

BROADSIDE COMPOUND

Mount Jackson, Virginia

Three floors above in his office, Carson West sat in front of his computer, watching as the camera zoomed in on the figure hiding behind the rock. With the satellite moving out of range, the feed from the Congo began to pixelate, the digital blurring making details of the face impossible to see.

The news of the helicopter being shot down had seemed to be the answer to his prayers. A solution to all his problems at Broadside, but at the sight of the figure on the sandbar, he wasn't so sure.

Besides mandatory Wednesday chapel services at the upscale Catholic prep school he'd attended, West had never been one for religion, but sitting there, waiting for the image to clear, he offered a silent prayer.

I don't know if you're up there or if you even care, but I'll build you a church or finance a fucking orphanage, whatever you want—just please let them be dead.

He waited, his heart hammering in his chest, as the picture buffered. Then he saw Lane's face on the screen. *You've got to be kidding me. How in the hell is he still alive?*

The fact that the former PJ was not only alive but capable of returning fire meant there was a good chance Jones might have survived. In an instant everything came crashing down around him, and his first thought was to run, grab his passport, empty his bank account, and get out of the States immediately. It was a tempting idea, but West knew running would only confirm what Taran already suspected.

Shit.

As he watched the unfolding firefight, a second thought came creeping through the fear—a way to handle all his problems at Broadside and keep his job once and for all. It was a bold plan, audacious even, but if he played it right, West knew there was a chance he could get Sterling to kill them all.

Like a spider spinning a web, West began to shape the plan. The key was to use the information he'd found out about Mia's time in Nairobi and her link to Angelo to convince Sterling she was there to expose his precious mine. Rip him from his lofty pedestal.

West did a walk around his office, his mind spinning as he examined the plan from every possible angle. It was risky to the point of being suicidal, but at the same time, it was brilliant because he knew that Sterling was such an arrogant ass that he'd never see it coming.

By the time he returned to his desk and picked up his cell phone, West's breathing had returned to normal, and his confidence was through the roof. *You can do this*, he thought, dialing the number.

The phone rang in his ear, and West waited, his mind sharp as a bear trap. *You've got to lay it on him, but not too thick.*

"Alexander Sterling's office, how may I help you?"

"Joanne, this is Carson West," he said. "I need to talk to Mr. Sterling. It's urgent."

"I'm afraid that's impossible, Mr. West—"

"If you don't get him on the phone in the next ten seconds, we're all going to jail," he snapped.

The line went silent for a second, and then Joanne's voice returned. "In that case, let me see if I can find him."

"Thank you," he said with some restraint.

West sat calmly, the tick of the clock on the wall behind him impossibly loud. While he waited, he wondered where Sterling was. *Malibu? The Caymans?* He didn't know, but of one thing he was sure: the man would not appreciate the intrusion.

True to form, when Alexander Sterling came on the line, the irritation in his voice snapped through the phone like a whip. "This better be good, Carson."

The tone put West instantly on edge, and he briefly considered hanging up the phone. Letting that silver-spooned son of a bitch clean up his own mess for once would be a pleasure. But West was a pragmatist at heart, and while he firmly believed that a rising tide raised all ships, he knew that worked both ways.

Shoving the irritation aside, West brought Sterling up to speed on what he'd already found out about Mia the day before. "I've just learned that Mia was on an FBI task force in Nairobi that was looking into Crimson Ridge."

"And?"

"Apparently she found a connection between the work Roos did in Kenya and his current position at the mine," he lied. "You have to call Botha, tell his men to kill them—all of them—including Mia Webb."

"Kill an FBI agent, are you crazy?"

"Sir, she's seen the mine. They all have. We've got to get rid of them."

"You'd let me kill your own people?" Sterling questioned.

"It's the only way to make sure the mine stays safe," West replied carefully.

"Well, it's about time you grew some backbone," Sterling chuckled.

CHAPTER 43

SANDBAR

Ubili, DRC

Lane hauled himself onto the sandbar, his chest heaving as he stared up at the helicopter hovering over the boulder. He wiped the water from his eyes, trying to understand what was happening, and then saw the man with the AK-47 leaning out of the troop door.

Instinctively, he ripped the Staccato from its holster and brought it up in a two-handed grip. He centered the dot on the man's chest and fired three quick shots, the pistol bucking in his hand at the same moment Mia stood up, her hand snapping forward as she flung something at the tail of the helicopter.

His bullets and her object hit at the same time. The spark of the stone off the tail rotor was followed a split second later by the man's body tumbling from the side. Then the helicopter was banking hard across the river, the retreating rotors covering up the muffled thump of the body slamming into the ground.

With adrenaline pumping hard through his veins, Lane holstered the pistol and sprinted over to the boulder just as Mia threw herself to cover. He collapsed beside her, the bite of the sand fleas combined with the hail of lead sparking off the rock grating on his strained nerves.

"I had the situation under control," she said.

He looked at Mia, then to the dead man lying facedown in the sand, and then back to her. "How about a thank-you for saving your life?" he asked.

"I'll thank you when you get those assholes to stop shooting at us."

"Not a problem," he said, fumbling a 40 mm grenade from the pouch on the front of his kit.

Brushing the sand from the breech, Lane inserted the grenade into the launcher and snapped it closed. Easing around the boulder, he sighted in on the group of fighters closest to the river and pulled the trigger.

The explosive arced through the air and after a short flight slammed into the ground, the resulting detonation leaving behind a cloud of black smoke and jumbled body parts. Lane mechanically ejected the empty casing, his fingers tiptoeing across the remaining rounds until they found the one he wanted.

Unlike the gold-tipped high-explosive round, this one was gray with a red band that marked it as tactical CS—the military's version of tear gas. Shoving the round home, he sent it, too, sailing across the river, toward the remaining fighters running for the trees. Like its predecessor, it found its target, but instead of a flash of flame and shrapnel, a dense cloud of noxious smoke marked the detonation.

That ought to give them something to think about.

The smoke spread across the riverbank, engulfing the fighters, who were either too stupid or too slow to make for the trees. Realizing that they were not going to die, a few of them lifted their rifles and sent a "fuck you" burst cracking across the river, but then the CS kicked in, the burning gas sending them running away.

"We can't stay here," Lane said.

"Tell me something I *don't* know."

"You good to use this?" he asked, handing her the rifle.

"Yeah—I think I can figure it out."

"Good," Lane said. "Then you won't have any problems dropping the next guy who takes a shot at us."

With Mia covering their rear, Lane keyed up on his radio. "Guardian 1, this is Guardian 5. How copy?" He waited for a response, and when none came, he repeated his transmission, the silence that followed telling

Lane that his team was either dead or unable to answer their radios. While he wasn't sure which one it was, both were bad, and needing to know the full situation, he switched over to the operation's frequency.

"Any station this net, this is Guardian 5. How copy?"

"Guardian 5, this is Davy Jones," an unfamiliar voice said. "What is your status?"

"Davy Jones, we've got a bird down. I repeat, Guardian 7 is down."

"Roger that," the man said. "What is your status?"

My fucking status? My team is likely dead, and I'm getting shot at by a bunch of assholes from the Lost Boys. That's my status.

Lane took a breath and, shoving the emotion aside, did his best to answer the question.

"Davy Jones, my team is down, and I am on the run with the package."

"Guardian 5, this is Davy Jones. Say again—you *have* the package."

"Roger that."

"Stand by."

"They put me on hold," he said.

"What? Are you fucking serious?" Mia asked.

Lane was about to respond when there was a crackle of static followed by an unfamiliar but authoritative voice coming up on the net.

"Guardian 5, this is Davy Jones actual," the man said, using the call sign for the TOC battle captain. "I need you to move to the crash site. Prepare to copy grid."

"What is he talking about?" Mia asked. "We're going back to the crash site?"

"Yep," Lane replied, digging the ziplock bag that contained the topographical map of the area from his pocket and spreading it on the ground.

"Look, I'm no survival expert here, but don't you think that's a bit obvious?"

"It's not my call," he said, while marking their current location on the map.

"The hell it isn't."

"Why don't you do your job and let me do mine?" he snapped.

If looks could kill, the one Mia gave him would have ended him right there, but before Lane could apologize, the voice was back on the radio. "Prepare to copy grid."

"Send it," he said.

Once he received the coordinates, Lane plotted them on the map, a quick range estimation telling him it was three kilometers from the sandbar to the downed helo.

Traveling alone and on flat ground, Lane knew he could cover the distance in under an hour, but considering the terrain and that he'd be traveling with Mia, he figured it could take twice that time. However, it wasn't how long it would take them to get to the crash site but how long they would survive if the enemy followed them across the river that mattered.

"Sir, what's the extraction plan?" Lane asked.

"We're working on that now."

"You're working on it?" Lane repeated. "Is that your way of telling me that we're on our own?"

"Believe me, son, we are doing everything we can to get you out of there," the battle captain said. "All you need to focus on is protecting the package and getting to the crash site."

Sitting safely in the TOC, a thousand miles away from the bullets and blood, it was an easy comment to make, but here on the ground, all it did was piss Lane off. Feeling himself on the verge of losing his cool, he took a calming breath and simply said, "Will do. Guardian 7 out."

With the conversation over, he turned his attention back to Mia. "Hey, I didn't mean to bite your head off a second ago."

"Yeah, you did," she said, "but we'll have time for me to be pissed at you later. Right now, we need to get moving."

"Fair enough," Lane said, "but we've got some pretty hard terrain ahead of us. Are you sure that you're up for it?"

"If you can make it, I can make it," she said, handing him back his rifle.

"Well, I guess we've got nothing else to talk about," Lane said, turning back to the river.

CHAPTER 44

SANDBAR

Ubili, DRC

Mia followed Lane to the bank, wishing she'd kept her mouth shut as she studied the rushing tributary rolling south toward the falls. At first glance the water appeared just as turbulent as its main trunk, but a look past the bend in the river showed the current slowing before forming a tranquil pool beneath a clump of mangroves.

Still, making it that far without being sucked under was not going to be an easy task. While she studied it, Lane slipped into the water and turned back to face her.

"Let me help you," he said, holding out his hand.

Mia ignored it and slid off the bank and into the water. The current moved faster than she'd expected, and as it swept her around the bend, she wondered if she'd made a mistake. Then just as she'd expected, the flow began to mellow as the water reached the shallows.

It was peaceful, almost tranquil, beneath the trees, and Mia felt her body relax. The earlier tension began to ease as she looked up at the sky. It was beautiful country, and for a moment she felt like she was taking a trip back in time to when the earth was young and untouched by the hands of man.

But the sight of the fat snake sunning itself on one of the low limbs above her head was quick to snap her back to reality.

"Relax, it's just a ball python," Lane said, catching up to her and pushing toward the river's edge. "It won't hurt you."

"Does he know that?" Mia asked, falling in close behind him.

"You don't seem like the type to be bothered by a snake," he commented as they sloshed through the knee-deep water.

"I don't care how tough you are; snakes are creepy."

"I can handle snakes. It's the spiders I don't like," he said. "When I was growing up, my sister and I stumbled on a whole nest of brown recluses in the barn. After that, just seeing one of those evil bastards gave me nightmares for weeks."

"We had those in Texas. My dad used to call them fiddlebacks. He said that their venom would rot away your skin," Mia said. "I always wondered if that was true."

"I've seen it happen," Lane confirmed. "It's not pretty."

They continued in silence, following the river until the water began to recede and the stone that lined the riverbed gave way to a soup of gray mud that made each step feel as if they were walking through wet cement. By the time Lane moved toward the tangle of roots protruding from the ground, Mia was breathing hard, and this time when he offered his hand after climbing up onto the bank, she took it and let him haul her up.

He studied her for a second and said, "You don't look so good."

"I'm fine."

"No, I'm serious," he said, taking her finger and pushing down on the nail.

"What are you doing?"

"It's called capillary refill," he explained. "You push down on the nail and wait to see how long it takes for the color to return."

"And what does that tell you?"

"It tells me you're dehydrated," he answered. "When was the last time you had anything to eat or drink?"

"They gave me a little food back at the mine," she said, "but it wasn't much."

"That's what I was afraid of," Lane replied, leading her over to a hummock of grass and dropping the E&E bag he'd taken from the helicopter.

"You sound like my dad."

"He must have been a smart guy," he said, unzipping the pack and pulling out water and a meal-replacement bar.

"Yeah, he was," Mia acknowledged as she took the items from Lane.

She cracked the top of the bottle of water and took a long gulp. The water hit the spot, but the protein bar was a different story. While the label claimed it was "honey walnut," the bar itself tasted like sawdust, and it took a determined effort and a gulp from the bottle of water to get it choked down.

"Take your time," Lane said. "We've got a few minutes to rest."

Mia nodded and took another sip of water.

"Throwing a rock at a helicopter, that was some real David-and-Goliath shit," Lane said, grinning.

"And here I was expecting you to take all the credit for saving me."

"Sorry to disappoint you," Lane said, "but that's not how I roll."

"Good to know," Mia said, taking another drink. She paused and studied him over the bottle.

"Something on your mind?" he asked.

"Are you sure we want to go back to the crash site?" she asked. "I mean, isn't that exactly what the bad guys would expect us to do?"

"Yeah, but if there are survivors, it's my job to take care of them," Lane said. "Plus, we're low on ammo, and I don't know if it's a battery issue or what, but my radio stopped working about a mile back."

"And you need the radio to call the cavalry?"

"I hate to break it to ya," Lane said, "but I am the cavalry."

"Wow . . . that's disconcerting."

"It is what it is," he said.

"So, I assume you were in the military, right?"

"Yeah, I was a PJ in the Air Force," Lane replied.

"A PJ . . . those are the guys who rescue the downed pilots, right?"

"That's one of the things we do."

"I was watching you treat Felix," she said. "I've been to some serious first-aid classes in my time, but I've never seen anything like that."

"Too bad it wasn't enough," Lane said quietly.

"You did everything you could."

"You can always do more."

With those words, Lane got to his feet.

"Finish your bar," he said. "We need to move."

She chugged the rest of the water and stuffed the bar into her mouth before getting to her feet. "Hey, I didn't mean to—"

"It's fine," he said.

It was an obvious lie, but Mia knew better than to say anything more. She fell in behind him as he moved forward. She wasn't sure if he just didn't want her talking or if he was eager to get to the crash site and check on his friends, but the pace was quick, and Mia was exhausted.

She wanted to ask him to slow down, but her pride wouldn't let her. Swiping at the swarm of mosquitoes buzzing around her face, she dragged herself through the tangle of wait-a-minute vines and over the gnarled roots that constantly threatened to send her sprawling to the ground.

By the time they reached the edge of the crash site, Mia was fading fast. "So . . . what happens when they come and get us?" she called out to Lane.

"We leave," Lane said without slowing down. "Get you home."

"Wait . . . no," she said. "We can't just leave him."

"Leave who?" Lane asked, glancing back at her.

"Sawyer . . . he's . . ."

"Like I said, my job is to get *you* out of here."

She came to a halt and tried to speak, but her mouth was bone dry and her mind sluggish. "No . . . they've killed people . . . They have to pay."

"What are you talking about?" he asked, coming to a full stop and looking at her directly. "I know those guys are bad news, but my mission is to get you out of here."

"No, Lane, you have to listen . . . I wasn't the only one being held at the mine," she said. "I've got . . . I've got . . ."

"You've got what?" he asked.

Mia shook her head to clear the dizziness, but her mind refused to cooperate. "S-something's wrong . . ." she said. "I think I—"

Then she passed out.

CHAPTER 45

EAST BANK
Ubili, DRC

Gavin Roos climbed down from the ridge and crossed the beach, his eyes darting from the coil of black smoke rising from the west side of the river, to Pieter and the rest of his men unloading the Zodiac Mark 3 from its trailer behind the RZR.

"What's with the boat, and where the hell is Rambo?" he demanded.

"Lying on the sandbar," Pieter replied.

"What?"

"The stupid bugger just got himself shot trying to take out the girl," Pieter said, handing Roos a pair of binoculars.

He took the binos, lifted them to his eyes, and turned toward the tiny island in the middle of the river. He did one quick pass of the sandy bank but failed to see anyone. Sensing the problem, Pieter moved to his side and pointed to the boulder on the left edge. "Look to the right of the rock."

Roos followed the man's direction, and as he thumbed the focus knob, he saw a black combat boot protruding from the curtain of river grass. Panning to his left, he followed up the man's leg and settled the glass on his face. Roos stood there, studying Rambo's sightless eyes and the confused look on his face, then handed the binoculars back.

"How the hell did this happen?"

"The girl's got skills." Pieter shrugged.

"What are you talking about?"

"She waited for the helicopter to get low enough and then threw a rock at the tail rotor," Pieter said. "Bought herself enough time to let one of the men who fell from the helo take Rambo out. Like I said, she's got skills."

"We'll see about that," Roos said. "Where are they now?"

"They're gone. Slipped off the back of the sandbar and headed downstream thirty seconds ago," Pieter said. "You should have sent me over there."

Roos knew Pieter was right, but there was nothing he could do about that now.

"Either way, it's good I grabbed the Zodiac when I went back to pick up Rambo's men," Pieter said.

"Smart thinking."

"Grabbed some more ammo too, and while the lads were loading it up, I did some poking around."

"And?"

"And I found *this* on the floor beside Liam's body," Pieter replied, digging a wrist-top computer about the size of a deck of playing cards from his pocket. "He must have cut it off whoever rescued the girl."

Roos took it and, after studying the thick rubber strap and the shockproof bezel protecting the screen, assumed it was one of the digital altimeters favored by the skydiving crowd. But then he pushed the button on the side. The screen flashed to life, and the moment he saw the topographic map overlaid with the blinking dot in the center, Roos knew exactly what he was looking at.

"A tracker," he said.

"Explains how they found her."

Roos was about to tell Pieter that it was high time they returned the favor when a Toyota Hilux pulled up behind the RZR and Tommy and the rest of his men climbed out of the passenger side.

"What's this prick doing here?" Pieter demanded under his breath.

Realizing he'd forgotten to tell him about Botha's decision, Roos instructed, "You two play nice."

"Play nice with that twat?"

"Pieter, I'm serious," Roos snapped. "We need his men, so be civil."

Pieter's disdain for Tommy in his neatly pressed uniform was obvious, but like the rest of Roos's men, his second-in-command was a pro, and Roos knew Pieter would do as he was told.

"What's going on here?" Tommy asked.

"Just a minor security situation," Roos said.

"A minor situation, eh? Does the boss know about this?"

"No, but I'm sure you can't wait to tell him," Pieter said.

Tommy ignored him, his eyes shifting from the boat back to Roos. "What are you planning on doing?"

"One of the prisoners has escaped," Roos explained. "We're heading across the river to get her back."

"That's not our job," Tommy said. "*Our* job is to stay here and protect the mine. The threat's gone. Why would we go after them?"

"Because I'm the one in charge and I'm telling you that's what we're gonna do," Roos barked.

Tommy stared at him for a moment and then shook his head slowly from side to side. "I'm calling the boss," he said, and with that he stepped away. "Watch 'em," he told one of his men before starting up the hill, where he'd get a clearer signal.

Roos stepped forward to follow, but one of Tommy's men was quick to block his path. "Get the hell out of my way," Roos snarled.

"Afraid I can't do that, mate," the man said, his fingers flexing on the foregrip of his rifle.

"Have you lost your fucking mind?" Pieter demanded.

"Nothing personal, just orders," the man responded.

Roos shook his head at Pieter and dug his cigarettes from his pocket. He lit one, his mind spinning, searching for his next move.

"Just say the word," Pieter said quietly. "The boys are ready."

Roos scanned the area, noting the position and readiness of each man. With Tommy's entire team spread out across the high ground, they had the tactical advantage. But his men had spent the last six months fighting and dying to secure this nasty stretch of jungle, while Tommy's men were untested. In a firefight, he was certain his men would win.

Still, he didn't want to have to kill the other team unless it was absolutely necessary.

Up near the RZR, Tommy was cutting circles in the sand as he spoke into the phone. Roos watched him, his mind running through the hundreds of ways this could go down. Before he could determine his next move, Tommy had turned and started back down the beach, the phone still pressed to his ear.

Roos studied the other man, searching his eyes for any hint of what was to come, but Tommy's face was unreadable.

Roos flicked away the cigarette and dropped his hand to his pistol. "Get ready," he hissed to Pieter.

Pieter stepped to the right and nodded to a third man, each of them suddenly taut as bowstrings as Tommy crossed the last few yards.

Roos took a breath and thumbed the retention band from his pistol. *Here we go.* But just as his hand closed around the grip, the hint of a grin at the corner of Tommy's mouth gave Roos pause.

"You've got the devil's own luck," Tommy observed, handing him the phone.

Roos took it, the pistol forgotten as he lifted the phone to his ear. "Yes sir."

"You were right to send men after Sawyer," Botha said.

"How so?"

"The girl he was with, Mia Webb," Botha explained, "is a federal agent with the FBI."

"And the men who came to rescue her?" Roos asked, his throat suddenly dry. "Do they work for the American government as well?"

"No, they are contractors for a company called Broadside," Botha replied. "Highly trained operatives who specialize in high-risk rescue operations."

Suddenly everything made sense. But the fact that his boss knew more about his operation than he did put Roos instantly on edge.

"How did you come by all this?" he asked.

"Because besides being highly capable, these men are also well equipped," Botha informed him.

"I'm not following."

"They have a drone overhead watching everything you do."

Roos instinctively looked up, his eyes squinting as he searched for the telltale glint of sun off metal. "Shit."

"Lucky for us, Mr. Sterling has a man on the inside, and he's agreed to cut their communications and drone feed," Botha said.

"So now what?" Roos asked, already knowing the answer to the question.

"Now you go to the crash site and kill them all."

"With pleasure." Roos smiled.

CHAPTER 46

Ubili, DRC

One second Mia was talking, and the next her eyes were rolling back in her head, knees buckling as she stumbled forward. Lane caught her before she collapsed and lowered her gently to the ground. He shook her shoulders and called her name, but after failing to get a response, Lane knew that she'd reached the end of her rope and the best thing he could do was carry her to the crash site.

Well, awesome.

He stood Mia up, lifted her into a fireman's carry, and then set off. The feeling of her weight across his shoulders took Lane back to indoc, the grueling nine-week smoke fest where all the wannabe PJs and combat controllers were sent to see if they had what was needed to make it in Air Force Special Operations. The first three weeks was the selection phase, and as the name implied, its sole purpose was to separate the groupies from the rock stars.

Most of the men who were going to quit dropped out during the pool phase, and those who survived couldn't help but hope that things got easier. They were of course wrong, a fact Lane and TJ discovered firsthand during the last week of training. Everything in indoc was about keeping the candidates mentally and physically stressed. Exhaustion, hunger, dehydration—these were all the tools the instructors used to ramp up the pressure.

It was during the third week that Lane learned all the different ways to carry a "wounded" man. Each one had its merits, but over a long enough distance, they all sucked. The key was to shut off your brain, go to your happy place, and forget the pain. Regrettably, with the enemy somewhere to his rear and half a kilometer of nasty terrain to his front, Lane knew he needed to stay present.

Like all PJs, Lane was used to working in austere and isolated environments, and before coming to the DRC, he would have considered the mountains of Afghanistan to be the most challenging environment on the planet. But struggling through the undergrowth, with Mia bobbing on his shoulders like a dead deer, Lane was quick to change his mind.

There was a treachery to the way the sunlight filtered through the canopy, its sallow half light creating a shadow world that hid the roots and vines coiling across the floor. If he were walking alone, it would have been hard enough to stay on his feet, but with Mia an extra weight, Lane knew the only thing separating him from a broken ankle or a blown-out knee was one careless step.

It was a slow, painful slog, and just when he thought it couldn't get any worse, Lane felt the ground rising beneath his feet. He paused at the bottom of the slope and took a long pull from his CamelBak. After drinking his fill, Lane capped the tube, then continued up the slope and down the other side, where the terrain narrowed around a fallen tree that blocked his path.

He paused, searching for the best way to negotiate the obstacle. There was no going around. It was either over or under. Lowering Mia to the ground, Lane slithered beneath the tree and then reached back, grabbing her under her arms and pulling her through. Once on the other side, he lifted her back onto his shoulders and continued—the added weight of her body on his med ruck causing the straps to dig even deeper into his body.

A short time later, the trees began to thin, the smell of smoke and spilled aviation fuel telling Lane that he was almost at the crash site. On cue, his mind shifted to the men on the downed helo. The questions flashed rapid fire through his mind. Had any of them survived, and if so, what were their injuries?

While Lane didn't know if anyone was alive, he was certain that *if* anyone had survived the crash, they were guaranteed to be on guard, ready to deal with unwanted visitors. To be safe, he stopped short of the clearing and lowered Mia to the ground, then turned his attention to the problem at hand.

He tried his radio again, hoping the batteries had dried out, but when he pushed the talk button, all he got was the garbled hiss of static. With no way to alert any survivors to his presence, Lane tugged the Vortex Recce 8x32 monocular from his ruck and glassed the clearing. He scanned the area for any hostiles that might have beaten him to the crash site, and finding it secure, he turned his attention to the helicopter.

He started at the nose, the Mi-17's crumpled cockpit telling him that the pilots had been killed on impact. Moving aft, Lane found two more bodies splayed out beneath the gaping hole that had been the troop door. The first was one of the door gunners; the other was Hunter, and from the amount of blood that stained the grass around them, Lane knew both were dead.

While he hadn't known either of the men long, they were still his teammates, and the sight of their bodies filled him with rage. The anger burned hot through his veins, but Lane knew this was not the time or the place to get swept up by emotion.

Instead, he panned the monocular to the tail of the helicopter and zoomed in on the ramp. He searched the interior for any sign of life, but the only movement was a tendril of smoke coiling up from the shattered engine. He was beginning to think that his entire team was gone and that he and Mia were alone, when a flicker of movement drew his attention to the man seated in the far corner.

"Jones," he muttered. "I should have known that you were too ornery to die."

With that, Lane shoved the Vortex into his pocket and moved back to the tree. He hoisted Mia onto his shoulder and then began working his way around the edge of the clearing to the downed helo.

CHAPTER 47

CRASH SITE
Ubili, DRC

Mako Jones lay inside the crippled helicopter, feeling like he'd been hit by a Mack truck. Biting down on the pain, he stared through the gaping hole where the door gunner had been. His vision blurred as he looked up at the trees.

Where the hell am I?

Then the crash came racing back—the slam of the missile into the side of the helicopter and Lane and the girl being sucked out of the back. He'd managed a glance up at the cockpit and seen the warning lights on the control panel, and then they were going down. As a testament to his skill, the pilot had somehow managed to bring the stricken bird down on its wheels, but the impact had bounced the helicopter like a basketball.

Then gravity took over, and they'd slammed into the ground nose first, the spray of glass from the windscreen slicing into the pilot's throat.

Jones remembered yelling, "Brace," and had been reaching for his radio, trying to call in a last-minute Mayday, when the main rotor found the trees. It exploded on contact, and the broken shards came hissing through the cargo hold like a box of axe blades, a four-foot section killing both Hunter and the door gunner on its way out the opposite bulkhead.

Then his world went black.

Shoving the memories aside, Jones coughed and tried to get to his feet, but the movement sent a lightning bolt of pain cascading up his back. If there was anything he'd learned during his time in the teams, it was how to deal with pain. It was a lesson that had started on day one of BUDS and continued through the back-to-back combat deployments that had become the mainstay of his career. The pain was always there, a constant companion despite the surgeries and the pills that had followed. Desperate to get to the medical pack and the bottle of tramadol he knew was inside, Jones grabbed onto the cargo net and tried to pull himself to his feet, but no sooner was his butt off the deck than he saw the bone sticking out of his leg.

That's not good.

Realizing he wasn't going anywhere with a compound fracture, Jones eased himself back down into a seated position. Panting, he laid his head back against the bulkhead, his mind still unable to come to grips with what had happened.

He wanted to blame Taran and Carson West for sending them out half-cocked, but Jones knew it was an excuse. No, he was the man on the ground, and the buck stopped with him. *Getting your ass kicked by a bunch of third-world mercs. Wait till the guys back at the teams hear about this shit.*

The thought made him laugh, but the pain and taste of blood on his lips that followed told him there was a good chance he wouldn't be around to tell the tale.

Maybe it's better that way.

Despite the aches and pains that had plagued him during the previous two years at Broadside, Jones had refused to admit that he was getting too old for the game. For him, age was just a number, but looking back at it now, he knew that he'd held on too long. But before he could follow the thought to its inevitable conclusion, the distant snap of a twig drew his attention to the trees.

The sound sent a double shot of adrenaline rushing through his veins, and with the pain forgotten, he snatched the Glock 17 from the holster on his chest. Pistol in hand, he scanned the trees, searching for the source of the sound, but there was nothing except the gentle sway of banana leaves in the wind. Thinking that his ears must have been playing a trick on him, he lowered the weapon and was trying to reach again for the med kit on the wall when he heard a low voice to his right.

"Damn, Chief, you look like shit."

CHAPTER 48

Mia didn't remember passing out, but when she came to and opened her eyes, she was sitting inside the helicopter, a section of tubing leading from her arm to the half-empty IV tacked to the wall. Across from her sat a member of Lane's team, a similar setup in his own arm.

"W-what happened?"

"Dehydration from the looks of it."

"Who are you?"

"I'm the team leader, Mako Jones, in charge of the mission to extract you from this godforsaken place. Things didn't exactly go as planned."

Mia nodded her head and looked around. Seeing a bottle of water sitting beside her leg, she grabbed it and took a long drink.

"Where's Lane?"

"He's out there," Jones said, nodding toward the trees, "checking the perimeter."

"So, you guys rescue people for a living?" she asked.

"That's right."

"Not very good at it, are you?"

"Got you out," Jones grunted.

"Halfway out," Mia countered. "How do you plan on getting us *all* the way out?"

"There's a boat in a village six miles south of here," Jones said.

"You're going to walk out, with *that* broken leg?" Mia asked.

"Listen, lady, I might be a bit banged up, but I can still fight," Jones growled.

Before Mia could reply, Lane ducked into the helo, a wry grin spreading across his face. "I see you guys are making friends."

"I don't think I like her very much."

"You don't like anyone," Lane said, bending to look at Jones's bandage.

"If I could walk, I'd—"

"*If* you could walk, we wouldn't be waiting around here to get our asses kicked," Lane responded.

"Touché."

"So, that's the plan?" Mia asked. "We're going to sit here and fight them off?"

"I didn't say it was a *good* plan."

"Why don't we strap him to the spinal board?" she said, nodding to the orange board clipped below the medical pack.

"And go where?" Lane asked. "It will be another twelve hours before Broadside can get a medical bird into the area."

"I could fly us out," Mia said.

"What?"

"I'm a pilot—"

"Well, unless you've got a helicopter in your back pocket, I don't think that's going to help us out much," Lane said.

"There's one at the mine."

"Absolutely not," Lane said.

"Hold on," Jones interjected. "You're a pilot?"

"Yeah, I've had my license since I was sixteen."

"Chief—*please* tell me you're not seriously considering this," Lane said.

"I don't know about you, but dying in the DRC isn't on my bucket list," Jones replied. "And since I'm still in charge of this team, you're damn right I'm seriously considering this."

"So how are we going to do that?" Mia asked.

Lane pulled the map from his pocket and spread it on the ground.

"These guys have training, which means they'll use basic infantry tactics to hit the crash site, two teams," Jones said.

"They'll want to grab the high ground before hitting the objective, which means one team will move around our flanks and set up a couple of machine guns on the hill I saw on the way in," Lane said, pointing to the terrain feature on the map. "Then once they're set, the second team will assault through."

"OK, now that we know what *they* are going to do," Mia said, "how do we beat them?"

"You see any choke points on the way in?" Mako asked Lane.

"A few," he answered.

"We've got a couple of Claymores and Hunter's SAW," Jones said. "We can set up an ambush. Hit them before they even get here."

"Maybe if we had the whole team," Lane said.

"Lane, this is not a request," Jones said. "It's an order."

"It's bullshit."

"Duly noted," Jones said. "Now go get your shit and make it happen."

"Fine, we'll do it your way," Lane said, grabbing the team's breaching ruck and slinging it over his shoulder. "But when I get back, we are moving your ass to the top of that hill and hiding you in the jungle."

"Why not leave him here?" Mia asked.

"Because once the shooting starts, they are going to put enough lead in this helicopter to turn it into a pencil," Lane said as he moved to the ramp. "At least from the top of the hill, he'll have a chance."

"What do you want me to do while you're gone?" Mia asked.

Lane looked around the helicopter and then reached down and grabbed one of the body bags from the box by the door. "Find everything that will go bang or boom and put it in this," he said, tossing her the bag.

Then he was gone.

CHAPTER 49

Once both of their teams were assembled, Roos pulled out a map of the area and spread it across the hood of the pickup. While he studied it, Tommy was quick to throw in his two cents.

"It doesn't take a tactical genius to figure out where they're going," he said, nodding to the tendril of smoke that marked the crash site.

"Says the asshole with the clean uniform," Pieter muttered.

Roos silenced him with a look and watched Tommy trace his finger across the map.

"We could land the boat here and head south," he said. "Since you and your lot know the area better than my boys, I figure you'll take point."

"Naturally," Roos said. "Then what?"

"We'll stop half a klick from the objective and slip around their flanks in order to set up a machine gun position on this hill," Tommy said, pointing to a spot on the map.

"Let me guess," Pieter interjected. "Once you and your pretty boys are nice and dug in, you'll give us a call to hit them from the front."

"Fine, then *we'll* take point," Tommy responded.

"You two knock it off," Roos growled.

"What? I'm just trying to help," Tommy said.

"All your helping is giving me a headache, so knock it off." Turning to Pieter, he said, "Get the lads ready to go. We're moving out in five minutes."

"Roger that, boss," Pieter said.

"He always was the good little soldier," Tommy said when Pieter had moved away.

"He's not the man you used to know," Roos said, folding the map. "None of them are, so *if* you want to survive, I'd suggest you keep your mouth shut and do what they tell you."

"These shit heels on the other side of the river really got you that worried?" Tommy asked.

The smile was back, and as much as Roos wanted to use his Browning Hi-Power to wipe it permanently off Tommy's face, he knew better. Knew that he needed everyone to work together if they were going to pull this off.

"I don't know what Botha told you about what we do out here," he said, "but this is the real deal. And the men we're going against have the skills and the experience to send you to the deep sleep."

"Oh, don't you fear, Gavin, my son. When the shooting starts, me and my boys will be the first to run to the sound of the guns."

"That's exactly what I am worried about," Roos replied.

Tommy studied him for a moment, then snapped to attention and fired off a crisp salute. "You just try to keep up." He grinned before turning and heading back to the RZR to draw his extra ammo.

Five minutes later both teams were loaded onto the Zodiac, and as they pulled away from shore, Pieter leaned into Roos and hissed, "That sniveling little fuck is going to get us killed."

Roos had been thinking the same thing and was desperately trying to come up with a way to turn the tables. But even more important than that, he needed to figure out how in the hell he was going to get the final shipment of ore to Colonel Yu and get out of the country with his life.

CHAPTER 50

Lane studied the trees around him and recalled the five-day man-tracking course he'd taken in the mountains of North Carolina. Growing up in Tennessee, Lane had spent most of his time outdoors, and whether he was hunting deer or turkey or just out exploring, he'd *thought* he knew his way around the woods.

But the tracking course had been quick to prove him wrong.

The first two days were spent in the classroom, listening to the weather-beaten instructors lecture them on the finer points of the craft of tracking. The rest was out in the field. Trying not to break an ankle while humping a fifty-pound rucksack through the swamps, he'd learned many valuable skills—chief among them that when confronted with unfamiliar terrain, humans, like animals, always sought the path of least resistance.

The easy way.

Remembering the fallen tree he and Mia had negotiated on their way to the crash site, Lane headed back toward the river, his senses alert for any signs of their pursuers.

The downed tree offered the perfect choke point, and knowing that the men would be forced to bunch up to make it past, Lane was quick to take advantage. Dropping the rucksack, he pulled out a pair of Claymores, and working with the practiced ease of hundreds of repetitions, he got them into action.

He staked them to the ground, and after making sure they were aimed where he wanted, he inserted the remote blasting caps and then slipped back under the tree. Careful not to make it too obvious, he scuffed up the bare dirt with his boots, leaving just enough of a track that anyone looking hard would see it. Satisfied with his work, Lane moved back to the Claymore, removed the safety wire, and eased back to the helicopter.

Inside the cargo hold, he found Mia topping off rifle magazines while Jones continued to work on the radio. "Any station this net, this is Guardian 7," he said.

"Anything?"

"Nope," Jones said, tossing the radio back onto the bench. "I checked the antenna and the signal, and both are good to go."

"Which means no one is at the TOC, or something happened to the feed."

"It's got to be the satellite," Jones said with a shake of his head.

"Either way," Lane said, pulling a syringe from his med ruck, "we've got to move."

"What's that?" Jones asked.

"Ketamine. It will help with the pain."

Lane stuck the needle into Mako's arm and pushed the plunger down, and then he and Mia lifted him onto the backboard that Mia had placed next to him.

"For the record, this is a *terrible* idea," Lane said, pulling the straps tight across Mako's chest.

"Yeah, I think you mentioned that already," Jones said, his teeth clenched against the pain.

It took ten minutes to haul Mako through the brush and up the hill, and while Mia pulled in a sharp breath every time the makeshift litter banged against a tree, Jones remained silent. Once they made it to the top, Lane unstrapped the man from the board and propped his team leader against a low boulder.

"Damn, that sucked," Jones said.

"Once the drugs kick in, you'll be right as rain," Lane said.

"If you come back for me," Jones panted, "then you're a bigger sap than I thought you were."

"Don't get all sentimental on me." Lane grinned. "You're not the first SEAL whose ass I've had to save."

CHAPTER 51

Seven thousand miles away, Carson West stood in his office, looking down at the TOC, while the techs tried to figure out why they couldn't reestablish the satellite link. For as long as he'd been working at Broadside, the techs had been refining the company's communications, seeking new and expensive ways to increase both the range and the reliability of the system.

They were masters at their chosen profession, and as such he knew it wouldn't be long before one of them figured out that the reason they weren't able to make contact with Guardian 7 was that someone had sabotaged the array. Eventually one of the techs would get around to looking at the mainframe's log, searching the list of people who'd accessed the computer that controlled the uplink, and once Granger saw West's name on the list, it wouldn't take him long to realize what he'd done.

Fortunately for West, he didn't plan on being around when that happened. With that thought in mind, he moved back to his desk and removed the thumb drive from his briefcase, then plugged it into his computer. He waited a few seconds for the drive to appear on the monitor and double-clicked it, revealing the data-destruction program he'd downloaded from the dark web for this very purpose.

With a flurry of keystrokes, West typed in the required commands and then launched the program; the computer hummed as it went to work erasing its drive. While he waited for it to complete its task, West leaned back in his chair, his mind turning to the next phase of his plan.

He'd grown up poor, and one of his earliest memories was watching his mother slice open a tube of Crest and scoop out the last bit of toothpaste for her toothbrush, which had barely any bristles left. Even later in life, when his father finally found a decent-paying job, his mother remained defiantly frugal.

Whether filling an empty ketchup bottle from packets she'd gotten at the local McDonald's or adding water to the shampoo to make it last longer, she'd steadfastly refused to throw anything away until she was sure that she'd used every drop. With this thought at the forefront of his mind, he had spent most of the morning moving small amounts of money from one offshore account to the next, bouncing his cash from the Caymans to Switzerland and finally to a crypto exchange in Macedonia, where it seemingly vanished.

The ding of the computer caught his attention. The program had completed its work, and with the hard drive now wiped, he pulled the drive from the slot, grabbed his keys and his briefcase, and walked out of his office.

West took the back stairs down to the loading bay and crossed to the slatted fence that surrounded the dumpsters. Whistling, he opened the gate and was about to toss his cell phones into the garbage when a voice froze him in place.

"Going somewhere, Carson?"

West spun to the left, in time to see Granger step into view.

"Oh, hey, Ron," he finally managed. "I—I didn't know you smoked."

"Gave it up after I left the army," Granger said, pausing to light the cigarette. "But you never really quit. Know what I mean?"

"Not really, but considering the stress you've been under, I can't say I blame you," West said, gauging the distance to his car.

Granger nodded and took a drag. "Jones was right about you, wasn't he?" he asked, blowing out the lungful of smoke.

"About what?" West asked.

"About you selling out the team in Mexico," Granger hissed. "Getting our men killed to help out your buddy, Sterling."

"That's bullshit and you know it," West bluffed. "Jones is a pillhead. A junkie who talks out of his ass."

"Maybe so, but at least he's not a traitor."

"I'm done with this conversation," West replied, fishing his keys from his pocket. "Get some sleep, Ron; you look like shit."

With that, he spun on his heel and started toward the BMW, but West hadn't made it more than a few paces when he heard the unmistakable *click-click* of a hammer being snapped back.

"When I called the boss and told him what we found, he said that you'd come in without a fight," Granger said.

"And if I don't?" West asked, holding still.

"It's a big compound. Lots of places to hide a body."

"You've never struck me as the kind of man to shoot a person in the back," West said.

"Are you sure you want to put that theory to the test?"

West stood there, the BMW so close that he could smell the leather. He studied the car, wondering if he could get away—wishing he had the courage to try. But in the end, both men knew that he didn't.

"Drop the keys and come back inside," Granger ordered.

West's shoulders sagged, and he took one final look at the car, then let the keys fall from his hand.

CHAPTER 52

WEST BANK
Ubili, DRC

After they beached the Zodiac, Tommy ordered Pieter to take point, but thirty minutes later he obviously found himself regretting the decision.

"Does he have to stop and check every bloody track he finds?" Tommy complained to Roos.

"You want to get there fast or alive?" he asked.

"Just keep him moving."

Roos nodded and rose to his feet, his rifle up and ready as he moved to Pieter's side.

"Tommy's getting anxious," he said.

"Well, he should be," Pieter said, his voice a whisper. "Man like that's got no business out in the bush."

"Just keep on with what you're doing," Roos said. "Eventually he'll grow tired of it and move his men to the front."

"Why don't we just do 'em now?" Pieter asked. "The boys are with you."

"Just stick to the plan," Roos replied.

"You're the boss," Pieter said, rising to his feet.

He continued to play his role like he was reading from a script, and after another lengthy stop, Tommy's impatience finally got the better of him.

"This is bullshit," he said. "We're actually moving slower now than when you talked to him."

"Keep your damn voice down," Roos hissed.

"I'm in charge here, *not* you."

"That may be, Tommy, but if you don't shut the fuck up, you're going to get us all killed."

"You know what I think?" Tommy asked, stepping forward. "I think you told Pieter to slow down."

"And why would I do that?"

"Maybe you're just getting old, losing a step," Tommy sneered.

"Listen to *me*, you little prick," Roos barked. "While you and Botha were back in Pretoria jerking each other off, me and my lads have been stacking bodies. So if you and your lot think you can do a better job, then have at it."

Tommy gave him a wink and then whirled around and headed back to the rear of the formation, where Rambo's remaining fighters were standing around, passing a joint. "Van Wyk, get those lazy fuckers up to the front," he shouted.

Five minutes later the line of march had been reorganized and the rebels were moving forward, the machetes glinting in the light as they hacked their way through the jungle.

"Subtle," Roos said as Tommy moved past him. "Real subtle."

"You just try and keep up."

With the doped-up rebels breaking trail, Tommy pushed hard for the crash site, and by the time they came across the fresh prints pressed into the dirt, Roos and the rest of his men were puffing like an engine with a broken manifold.

"We've got tracks by the tree," one of the rebels advised. "They're fresh."

Roos scanned the scene, his gaze lingering on a fallen tree resting against a large boulder. The dull yellow color of its splintered trunk told him that it had fallen naturally, but with high ground to both the left and the right, it screamed ambush. As the first two men ducked beneath the tree, Roos dropped his head and opened his mouth, preparing himself for the explosion he knew was to come.

But nothing happened.

Confused, he turned his attention to the rocky ridge twenty yards to his left and searched the dappled shadows, sensing the danger, knowing that it was lying there just out of sight, but unable to divine its source.

"This is wrong," Pieter said. "We need to get out of here."

Roos agreed, but before he could do anything, Tommy keyed up on the radio.

"You coming or what?"

"Don't do it," Pieter warned.

It was the right call, but both men knew that they had too much on the line to turn back now. Roos waited a moment, certain they were all headed into a trap, and then he lowered the binos. *Fuck it. If this is the day, then let's get it over with.*

And with that thought he was moving, his skin crawling as he started toward the fallen log.

CHAPTER 53

Twenty feet to the left of the tree, Travis Lane lay on his stomach, Hunter's machine gun locked and ready to fire. He pulled it close and snugged the buttstock to his shoulder, the nitrobenzene smell of the gun oil he'd placed on the bolt in sharp contrast to the earthy scent of the jungle. Lane watched the men approach and idly rubbed his thumb and index finger together in anticipation of the killing he knew was to follow.

Just a little closer.

The first element did exactly that, and Mia disengaged the safety catch on the detonator as their point man stalked purposefully toward the fallen tree. She waited for Lane to give the signal to initiate the ambush, and with more men scrolling into the kill zone, he was tempted to give her the nod, but something wasn't right.

In his experience, the best-trained men were always positioned at the front of the element, but with those men seemingly unaware of the danger facing them, Lane shifted his attention to those in the back. Swinging the barrel to the right, he scanned their faces, searching for the one in charge.

Seeing an alert man with a large knife strapped to his back, Lane studied his prey through the optic. He thumbed the selector to fire and centered the reticle on the other man's chest, wanting to take the shot.

But with his target partially obscured by the trunk of a gnarled sapling, Lane couldn't guarantee a kill.

The seconds ticked by impossibly slowly while the man stood there, still as stone.

"What are we waiting for?" Mia asked in a whisper.

"Not yet," Lane hissed.

Move, dammit, he begged, but his target remained still.

Resigning himself to the fact that the man was going to stay out of his line of fire, Lane was about to swing the machine gun back to the fighters at the tree trunk when the man with the knife finally stepped off.

With his target moving, Lane began the countdown. "Ten . . . nine . . . eight," he mouthed. He waited for Mia to take up the count and then dropped his eyes to the sights, waiting for her to spring the ambush.

Seven . . . six . . . five . . .

Then the man with the scarred face stepped into view, a pair of binoculars hanging from his neck. As Lane watched, the man stopped and lifted the binos to his eyes, sweeping them across the trees before settling on their position. Despite the distance, he felt the man's gaze on him and knew in an instant that he'd picked the wrong target. But before he could do anything about it, Mia squeezed the detonator, and the clack of the firing mechanism was followed by the resounding crash of the Claymore's explosion.

A split second later Lane opened fire, the spray of lead catching his original target full in the chest. The man dropped like a stone, and Lane swung the barrel to the left, searching for the man with the scarred face, but he was gone.

Shit.

With the smoke from the firefight billowing around them, picking out individual targets was no longer possible. He held down the trigger and swept the barrel back and forth across the kill zone while Mia rose to a knee and opened up as well.

But she hadn't made it through half a magazine when the first volley of return fire came snapping overhead.

"Get down," he shouted.

Mia dropped to the dirt just as a grenade was thrown toward them. It landed short, but the rush of the concussion followed by the smack of bullets into the rocks told Lane they'd lost the advantage.

Tugging a frag of his own from his kit, Lane pulled the pin and flung it over the edge. "Let's move," he ordered.

Leaving the empty machine gun where it was, he grabbed Mia by the arm and pulled her down the back of the ridge. They jogged through the woods, skirting the edge of the crash site. Lane paused to cast a final glance at the hilltop fifty yards to his left, where he'd left Jones, and offered a silent prayer.

Good luck, pal.

Then they were running, their weapons and gear rattling against their bodies as they raced east toward the river.

CHAPTER 54

RIVER CROSSING

Ubili, DRC

It was four miles to the river crossing, and Lane pushed hard, praying the men followed them and stayed away from Jones and the hide site they'd made for the man on top of the hill.

He could hear Mia panting behind him, and he slowed to grab the pack from her shoulders. "We're almost there," he said. "Keep going." One look at her face and Lane knew she was hurting, but instead of asking him to slow down, she matched him step for step. The woman was tough; he had to give her that.

By the time they'd sloshed across and arrived on the far bank of the river, the sun was on its way down, and they were both exhausted. Once clear of the bank, they slipped into the trees.

"They've got to be dead," she said. "I mean, no one could have survived that, right?"

"I saw at least three, maybe more, escape alive," he said, snapping a limb from a tree.

While Mia guzzled water from the CamelBak, Lane moved to the riverbank and used the branch to sweep away their tracks. During his time in the 24th, Lane had never once doubted himself, but suddenly he wasn't sure. This was an entirely different mission, and considering everything that had gone wrong, he was starting to think this entire op was cursed.

Maybe Mako is right, and we should just get the hell out of here while we still have a chance.

In combat, doubt was just as lethal as a bullet, and standing there at the riverbank, Lane took a breath and forced his focus back to the mission at hand. During Green Team they'd told them to concentrate on what they could control, but with the jungle towering over him like a primordial beast, it wasn't control but staying alive that held Lane's attention.

Finishing up his task, he moved back to the trees and, after tossing the branch into the undergrowth, pulled out his compass and turned his attention to their next move. They had six more miles to the mine, but with the shadows already stretching long over the jungle, he figured they could cover half the distance before he would let them stop for a short rest.

After taking a quick azimuth, he grabbed the Benelli shotgun he'd taken from the helicopter and motioned to Mia. "Let's go."

It took them an hour to get to the position he'd picked out on the map, the monotony of the forced march broken every kilometer by Lane suddenly changing their direction of travel or circling back to check their back trail. It was hard going, but by the time he reached their destination, Lane was confident that they weren't being followed.

"We stop here for food and a short rest," he said, dropping his pack.

"Thank God."

The spot was exactly what he'd hoped for: a sliver of dry ground in the middle of another swamp. Mia, on the other hand, wasn't quite so forgiving.

"You sure know how to show a girl a good time," she said, falling to the dirt.

She tugged off her boot and, sucking air between her teeth, gingerly peeled off her sock to reveal a blister the size of a silver dollar.

"That's a nice one," he said. "Let me guess: you don't do much hiking where you're from."

"If this is hiking, you can keep it," she said. "Damn, this thing hurts."

"Here, let me take a look," he said, grabbing a pair of latex gloves from his med kit.

"Easy," she said as he picked up her foot and gently pressed the blister.

"We're going to have to pop it," he said.

"Awesome."

Lane grabbed the chest-decompression needle and held it up near her foot.

"Got anything bigger?" she asked.

"I can look," he said, grinning.

Before she had a chance to reply, he lanced the blister, and Mia's hiss of pain was followed a second later by a sigh of relief as the fluid jetted from the tiny hole.

"Better?"

"Yeah, thanks."

Lane recapped the needle and, after applying a dressing, pulled a fresh pair of socks from his pack. "Might be a little big, but they're dry," he said, handing them over.

"So this is what you did in the military? Took care of people with blisters?"

"More or less," he said. "What about you?"

"What do you want to know?"

"Maybe start with how you ended up locked in a conex box."

"I was going after a colleague of mine. He was a UN worker named Angelo Garza, and he was murdered while investigating an illegal mining operation in Ubili," Mia said.

"The mine where we found you?"

"Yeah." Mia nodded.

"Who killed him?"

"Gavin Roos and the men from the NorthStar Mine."

"Is that the man with the scarred face?" he asked.

"That's him."

"Besides being an asshole, why would he risk the heat of killing a UN worker?" Lane asked.

"You've been to Afghanistan, fought the Taliban, right?" she asked. Lane nodded.

"Well, Roos and the rest of his people at the mine are just like the Taliban, but instead of killing for religion, they kill for money."

"So that's what this is all about?" Lane asked. "Money?"

"For them," Mia said.

"What about you?"

"For me, it's personal," she replied. "These assholes killed my friends, and I want them to pay."

"And how are you going to do that?"

"By getting Sawyer to testify against Sterling and everyone else involved with the mine."

"And let me guess—you want me to help you bust him out?"

"That's right."

"Well, shit," Lane said.

They fell silent for a moment. Then Lane handed her an MRE, and after showing her how the chemical heater worked, he grabbed his entrenching tool and started digging a fighting position.

"Do you have ADHD or something?"

"What do you mean?"

"You never sit down," she said between bites of beef stew. "You're like a human border collie, always on the move."

"Yeah, well, this is how you stay alive," he said, attacking the dirt.

By the time Mia had finished her food, Lane had dug the hole and piled dirt around the front to form a barrier.

"You think both of us are going to fit in that?"

"Nope, just you."

"Where are you going to sleep?"

"Don't worry about me," he said, grabbing his night vision goggles.

He waited for Mia to settle and go to sleep and then dug a tube of amphetamines from his pocket. Lane popped one of the pills into his mouth and then doused himself with a liberal amount of mosquito dope. The repellent seeped into his pores, burning his skin from the inside out, but it was better than being eaten alive.

Digging a section of netting from his bag, he draped it over his face, laid the shotgun across his thighs, and leaned back on his rucksack. Their arrival had disturbed the natural order of the swamp, but with Mia asleep and Lane sitting still as a stone, life returned to normal.

It was a moonless night, and even with the night vision, it was hard to see anything but the reeds swaying before his face. Thanks to the government-issued speed, Lane was wide awake, but with nothing to do but wait and watch, his mind began to wander. Starved for stimulation, his senses began to play tricks on him: the bushes turning to figures, the gentle plops of the bullfrogs in the water sounding like footfalls in the distance.

It took discipline to stay focused, to sit still and not react to every sound, but Lane was well practiced. At three in the morning, he finally allowed himself a little stretch and was working the tension out of his neck when the gentle *tink* of metal on metal came echoing out of the darkness. Instantly on guard, he lifted the shotgun and scanned his surroundings.

But there was nothing.

Lane was about to chalk it up to the speed when he heard a metallic *tick* from his left. Turning his head, he tracked the sound to its source, but without the moon all he saw was the ambiguous outline of the reeds. Taking his left hand off the shotgun, he slowly reached up and toggled his night vision from IR to thermal.

There was a microsecond of darkness; then like a mechanical blink, the shadows were gone and replaced by the glowing orange shapes of men creeping toward their position.

How the fuck did they find us?

Before Lane had a chance to consider the answer, the first grenade came tumbling through the air.

CHAPTER 55

Mia was sound asleep when the boom of a grenade brought her back to the land of the living. She lay there, struggling to make sense of the bare earth walls before her. *Where am I?* Then it came rushing back. Roos, the swamp—*Travis.*

The realization that they were under attack shoved her sluggish mind into overdrive, and Mia grabbed her rifle, the geyser of dirt and frag kicked up by the exploded grenade impacting around her. She got to her feet and surveyed the scene over the lip of the fighting position. The reeds were on fire, and the dancing flame provided just enough light for her to see shadowy figures wading through the swamp. But it was the crumpled body lying near her that immediately grabbed her attention.

Lane had told her that if they got hit, she was to take the sat phone that they'd retrieved from the downed Mi-17 and head south to the village, where a Broadside team would come pick her up. But too many people had died already, and Mia would be damned if she was going to add his name to the list. Ignoring the snap of bullets overhead, she rushed over to Lane and shook his shoulder.

"Get up. We've got to move."

But the man was out cold.

Realizing she had no one to depend on but herself, Mia bent down and scooped one of the frags from Lane's open pack. She ripped the pin free and hurled it toward the men on the left. The grenade detonated, the flash of the explosion revealing Lane's night vision goggles lying on the ground.

Mia scooped them from the dirt and pulled them over her eyes, fingers fumbling over the housing as she searched for the power switch. *Where the hell is it?* She found it and, remembering the Claymore mine she'd watched him set at the edge of their camp, began searching for the detonator. Aided by the green glow of the night vision goggles, she saw it lying next to his shotgun. She clacked it together just like he'd told her, but instead of the boom she'd been expecting, there was nothing but the slosh of boots moving through the water.

"There she is. Grab her," a voice said.

Frantic at how close they were, she tried the detonator again, and still nothing happened.

With her heart hammering, she was turning for her rifle when she saw the disconnected firing wire lying on the ground. She picked it up and blew off the dirt, her hands shaking as she inserted it into the bottom of the device.

The calm that followed was like nothing Mia had ever experienced. Like a spectator in her own body, she watched herself hold up the detonator and felt the smile spread across her face as she squeezed it together.

The Claymore erupted with a spray of water and lead, the ball bearings packed inside blowing the men off their feet. At the same time, the moon peeked out from behind the clouds, and in its silver light, Mia could see everything: the seven mercs moving methodically up the left side and the rebels hunkered down on the right. Realizing what she had to do, she grabbed Lane's AK and dropped to her knee.

She pulled the trigger to the rear and worked the muzzle back and forth like a fire hose, the wall of lead sending the advancing rebels diving for cover. Mia kept it up until she ran the magazine dry, then turned to run while the two groups began shooting at each other.

Taking advantage of the chaos, Mia snatched the tattered rucksack from the ground, strapped it onto her shoulders, and moved back to Lane.

She grabbed him by the back of his plate carrier and dragged him into the water. He was heavy, and Mia hadn't made it more than fifty yards downstream before her legs were shaking, lungs burning from the effort.

She thought of John and Angelo. How each man had given his life to get her here. The rage stirred within her, and Mia stoked it, letting it build until it was coursing through her veins like lava.

You can do this.

With her mind clear and her focus sharp, Mia pulled Lane up the slope and into the undergrowth, her eyes searching the shadows for someplace to hide.

Mia laid Lane down and stepped back to take a breath. The trip of her foot on a stone almost sent her tumbling backward into what appeared to be a small cave. Realizing this space was their only place to hide, Mia yanked Lane inside and collapsed onto the ground beside him, her body quivering as she struggled to calm her breathing.

The firefight was still going on, the men shooting at targets that were no longer there. She could hear a hoarse voice barking orders, trying to stop the shooting, but it wasn't until a pop flare went hissing skyward that the gunfire slowly melted away.

The flare lit up the swamp, and Mia threw herself across Lane, her fear turning to terror when she realized that his chest wasn't moving. Trying to remember her first-aid class, Mia tilted his head up and back and pressed her cheek close to his mouth. Failing to feel or see any signs of breathing, she turned to his medical bag.

There's got to be something in this fucking pack of his.

Mia opened the flap and used a tiny red-lens flashlight she found to study the contents. Most of the names printed on the bottles and vials meant nothing to her, and she was about to give up when she saw the black auto-injector with *Epinephrine* printed on the side.

Growing up, she'd had a friend who'd been prescribed an EpiPen, and Mia had been taught how and when to use the injector. However, looking at the military-grade item in her hand, she was pretty sure this wasn't to be used in case of beestings. But with Lane's lips now beginning to turn a pale shade of blue, Mia knew she was running out of time.

Well, here goes nothing.

She prepped the auto-injector the same way she'd been taught years ago, and after removing the storage cap, she held it against his thigh and pressed the button until it clicked.

CHAPTER 56

The rush of epinephrine hit Lane like a stick of dynamite, and he sat straight up, his heart threatening to burst from his chest. His sudden return to consciousness left him confused, and his eyes shifted rapid fire from Mia to the mouth of the cave and finally to the auto-injector stuck in his leg.

"W-what happened."

"You stopped breathing," she said.

He pulled the auto-injector from his leg. "Epinephrine, smart."

"I figured you'd be pissed that I didn't listen to you." She grinned.

"Hard to be mad at someone who just saved your life."

"We make a good team," she said, scratching at her own leg.

With the synthetic adrenaline coursing through his veins, the exhaustion of the previous twelve hours vanished, and Lane leaped to his feet. Mia looked up at him, her mouth open.

"What?" he asked.

"A second ago you were dead, and now you're walking around like nothing happened."

"That's what a good shot of epinephrine will do for you," he said, moving to look out the mouth of the cave.

Seeing no movement close by, he shifted back into the enclosure and sat down, picking up the small flashlight Mia had left on the ground.

Handing it to Mia, he said, "Help me out."

He turned toward her, allowing the light to shine on the sliver of shrapnel sticking out of his bicep. "That doesn't look good," she said.

"Yeah. I really hope I put some lidocaine in this thing," he said, reaching for the ruck.

Lane opened it up and pulled out a pair of latex gloves, a bottle of iodine, a surgical stapler, and an assortment of gauze bandages. But no lidocaine.

He pulled on the gloves, opened the bottle of iodine and set it on the ground, and then turned to Mia. "This might get messy," he said. "Do you have a weak stomach?"

"Nope."

"Good," he said, grabbing the end of the metal shard and pulling. Pain washed over him, the skin around the wound bulging as he worked. "Shit, that hurts," he grunted.

Beside him, Mia's eyes went wide, and the light began to shake. "I . . . I . . . think I'm going to be sick," she said, lifting her left hand to her mouth.

"Just hold it steady," Lane ground out.

The last few centimeters were the hardest, and by the time he finally got the shrapnel free, his face was slicked with sweat. He dropped the shard on the ground and reached for the bottle of iodine, his hands shaking as he poured it into the wound.

"Now for the *really* fun part," he said, handing Mia the surgical stapler.

"W-what do you . . . ?"

"Someone has to hold the wound closed while the other staples," he said, "and since I've got the only pair of gloves, it looks like you're stapling."

"Please tell me you're joking."

"Afraid not."

"Fine, show me how to use it," she said, handing him the light.

"It's simple. Just press the front to the wound, look through the little window to make sure the staple is going where you want it to, and then squeeze the handle."

"OK."

Holding the light in his mouth, Lane pinched the skin together and then nodded to Mia, who pressed the stapler to his skin. She squeezed the handle, the metallic *click* of the stapler making her flinch.

Lane reached up and took the flashlight from his mouth. "It's crooked," he said.

"Cut me some slack; I'm new to this," Mia replied.

"Let's see if we can get the next one straight."

"Just shut up and hold the light," Mia said.

She delivered the next two with confidence, both of them arrow straight. "I think you missed your calling," Lane commented.

"Well, after the FBI fires me, maybe I can become an EMT."

Lane frowned and placed two gauze pads over the wound before handing Mia an ACE bandage to hold the dressing in place. "Why would they do that?" he asked.

Instead of answering, she focused on wrapping the wound. He was about to repeat the question when she finally spoke.

"There's something you need to know," she said without looking up. "Something I should have told you before." And then she went quiet, seemingly unwilling to say more.

Lane resisted the urge to break the silence and waited patiently for Mia to find the words.

She secured the end of the bandage and then looked up. "My boss doesn't *exactly* know where I am."

"Is that a good thing or a bad thing?" Lane asked.

"Well, I guess that depends on how all of this turns out," she said. "But judging from our current circumstances, I doubt I'll be getting promoted."

"And if we bring Sawyer back?" Lane asked. "Get him to testify against Sterling and Crimson Ridge?"

"That would definitely help," she said. "Do you think we could pull it off?"

Lane didn't know. Tactically speaking, returning to the mine to rescue Sawyer and steal the helicopter was a terrible idea. Especially when he thought about how Roos and his merry band of bloodthirsty mercs had been one step ahead of them the entire way. In fact, he still couldn't figure out how the fighters had found them in the swamp, especially after everything he'd done to throw them off their trail.

CHAPTER 57

SWAMP
Ubili, DRC

By the time the Huey returned to the swamp, the sun had breached the horizon, its yellow light struggling to pierce the fog that hung over the low ground like a shroud. Roos stood in the center of the scrub, blood seeping through the field dressing he had tied over the ragged bullet wound to his shoulder.

Pieter was dead, and the rest of the wounded had already been ferried back to the mine. All that was left of his team was the shredded remains stuffed into the three body bags lying at his feet. He closed his eyes, suddenly exhausted, the rushing downdraft from the hovering helo tearing at his salt-stained cammies.

The night ambush had been a mistake, a tactical blunder fueled partly by Roos's ego but mostly by his need to bring this entire shit show to an end. *Bloody stupid,* he cursed himself. But the damage was done, and with the Huey on the ground and two burly men leaping from the cargo hold, Roos knew it was up to him to salvage what was left of his plan.

Resolved to do exactly that, he helped the men load the body bags into the hold and then took one last look over the blood-slicked killing ground. Vowing to himself that the death of his men would *not* be in vain, he climbed into the helo, his body exhausted.

That he had made it out alive was nothing short of a miracle. But with the deadline for delivering the final load of coltan to the Chinese a short three hours away, his survival seemed more like a cruel joke than anything else.

If Roos had been dealing with a reasonable man, he would have explained the situation and asked for more time. Unfortunately, Colonel Yu was neither reasonable nor forgiving, and considering his long reach, running wasn't an option. Which was why Roos had left Costa and Oskar at the mine when the rest of them had gone after Mia and her guardian angel.

"Well?" he asked the brown-haired man.

"We've got three of the sling loads ready to go," Costa said.

"How long on the last one?"

"Few more hours."

Roos nodded and settled back in his seat, his hand finding the wrist-top computer in his pocket. He pulled it out, wiped the mud and grit from the face, and studied the blank screen. There was a part of him that wanted to assume the lack of a blinking red dot meant his quarry was dead, blown to hell by one of the many grenades that had gone off during the ambush, but Roos hadn't made it this far by leaving anything up to chance.

"Let's do one more pass before heading back," he told the pilot.

The man complied and pulled the helicopter into a sweeping turn over the area. "Keep your eyes open for the girl," Roos told the men.

They nodded and leaned out, eyes locked on the ground, but there was nothing.

"Boss, we need to go," Costa said.

Leaving an enemy on his back trail went against every ounce of Roos's training, but with the certainty of what would happen if he missed his deadline, he knew that he didn't have a choice.

"All right," he said, "let's head back."

It was a short flight to the mine, and when they landed, Roos found it exactly as Costa had said. He climbed out of the helicopter and brushed past the men who were waiting to unload the body bags containing the dead mercenaries. While they got to work, he stepped over to the cargo nets stuffed with the burlap bags full of ore and checked the rigging, making sure they were secure, before turning to the ground crew.

"I want the helicopter fueled and ready to go in twenty minutes," he said. "And Costa, I need you to send someone to sanitize the office. If it will burn, I want it gone. Nothing gets left behind, you hear me?"

"Yes, boss."

With that done, Roos started down the hill, pausing at his room for the bottle of Johnnie Walker Red before continuing toward the clinic.

"You've got the devil's own luck," the nurse said when he walked inside.

Roos dropped onto one of the neatly made beds with a grimace and uncorked the bottle with his teeth. He took a long pull, the blended whisky warming him from the inside, and when he finally came up for air, his face was flushed. "We've got a deal, the devil and I," he said, his voice raspy from the booze. "Now go get the doc."

"He's tending to the rest of your men right now," she said. "So you're going to have to wait."

Humbled by her words, Roos nodded and looked down at the floor. "How are they doing?"

"It doesn't look good."

"I know you don't owe me anything," he said, "but do what you can for them."

"You want to help them?" she asked.

"Yeah." He nodded, taking another pull from the bottle.

"Then end this now," she said. "Leave this place before you kill anyone else."

He looked up, wishing he could take her advice but knowing that if he didn't deliver the promised ore to the Chinese, those he'd managed to save from the ambush wouldn't last the week.

"Wish I could," he said. "But it's not up to me."

"Before coming here, I'd never met a person who I thought wasn't worth saving," she said, her blue eyes hard as diamonds. "But you, Mr. Roos, are one heartless son of a bitch."

"Tell me something I don't know," he said, taking another pull of the bottle.

CHAPTER 58

Fifty yards to the south on the side of a hill, Lane and Mia lay hidden behind a log, their eyes on the Huey hovering over the third sling load. While the pilot held the helicopter steady, the two mercenaries they'd been watching stepped out, one man using a static wand to hold the hook while the second attached it to the thick strap connected to the top of the cargo net. When it was secured, both men moved away and the pilot lifted off, the cargo net full of burlap bags dangling beneath the helicopter as it flew east.

Mia activated her stopwatch. "Twenty minutes on the clock," she said, lifting the Vortex monocular to her eyes.

"What do you see?" he asked.

"Besides the two shitheads at the helo pad, we've got a third guarding the workers and no sign of Roos."

Lane wasn't a mining expert, but looking at the equipment arrayed outside the buildings, he found it easy enough to guess their functions. Ignoring the damaged maintenance bays and fire-blackened storage sheds, he followed the smell of smoke to the smoldering fifty-gallon drum sitting in front of the building with the antennas on top.

"What's that smell?" Mia asked.

"Looks like they're burning paper."

On cue, a fourth mercenary crossed into view with an armful of files.

He carried them to the barrel and dumped them inside, then stepped back as the flames leaped skyward. The guards plus the burning documents told Lane that Roos and his men were not planning on sticking around, and with the clock ticking, it was imperative that they find Sawyer.

But where was he?

If he was still alive and as valuable as Mia said, it was only logical that he'd be heavily guarded, and with that thought in mind, Lane turned his attention back to the three mercs smoking and joking near the L-shaped building in the middle.

Bingo.

"We've got three guards at the front and another two on roving patrol," he said. "Still no sign of Roos."

"What's next?"

"We're going to need a diversion," he said.

"Do you have any more party favors in that bag of yours?"

After absorbing most of the grenade blast, Lane's battle-scorched ruck had definitely seen better days. The med kit strapped to the outside was gone, and so were the entrenching tool and the satellite radio, but somehow Felix's breacher bag had survived the explosion. Lane pulled it out and inspected the two blocks of C-4 along with the reinforced plastic box that held the M7 blasting caps.

He popped the lid and looked inside, breathing a sigh of relief when he found the fragile blasting caps undamaged. How they had survived the explosion was beyond him, but never one to look a gift horse in the mouth, Lane got to work building the charges.

Using his knife, he cut the blocks into six equal squares and then prepped the caps.

"Just in case you were wondering, this is *not* the preferred way to handle explosives," he said.

"Good to know," she replied. "So, what's the plan?"

"Well, it's a good-news, bad-news kind of deal," he said. "The good news is that *if* we do this right, I think we might just pull it off."

"And the bad news?"

"We're going to have to split up," Lane said.

"Wait, what?"

"You said the helicopter was going to have to land and fuel up before the last flight, which means we need to hit the helo and that L-shaped building where I'm sure they are keeping Sawyer at the same time. If we don't, we risk spooking the pilot and having him fly off, leaving our asses here."

"There has to be another way," Mia insisted.

"There isn't," he said with a shake of his head. "The helo pad is on the south, and the prison is on the north. They're just too far apart."

"So how do we do this?"

"You take the south, put the charge on the propane tank, and wait for the helo to land. While you're doing that, I'll make my way to that big shipping container on the side of that maintenance bay," he said, pointing at the large crate. "From there I'll have an easy shot on those two mercs, and then I can go in and rescue Sawyer."

"That's a great idea, but I don't know anything about using explosives. How am I going to blow up the propane tank?"

"I'm going to teach you," he said, handing her the block of C-4.

Mia looked at him for a long moment and then nodded. "Fine, show me how to do it."

It was a down and dirty introduction to explosives, but Lane explained it in a way that was easy to understand, and when he was done, he made her walk him through the required steps. "First I strip the film off the tape and slap the charge to the bottom of the propane tank," she said. "Then I stick in the blasting cap, unwind the shock tube, and once I'm behind the building, I put the free end of the tube into the igniter, and when I'm ready to blow it, I remove the safety wire and pull the firing ring."

"And then what?"

"I stay behind cover until all the shrapnel hits the ground, and then I take out the pilot."

"Like I said, you're a natural."

"Thanks, Coach," she said, picking up her rifle.

"How are you on ammo?" he asked.

"I've got two magazines and one grenade."

"Here, take this," he said, handing her an additional magazine. "And one last thing. No matter what you hear going on from my side of the mine, you stick to the plan."

"Got it."

"I'm serious, Mia," Lane said.

"Yeah, I heard you."

"All right then, let's do this."

CHAPTER 59

Lane watched Mia slip through the trees, waiting until she was out of sight before turning his attention to what he needed to do. He'd told her that he was fine, but it was a lie. He was hurting, and with the epinephrine long since worn off, Lane's wounds were beginning to throb.

He dug the bottle of Dexedrine from his pocket, and ignoring the warning not to exceed one pill in twelve hours, he shook two more into his palm. He swallowed them dry and then grunted to his feet.

It was twenty yards from the log to the back of the building with the satellite array, but the jungle was thick, and negotiating the dense undergrowth without alerting the men guarding the mine took time. Lane's progress was slow and painful, and when he eventually crawled into the thicket adjacent to his destination, he was smoked, his assault shirt soaked through with sweat.

Lane sipped water from the hydration bladder, and a quick check of his watch showed that he had five minutes until the helicopter came thundering over the trees. He lay there a moment, feeling the tingle of the speed kicking in and watching a man continue to feed documents into the burn barrel.

The flicker of flames gave Lane an idea, and he rolled onto his side, pulling a fragmentation grenade and the roll of electrical tape he always carried with him from his kit. He picked the end of the tape free of the roll, stuck it to the frag, and then began wrapping the tape around the spoon. With the spoon taped, the grenade wouldn't detonate when he pulled the pin, which was usually a bad thing. But Lane didn't want the grenade to blow up when he pulled the pin; he wanted it to go off after he dropped it into the burn barrel. Preferably after he was safely behind the L-shaped building. The only problem was he didn't know exactly how long it would take the smoldering flames inside the barrel to melt through the tape and release the spoon.

Erring on the side of caution, he wrapped the tape around the frag three times and then ripped it free. Returning the grenade to its pouch and the tape to the carabiner clipped to the front of his kit, Lane checked his watch and saw he had three minutes until the return of the helo. Unfortunately, the man in front of him was oblivious to his surroundings and continued to methodically feed the burn barrel.

With the seconds slowly ticking by, Lane was beginning to think that he was going to have to shoot the guy when he dropped the final folder of documents into the barrel and headed back inside the building. The moment he was out of sight, Lane was on his feet. He grabbed the grenade from its pouch, yanked the pin free, and crossed to the burn barrel.

Lane dropped the frag inside and then moved to the line of trucks on the left side of the roadway, which would block him from the view of the mercs standing in front of the target building. He shifted around the tailgate of one vehicle and then eased down the driver's side of the truck, pausing at the nose to sneak a quick look back. Finding the mercs exactly as he'd left them, Lane continued forward, past the pair of Land Cruisers, before stepping out of cover and racing for the long side of the L-shaped building.

Pressing his shoulder against the wall, Lane took a second to catch his breath, then stepped forward carefully. He could hear the men standing around the back talking, their bored voices making him confident that they had no idea he was there, and he continued the final few feet to the corner. Inching out, he took a quick look and found the two mercs who were supposed to be guarding the metal door sitting on an empty cable spool, their rifles against the wall while they shared a half-empty jug of palm wine.

With his targets identified, all that was left to do was wait. A quick look at his watch showed that thirty seconds had passed since he'd stepped out of the trees. He could hear the Huey now, the rhythmic beat of its rotors sounding like distant thunder, yet it wasn't the sound of the helicopter but the impending blast of the grenade that had his attention.

For this mission to succeed, Lane knew he had to be in position to engage the mercs guarding the pad before Mia blew the propane tank. He'd hoped that the grenade blast would keep the guards at the front of the building occupied while he went to work, but apparently he'd used too much tape.

Out of both time and options, Lane double-clicked the radio, the signal to Mia that he was ready to start the show. He waited for her to respond and then lifted his rifle and was about to take the corner when the grenade finally exploded.

As diversions went, the explosion wasn't as loud as Lane had hoped it would be, but the pained scream that followed more than made up for it. Hearing the subdued shouts from the fighters at the front of the building, he rounded the corner and found the men trying to get to their feet.

Lane fired on the move and gave each man a double shot to the chest before running past. He moved swiftly across the open ground, his eyes on the large shipping crate he'd seen from his hide site. He placed his rifle on top of the crate and pulled himself up, the movement threatening to rip the staples from his wounded arm.

Biting down on the pain, he kept at it, using the toes of his boots to push him over the lip of the crate. By the time he made it to the top, the helicopter was almost to the landing pad. Lane crawled to the edge and stripped his final HE round from his kit. Snapping the breech closed, he flipped out the leaf sight and lined up the shot. He made a slight correction for the wind and slipped his finger around the trigger.

It's showtime.

CHAPTER 60

NORTHSTAR MINE

Ubili, DRC

Mia moved into position and took a second to catch her breath before darting from cover. It was a short dash to the propane tank, and she made it into position and dropped to a knee. Wiping her sweaty palms against her pant leg, she fumbled to strip the film from the Breachers tape.

C'mon . . . C'mon.

Finally, she got the corner free and peeled the film away, then slapped the charge to the base of the tank. Remembering what Lane had told her, she pressed the blasting cap into the C-4 and headed back the way she'd come, the length of shock tube trailing behind her. Once again behind cover, she inserted the free end of the tubing into the M81 igniter and checked her watch.

Two minutes.

Her mind filled with the hundreds of things that could go wrong. What if she'd screwed up the math and the helicopter didn't need fuel? What if she'd messed up the charge and it didn't blow? A metallic *clang* from the pole building adjacent to the helo pad drew Mia from her worry, and she looked up, her mind instantly put at ease by the sight of the ground crew rolling the barrel of aviation fuel up to the helicopter pad.

Mia could hear the helicopter now, and she craned her head to the left in time to see the Huey come sliding over the trees. The pilot brought it in for a textbook landing, the ground crew waiting for him to shut off the engine before starting the refueling process.

Mia looked down at her watch. *Twenty seconds.*

The pilot was out of the cockpit and, after a long stretch, unzipped his flight suit and moved to the edge of the landing site to take a piss.

At the ten-second mark, Mia pulled the safety wire from the igniter and slipped her finger through the pull ring. *Here we go.* She gave it a sharp tug, feeling the tension of the internal firing pin as it was shoved against the primer. It gave with a barely audible pop, and the resulting spark lit the explosive powder that lined the hollow shock tube.

A split second later the propane tank erupted, the pressure wave from the explosion knocking Mia off her feet. She landed on her hip and immediately rolled onto her stomach and covered her head with her hands. Mia stayed down, feeling the rush of the heat and hearing the metallic *clangs* of the ruptured tank raining down on the surrounding buildings.

When she finally hazarded a look at the scene around her, what she found was almost apocalyptic, the thick black smoke and muted orange flames flickering in the premature twilight like something out of Dante's *Inferno.*

Mia scrambled to her feet, grabbed her rifle, and was moving around the back of the building when she heard the *crump* of Lane's 40 mm round exploding.

"You're clear," he said over the radio. "See you in five minutes."

Mia acknowledged the transmission and rushed toward the helo pad, where she found the bodies of the dead mercs crumpled on the ground near the sling loads. Mia slowed and scanned the area, searching for the ground crew, but all she saw was the abandoned fuel hose still connected to the Huey.

She lowered her rifle and was moving to disconnect the fuel hose when the dazed pilot came staggering around the nose of the helo. Mia snapped her rifle onto target and stepped forward.

"Hands up!" she shouted.

The pilot froze, his mouth forming a silent O as he stared at her.

"Don't do anything stupid," she said, taking a step closer.

The man nodded and stepped forward, and for an instant Mia thought he was going to comply, but then his fingers twitched as he reached for the pistol in his shoulder holster.

"Stop!"

Before his fingers found the grip of the pistol, Mia fired. The bullets hit his chest, the impact spinning him to the ground. She hadn't wanted to kill him, but he'd given her no choice.

Offering a silent prayer of thanks to her father, Mia turned her attention to the Huey. She turned off the fuel pump, disconnected the nozzle from the helicopter, and then used the crank on the side of the pump to reel in the hose. When it was secure, Mia wiped her hands clean against her pant leg and was about to start her preflight checks when the first bullets came snapping overhead.

She threw herself to the ground and rolled behind the empty fuel barrel just as the mercenary who'd been guarding the workers fired two more quick shots. The rounds hit the barrel and punched through, the star-shaped holes six inches above Mia's head telling her she needed a better place to hide.

CHAPTER 61

By the time the doctor showed up, the bottle was half-empty and Roos was half in the bag. "What the hell took you so long?"

"I was taking care of your men," Lars said.

For once Roos didn't have a comeback, and he lowered his head and offered a slurred "Thank you, Doc."

The man nodded and began unwrapping the bandage covering the bullet wound in Roos's shoulder. "I'm going to need to irrigate this before I sew it up," he said. "Would you like something for the pain?"

"No," Roos said.

"Fine with me." The man shrugged.

He turned back to the stainless-steel tray and picked up a syringe full of saline. Roos swore he saw a smile when the doctor shoved the tip of the syringe into the jagged wound. "Here we go," Lars said, placing his thumb on the plunger.

The jet of liquid saline rushed across his ragged nerves like a vial of acid, and Roos's vision went white. He squeezed the neck of the whisky bottle and bit down on the pained groan crouched at the back of his throat.

Dr. Lars lifted the curved needle to the light and, after inspecting the catgut, moved back to Roos's side. Roos took a final pull from the bottle and watched as the man deftly sewed up the wound.

"You might be a spineless prick," Roos said, "but you've got a sure hand."

"Is that a compliment?"

"Take it however you want," Roos said, his eyes drifting to the window that looked out over the mine.

"What is your man burning out there?" Lars asked as he stitched.

"Papers," Roos said, watching as one of the boys carried another load to the burn barrel.

"You mean evidence."

"Don't get all high and mighty on me now, Doc," Roos sneered. "You're making pretty good coin for a man with no medical license."

Lars stopped in midstitch and looked down at his patient. "You know about that?"

Roos was about to reply when the burn barrel exploded, the ball of fire and chunks of steel catching the man with the papers full in the face. He stumbled backward, his clothes on fire, mouth opened in a long, agonized scream.

Roos leaped to his feet, the last suture still trailing from his arm. He tugged his shirt over his head, then strapped on his plate carrier and checked his pistol. By the time he was ready, the nurse was running for the door.

"No!" he shouted. "Don't go out there."

She opened her mouth to protest, but before the words were off her lips, the *thwack-thwack* of a suppressed rifle came bouncing across the mine. Roos had no idea who was shooting, and he didn't care. All that mattered was the safety of the helicopter and the remaining ore, and this thought sent him racing for the door.

Roos yanked it open and hustled down the steps, hurtled over the screaming man writhing on the ground, and raced across the roadway. He stopped at the edge of the building and looked south. The sight of the Huey sitting safely on the ground and the pilot pissing off the side of the pad put him instantly at ease, and Roos let out the breath he hadn't realized he was holding.

Shoving the pistol into its holster, he turned toward the L-shaped building where Sawyer was being kept. *I should have killed that fucker a long time ago.*

"Go check the prisoner," he barked at the mercs near him.

Roos jerked the radio from his kit and was bringing it to his lips when the propane tank detonated. Transfixed by the sight of the giant fireball, he stood there, braving the heat and the rush of black smoke that came tumbling across the camp.

What in the hell?

Eventually the acrid burn of the vaporized gases overcame him, and he lurched back inside the clinic. Coughing, he keyed up on the radio. "Ryk . . . Oscar, what's going on?" he demanded. "Someone answer me."

But there was nothing, and the silence told him everything he needed to know.

They're dead.

He was turning to go find the shooter when the smoke lifted and he saw Mia burst from cover, her arms and legs pumping as she sprinted for the helicopter.

Realizing what he had to do, he hustled over to the Toyota pickup and yanked open the back door. He grabbed the .308 Truvelo from the back seat and moved around to the front of the truck, deploying the bipod before laying the rifle across the hood. Once it was in position, he dropped his eyes to the scope in time to see the pilot go for his pistol as Mia held her gun on him.

It was a stupid move, especially considering the girl had him dead to rights, but like Roos, the pilot clearly assumed that Mia didn't have the stones to pull the trigger. They were both wrong, and a second later the pilot was splayed out on the ground. That he'd consistently underestimated the feisty American agent was now painfully obvious, but looking through the scope, Roos was determined that this would be the last time.

It was four hundred yards from his position to the Huey—an easy shot for a stationary target—but with Mia on the move, getting a first-round hit required Roos to shoot not where she was but where she was going to be when the bullet finally arrived. At its core, long-distance shooting was just a series of math problems: adjusting the scope's elevation to compensate for the drop of the bullet at distance and the windage for a moving target. But as much as Roos wanted to wait for that one perfect shot, the spit of the suppressed rifle from inside the L-shaped building told him there was simply no time.

Roos flipped off the safety and lined up the crosshairs, setting the tick mark in the center of the reticle up and to the right to compensate for the range and the fact that he was shooting at a moving target. He tracked her across the helo pad, the rhythmic rise and fall of the reticle on the target matching his heartbeat. Roos was waiting for the sight picture to still when Oskar came panting up the hill to the left of the helo pad, his rifle spitting flame.

Roos fired a split second later, the rifle bucking against his shoulder, and he lost the sight picture as the barrel recoiled skyward, but he didn't need to see his target to know that he'd missed. "Oskar, you fucking twat," he cursed.

He worked the bolt and chambered a fresh round, but by the time he got back on target, Mia was throwing herself behind one of the barrels. Roos waited, praying she would come out, but with Oskar now actively engaging her, he knew it wasn't going to happen.

Realizing he had to get closer, Roos cleared the rifle and was about to put it in the back seat when he saw Mia's guardian step out from behind the L-shaped building, Sawyer's arm over his shoulder.

I've got you now.

CHAPTER 62

The moment the 40 mm hit right between the two men, the blast bowling them over like ninepins, Lane ejected the empty casing and keyed up on the radio. "You're clear." Without waiting for Mia's response, he clambered down from the crate and moved to the target building.

He tried the knob, and finding it locked, he stepped back, fired three shots into the lock, and then kicked it open. Lane stepped inside and found himself in a narrow hall with a row of open doors on each side. Lane dirty cleared the first room to his left and stepped inside.

The room was small but neat. The pair of metal bunk beds and the lockers full of weathered fatigues hung dress right told him that he'd found the Crimson Ridge barracks. Before Broadside the only thing that he'd known about contracting work was that site security was a crap job that usually consisted of twelve-hour shifts standing around doing nothing. Any other time Lane might have been worried about waking any sleeping contractors, but since he'd spent the last twenty-four hours killing most of the men who'd slept here, Lane was confident that the rooms were now unoccupied.

Still, if there were any fighters remaining, there was no sense in giving himself away, and with that thought in mind, he slung the rifle, pulled the Staccato from its holster, and spun the suppressor onto the threaded barrel.

Now properly armed, Lane stepped back into the hall and continued his search. As he suspected, most of the rooms were empty, but as he neared the front of the building, he found a closed door secured with a thick padlock. Knowing how soldiers worked, he reached up and ran a hand across the top of the frame and was rewarded with a key. *Got to love lazy.*

He unlocked the padlock and opened the door, the smell of blood and stale urine overpowering his senses. Seeing the figure zip-tied to the chair in the center of the room, Lane figured he had found Winston Sawyer. The man groaned and looked up, his scabby face bruised and beaten.

"Who are you?"

"I'm a friend of Mia's," Lane said, moving behind the chair. He holstered his pistol and pulled out his knife to release the zip ties. "Can you walk?"

The man stood up, his legs unsteady as he rubbed his chafed wrists. "I can run if that's what it takes to get out of this shithole."

Looking at the man, Lane wasn't so sure. He was in bad shape, his legs and ankles swollen from the time spent strapped to the chair. For a moment Lane thought he might have to carry him, but after a few awkward stretches, Sawyer stood up straight with a fire in his eyes that dared Lane to doubt him.

"Well then, let's go," Lane said.

They stepped out of the room and were heading down the hall when Lane heard the *bang* of the front door being thrown open, followed by the rough voices of the few surviving mercs.

He shoved Sawyer into the next open room. "Stay here and wait until I come back," Lane said, pulling his last grenade from his kit.

Holding the frag in his left hand and the Staccato in his right, he moved to the door and waited for the angry voices that would tell him the mercs had found the now-empty cell. It didn't take long, and as soon as Lane heard the frantic shouts, he pulled the pin and let the spoon fly.

It took less than two seconds to reach the open door on his left, and he stopped short and tossed the grenade inside. Slamming the door shut, he bent down to retrieve the fallen padlock, then hooked the lock through the hasp and snapped it closed, ignoring the frantic beating on the door as he moved to the front of the building.

The grenade exploded, the flex of the wall combined with the resounding *boom* of the explosion drawing the last two mercs into the building. Lane waited for them to step inside before shooting them both and heading back to retrieve Sawyer.

"Let's go."

By the time they made it down the hall and out the back door, Sawyer's strength had begun to fail him, and Lane realized that walking back to the helicopter wasn't an option. Remembering the trucks at the front of the building, Lane ducked under the man's arm and half dragged, half carried Sawyer around the corner.

There was less than ten feet to go, and despite the extra weight, Lane was feeling strong, when Roos came stalking around the hood of the Toyota Hilux. If the man hadn't stopped to gloat, he would have had Lane, but instead of shooting, the scarred mercenary had to feed his ego.

"You *almost*—"

Lane fired from the hip and shoved Sawyer toward the Land Cruiser. A split second later, Roos opened fire, the first round hitting Lane in the chest plate and spinning him to the ground.

He landed on his side, his ribs feeling like he'd been kicked by a mule. Lane pushed the pain away and, since he was already on the ground, took aim at Roos's legs and fired as the other man skittered back to the truck. Due to the angle, Lane couldn't get a clear shot, and the first three rounds ended up as puffs off the dirt. But the fourth one found flesh, the lucky ricochet catching Roos in the calf as he was climbing behind the wheel of the truck.

Lane scrambled to his feet, intent on ending the fight, but before he had a chance, Roos cranked the engine. The Hilux turned over on the first try, and he shoved it into gear, then stomped on the gas. The tires spun, and Roos pulled away, Lane firing at the truck as the mercenary yanked it into a hard turn and raced off in a cloud of dust.

Lane had little doubt about where Roos was going, and he limped back to the Land Rover as quickly as he could. "Get in the truck," he told Sawyer, "and put your seat belt on."

Unlike the Toyota, the Land Rover did *not* start on the first try.

"Come on, you son of a bitch," he shouted.

Finally, the engine coughed to life, and without waiting for it to warm up, Lane shoved it into gear and then pressed down on the gas. He swung the truck around the back side of the building and let the rpm sweep into the red before shifting into second.

Off the jump, the Land Rover was slow as a barge, but once the engine got spooled up, it began to pick up speed. "C'mon, baby, you can do it."

He shifted through the gears, a glance through a break between the buildings showing Roos had a sizable lead, but when he returned his gaze to the front, Lane quickly realized he had another problem—namely the massive earth berm thirty yards ahead that marked the end of the road.

That's not good.

With the end of the line looming large in his windshield, Lane had less than a second to decide whether he should try to squeeze the Land Rover through the upcoming alley or leave the roadway entirely and try to make it down the back side of the hill. Determined not to let Roos beat him, he shifted into fourth gear. "Hold on," he said, pressing down all the way on the gas.

The engine groaned in protest, but Lane ignored it and aimed the hood toward the flat-topped mesa between the berm and the L-shaped building. Beside him, Sawyer grabbed onto the "oh shit" handle.

They raced up the side of the hill at fifty miles an hour, and the truck zoomed skyward. For a moment they were weightless, and he saw the gear in the back of the vehicle levitating above the back seat, heard the motor revving as the truck sailed through the air.

Then the Land Rover slammed into the ground, a geyser of ferrous red earth cascading over the hood and onto the windshield. Lane was driving blind, and his survival instincts screamed at him to hit the brakes, slow down long enough to see what was ahead of him. Instead, he flicked on the wipers and kept the pedal to the floor as the Land Rover raced across the top of the mesa.

The wipers swiped away the dirt, leaving a streaked arc of clear glass through which Lane saw the burnt-orange bucket of the excavator looming before him.

"Watch out!" Sawyer cried.

Lane cranked the wheel hard over and swerved beneath the bucket, wincing as the rusted teeth tore across the roof of the vehicle like the claws of a prehistoric beast. The sudden maneuver sent the top-heavy Land Rover leaning onto its side, its weight pulling the passenger-side tires off the ground.

He downshifted and, realizing he was on the verge of a rollover, cut the wheel to the right. He'd no sooner managed to get all four wheels back on the dirt than the ground dropped away, and the Land Rover went racing down the other side of the mesa. Lane caught a brief glimpse of Roos's truck on the road below and adjusted his course to intercept, but unlike the flattened peak, the back side of the hill was heavily eroded, its surface a lattice of axle-breaking gullies and tire-swallowing holes.

The Land Rover bucked like a mustang, the sudden play in the steering wheel telling Lane that the alignment was gone. That plus the ragged miss of the motor told him that the truck was on its last leg, but it didn't matter. All he needed was for the thing to hold together for another fifteen yards.

Realizing he was only going to get one shot at this, Lane aimed the hood two vehicle lengths ahead of the speeding pickup and yelled to Sawyer, "Hold on."

The engine coughed and sputtered as it bounced down the hill, and it was all Lane could do to keep it straight. He held on to the wheel, the distance between the two vehicles shrinking by the second.

Ten yards. Now eight. Five. Four. Three. Two . . .

A second before impact, Roos's head snapped left, his eyes widening when he saw the truck bearing down on him.

"Surprise, asshole," Lane said.

CHAPTER 63

NORTHSTAR MINE

Ubili, DRC

The Land Rover crashed into the side of the pickup at forty miles an hour, the sudden stop catapulting Lane forward in his seat. The seat belt snapped taut across his wounded bicep, but before his nerves could register the pain, his head slammed into the steering wheel.

His vision went white and he slumped in his seat, his mind hovering somewhere between the worlds of the living and the dead. Slowly his surroundings came back into focus, the taste of blood in his mouth and the sound of coolant from the shattered radiator hissing off the engine block.

He lifted his head, first checking on Sawyer, who sat looking pale as a ghost beside him, and then turning his attention to the pickup in time to see the passenger-side door swing open. Roos staggered out of the cab, blood staining the front of his shirt. The man took a step; then his legs gave out and he dropped, the pistol in his right hand clattering across the road.

Lane unclipped his seat belt and shoved the door open. "I'll be right back," he muttered, drawing his pistol.

He hauled himself out of the truck, the effort sending the world spinning before his eyes. Shaking his head to clear the dizziness, Lane spit a mouthful of blood into the dirt, aware of Roos scrambling across the road for the fallen gun.

This asshole just won't quit.

Lane tugged the Staccato from its holster and fired. The bullet slapped into the ground next to Roos's hand, the shower of dirt spraying across the man's blood-soaked face.

"Next one has your name on it," Lane warned.

Roos studied him for a second, but Lane kept his gaze unreadable as he advanced on the wounded mercenary. In one smooth motion, he kicked the Browning Hi-Power pistol into the weeds and dropped a knee onto Roos's back. He holstered the pistol and reached for a pair of flex cuffs strapped to his kit.

"Whoever you're working for, whatever they are paying you," Roos panted, "the men I am working for will double it. Just let me deliver that last—"

"I'm not interested in your money," Lane said, looping the plastic cuffs around the man's wrists and pulling them tight.

"Then what *do* you want?"

"I want you to shut your mouth and stand up."

Roos wobbled to his feet, and Lane grabbed him by the back of the shirt and spun him around just as Mia came running across the road.

"Holy shit!" she shouted. "When I saw the crash, I *knew* you were dead."

"Not yet," Lane said.

He shoved Roos toward her, then moved back to the stricken Land Rover and pulled open the passenger door. Lane helped Sawyer out of the truck, and they limped around the hood and started toward the helo. By the time they got to the edge of the pad, Mia had already shoved Roos into the cargo hold and belted him in. For a second, Lane thought she was going to come down and help them the rest of the way. But instead of doing so, Mia turned and placed her hands on her hips.

"What are you waiting for?" she demanded. "We've got to go."

Lane wanted to tell her to pound sand, but before he had a chance, Mia was climbing into the cockpit.

"This is bullshit," he muttered.

"You got that right," Sawyer said.

Realizing no one was going to help them, they hobbled the final ten yards to the Huey. Using the last of his reserves, Lane boosted Sawyer into the cargo hold and climbed in behind him. With no strength left to belt himself in, he pressed his back against the bulkhead, savoring the rush of air across his face as Mia yanked the Huey skyward.

CHAPTER 64

Atlantic Ocean

Travis Lane opened his eyes, his mind hazy from the pain meds he'd been given in Goma. He blinked the world into focus, the off-white walls and the antiseptic smell of the air reminding him of a hospital. Sitting up, he took stock of his surroundings, confused as to exactly where he was until he saw Mia staring at him from the leather couch on the right side of the Global 7500 cabin.

"Welcome back," she said.

"How long was I out?" he asked, grabbing the bottle of water from the cup holder.

"Almost ten hours," she said, "and *man*, you can snore."

Lane rolled his eyes and, when he'd gulped his fill of water, screwed on the top and returned it to the cup holder. "First off, I don't snore," he said. "And second, after what I just went through, I think I deserved some sleep."

"Hey, I'm not judging." She smiled. "I'm just glad you woke up before we landed."

"Where are we?" he asked.

"Beginning our descent into DC," she said. "How's the arm?"

Lane lifted his arm and gingerly flexed his shoulder, the neat row of sutures beneath the gauze four-by-four itching like hell. Happy with the range of motion, he turned his attention to the window, his eyes drifting over the landscape below.

"So, what happens now?" he asked, turning to Mia.

"Well, my hearing is this afternoon. Mike says I'll be fine, but I don't know."

"It's funny to think you'd be nervous after everything you've been through."

"I'm not so much nervous as . . ." She paused, her eyes ticking toward the window as she tried to find the right words. "I guess after everything that happened, all the death and suffering we saw, I just want it to matter."

"You mean Sterling?" Lane asked.

"Yeah."

"Well, with Roos and Sawyer having agreed to testify, I don't see you having much of a problem."

"You never know," Mia said, her eyes drifting to the window.

They landed in silence, and while the pilot taxied to the Dulles Jet Center, Lane spent a frantic second searching for his rifle before realizing it wasn't there. While Mia gathered her things, he waited for the pilot to pull the Bombardier into the hangar and then got to his feet.

Outside the aircraft a pair of black vehicles sat idling on the tarmac. "I think that one is yours," Lane said, pointing to the SUV with the serious-looking agent in dark aviators standing near the hood.

"Yeah," Mia said, stepping in for a hug. "You take care of yourself, Travis Lane."

"No promises." He grinned.

Lane helped her into the back of the truck and closed the door, and she offered a final wave before pulling off. Now alone, he slipped a pair of sunglasses over his eyes and turned to the Broadside support officer who was serving as his driver.

"Where are we headed?" Lane asked.

"Walter Reed," the man said.

"Did they end up having to take the leg?"

"Below the knee," the man said. "But if it's any consolation, the surgeon said they would have had to take the whole thing if it hadn't been for you."

"Good to know."

Lane climbed into the back seat and shut the door, and while the driver followed the access road to the interstate, Lane pulled out the cell phone they'd given him before leaving Goma. He typed out a quick text message to Abby saying he'd be home soon and, after sending it, settled in for the ride.

They drove east on SR 267, the big V-8 purring like a jungle cat as the driver merged with the traffic. The truck rode smoothly, and the hypnotic whine of the tires on the roadway sent Lane's mind circling back to the DRC.

It was a short hop from the mine to the crash site, and he had been physically unable to do much more than watch as Mia helped Jones take a seat on the cargo floor beside him. The other man eyed the two new faces next to him as he pulled a pair of headphones from the hook and pulled them over his ears. "Damn, bro, you look like shit!" he said over the internal radio.

"Tell me something I don't know," Lane managed.

"All right," Mako said. "Not many people would have done what you did. Coming back for me like that . . . I owe you."

"Just doing my job," Lane replied.

There was silence between them as Mia climbed into the cockpit and pulled on her helmet. "You guys ready to get the hell out of here?"

"Yes ma'am," Jones said. "But before we go, I've got *one* question."

"What's that?" Mia asked.

"Which one of you wants to tell me why this asshole is still breathing?" Jones asked, nodding at Roos.

"Let's just say that between him and Sawyer," Lane said, "they've got enough dirt to put Sterling and your buddy West away for a long time."

"If that's the case, then good job," Jones said.

They'd been greeted at Goma International by a Broadside medical support team and a scrum of federal agents in navy-blue blazers who'd been quick to take Roos into custody as soon as they touched down. While Lane had been left to fend for himself, the medical team had loaded Mako onto a gurney.

"Catch you on the flip side," he'd told Lane before they'd wheeled him to the waiting Orbis MD-10 Flying Eye Hospital that would take him back to the States.

The driver pulling off the highway put an end to the memory, and Lane leaned forward in his seat to see the ivory tower that marked the front of Walter Reed National Military Medical Center. The SUV stopped at the side entrance.

"I won't be long," Lane said.

"Take all the time you need. I'm getting paid by the hour."

Lane closed the door and went inside, and after getting directions from one of the nurses, he followed the signage to room 204. He knocked on the door and stepped inside to find Jones lying on the bed, a massive bowl of chocolate pudding on the tray table in front of him.

"Well, look who it is." The man grinned.

"What's going on, Chief?"

"Oh, you know, just chilling out and catching up on my stories," he said, ladling a huge bite of pudding into his mouth.

Lane followed his gaze to the TV and frowned when he realized what the man was watching. "Is that *The Young and the Restless*?"

"You know it."

"Damn," he said, turning his attention to Jones's IV stand. "What kind of drugs are they giving you?"

"Don't knock it till you try it."

Lane flashed him a grin and lowered himself gingerly into one of the seats. "Sorry to hear about your leg."

"Don't be," Jones said. "The docs told me that it will cut my rehab time in half."

"Yeah, still . . ."

"Don't do that," Jones said, suddenly serious. "You did a hell of a job out there."

Lane looked down at the floor and rubbed the back of his neck. "Doesn't feel like it."

"It never does, but that doesn't change the fact that none of us would have made it out alive if it wasn't for you."

While he appreciated the sentiment, Lane wasn't sure if it was true. He let the silence build until Jones hit the pause button on the television and turned to face him.

"Something on your mind?" he asked.

"Not really, I just wanted to stop by and see how you were doing," Lane said, getting to his feet. "You know, make sure you had everything you needed."

"Well, as you can see," Jones said, taking another bite of pudding, "I've got everything I require. But before you go, I was talking to Mr. Carter this morning, and seems like both of us have the same question."

"Oh yeah?" Lane asked. "And what's that?"

"When are you taking over Guardian 7?"

ACKNOWLEDGMENTS

I'd like to thank my family for putting up with me during this book and everyone at Blackstone for their patience. I'd also like to thank my editor, Jennifer Fisher, whose tireless effort saved both my sanity and my career. I owe you all a debt I can never repay.